# ABOUT THE AUTHOR

Lexie Winston has been an astronaut, rock star, princess and time traveller. In her dreams. But none of the dreams have lived up to what becoming an author has been like. She gets to live in a world of pure imagination, and her heroines get to do the things she's always wished she could.

When not writing books, Lexie is a mother of two gorgeous teenagers and the wife to a patient and understanding man. They live in Western Australia and are lorded over by a black toy poodle. She loves camping, reading and if her Kindle was stolen, her world would explode.

And you can find all links at

www.lexiewinston.com

# SPECTACLE

**LEXIE WINSTON**

# ALSO BY LEXIE WINSTON

**The Collectors Division**

(Paranormal Reverse Harem Series)

Guardian

Guardian's Blood

Guardian Ascending

Collector's Division Omnibus

**Neighpalm Industries Collective**

(Enemies to Lovers Reverse Harem)

Abandoned Girl

Broken Girl

Tormented Girl

Wanted Girl

Cherished Girl

Loved Girl

Superficial Girl - Jacinta's Story Part 1

Superficial Girl - Jacinta's Story Part 2

Neighpalm Industries Collective 1-3

Neighpalm Industries Collective 4-6

**Seductive Sins Collection**

(Reverse Harem Series)

Glorious Gluttony

Gangs, Guns, and Glory

Glory Glory Hellelujah

Crowning Glory

What's the Story, Morning Glory?

(Seductive Sins Omnibus)

**Galaxy Circus**

(Sci-Fi Reverse Harem Series)

Apprentice

Stagehand

Whisperer

Mama - Galaxy Circus Novella

Performer

Ringmaster

Interlude

Spectacle

Ovation

A Night Most Wicked - Galaxy Circus Novella

**Broken Promises**

(Dark Poly Romance Series)

Secrets Kept

Lies Untold

Trust Broken

**M.I.T.H.O.S**

(Contemporary RH)

Spies Like Me

Spies Like Us

**Storm View Stories**

(Contemporary Standalone RH)

Ice Me Out

First published by Neighpalm Publishing in 2024



Spectacle

Mobi format: 978-1-7636228-1-4
Print: 978-1-7636228-2-1
Cover design by Raven Ink Covers

Editing by Elemental Editing

# FOREWORD

I decided not to add a glossary in this book. I had complaints whether I put it in the front or the back. So if you need a refresher on our cast of characters the main ones are listed on the next page. Everything else you can find by scanning the QR code which will take you to my website Galaxy Glossary

# MAIN CHARACTERS

Lila Adams
Caspian
Link
Saxon
Xavier
Echo
Maxsim
Tirrian
Silac
Nikos
Ghosie
Brannock
Zeydan

# CHAPTER ONE

### Lila

"Why is the goddess of life in the box instead of my grandma?" I feel sick, like everything we did to get here was a waste of time. My poor grandpas are going to be heartbroken and devastated. How did Zamala get it so wrong?

I watch as the earth god cradles the small woman against his chest like she's the most precious thing in the world to him, and a sharp stab of jealousy burns inside me. Who is this goddess to him? He claims she is like his sister, but there is no blood relation, so maybe their relationship bloomed into something more.

He seems to be stunned into speechlessness, so I turn my attention to the others who seem just as bewildered as I am.

"None of us have been with the circus as long as

she's been missing, and I don't remember meeting her when I was a child. I couldn't tell you if this is her or not," Xavier says unhelpfully. "I suggest we return to the ship and let Link assess her, and maybe then we can get to the bottom of this."

"It's obviously not her from his reaction." I stab a finger in Zeydan's direction. He is muttering under his breath, and I briefly wonder if he's trying to wake her when I process what Xavier suggested. "Can we hide our return from my grandpas? This is going to break their hearts. They had so much hope. I could skin Zamala alive for giving them that." The last bit comes out in a growl, and smoke wafts out of my nose as scales ripple across my arms.

"Easy," Tirrian murmurs softly, approaching me from behind and stroking his hand over my back. "Your dragon is still new, and if you aren't careful, she will burst out of your skin unbidden. Take a deep breath and breathe in and out slowly."

"That's easier said than done," I tell him but do as he says, closing my eyes and breathing in and out a few times. When I feel more settled, I wait for Xavier's answer.

"I think maybe we shouldn't hide it from them. There must be a good reason why Zamala claimed your grandma was in the box. Maybe she's wearing a glamour."

"Xavier's right," Tirrian chimes in. "Zamala has never been wrong with her predictions."

"There's always a first time, and with our luck, this

is it," I reply stubbornly, crossing my arms to comfort myself. I'm feeling all out of sorts and slightly shaky. I think I might need some blood.

"She is not wearing a glamour. I would feel it if she was," Zeydan says, looking up from the goddess, but then his gaze returns to the glyphs on the box. "I didn't want to say anything before, but I recognize those glyphs. That box was created by the goddess of death, Vivax. I'm afraid she has something to do with Lilessa being in there, and if she does, then she now knows the box has been breached. We should leave now, just to be safe." I don't like his panicked tone. For fuck's sake, he's a god, so that means we really need to be concerned.

"But what about the halla harvesters?" I remind him, and he quickly shakes his head.

"They can return at another time. I will send them away. They will not question me," he replies with an arrogance that doesn't surprise me.

"Alright then, I'll contact the ship and let them know we're ready to teleport aboard." Silac moves slightly away from us, and I watch as he uses the communicator on his wrist to radio the ship. A wave of exhaustion flows through my limbs, and I sway. Ghosie starts to put his hands up to support me but quickly drops them with a huff of frustration.

"I'm sorry I can't help you," he murmurs, gesturing to his fur.

Before I can reply, Tirrian wraps an arm around

me. "I've got her," he tells the bear, who nods with a sad look in his eyes.

"Thank you for retrieving her, even if she isn't my grandma," I say to Ghosie, offering him a reassuring smile. "We appreciate everything you've done for us."

"Yes, thank you. Maybe once she wakes, she can shed some more light on the situation," Zeydan chimes in as Silac waves us together into a huddle.

"Okay, Rick, we're ready. Beam us straight to the medical bay please."

Tirrian's arm is tight around me as we dissolve into particles and fly through space before reforming in the medical bay on the ship.

Link is there, as is Saxon, and both are standing over a groaning Maxsim, who is lying on one of the medical beds. I look around for Echo, but I don't see him.

"Should I get Echo?" I ask as Zeydan lays Lilessa down on one of the spare beds.

"No," Maxsim rasps as I hurry over and take his hand. Link is sealing his wound with some kind of laser tool. There is also a line of blue blood running into his vein from a bag hanging next to the table. "I don't want to worry him." His eyes roll back in his head and his hand goes limp in mine as he loses consciousness,

"Lila!" Link sounds relieved. "Thank goodness, I was just trying to close the wound. He's okay, but he lost a significant amount of blood. I thought if I closed the wound, he would be alright until you returned, but

I'm having trouble sealing it." He sounds a little panicked. Today has been a clusterfuck. Both the god and the cool-headed cyborg are panicked, so this doesn't bode well. I feel my heart start to race as my panic joins Link's.

"Why me?" I ask, feeling more tired than I should after my bout of sex with Brannock. I should be completely recharged, but I'm still flagging on energy.

An amused grin crosses Link's lips, and my eyes get stuck on them for a moment. I feel my fangs descend and consider taking a bite out of him. I reach for him, but Xavier grabs me around the waist.

"Whoa, hang on. No eating the doctor until all his patients have been seen to," he murmurs quietly into my ear, his breath brushing across the lobe.

"Can you shift into your Celestian form and heal him before we go any further?" Link pulls the tool away and gestures to the gaping wound. It's oozing blue blood, and there's a foul smell coming from it. Fuck, now my heart is racing even faster. I put my hand against my chest like that will slow it down, then I shake off the bloodlust and return my attention to his words about shifting to Celestian form.

"Oh, of course. Shit, I forgot I could do that." I strip off my clothes and allow my Celestian form to appear. Xavier conjures me a shift dress in his favorite lavender that allows my wings freedom to move. I stretch them wide, and both Link and Saxon duck out of the way. The slight ache I feel whenever I assume this form dies away with the movement. My wings are the same color as my hair in normal form—shimmery white opal with veins of orange, pink, and blue. They are so pretty.

Stepping closer to the table, I place my hands over the wound in Maxsim's body. "I thought shifting would fix this," I remark to Link, who moves around to the other side of the bed and watches as my hands heat and white light emits from them, covering the wound.

"Normally it would, but I think the Madovians must secrete something from their claws that stopped it from healing." Link watches with wide-eyed amazement as the wound expels some kind of black toxic ick. He quickly grabs a vial from a tray behind him and scoops some of it up. The layers of tissue, muscle, and flesh heal beneath my glowing hands before the skin knits back together, mending the wound completely. I go to pull my hands away but stop when I notice little tufts of fur pushing through the dermal layers, covering the wound with new fur. It's like he wasn't even wounded to begin with.

His heavy breathing eases, and his eyes flutter closed as he starts to breathe steadily. "He's all healed, but he's going to need to sleep for a little while." I instinctively know this, which is kind of cool. The glow disperses, and I pull my hands away. "Can someone go get Echo to sit with him?" I ask, looking at the gathered men. There really are too many of us in here.

"He didn't want him to know because of the

babies," Saxon explains. "He didn't want to stress him out."

"Let's downplay the injury then and explain that he's all better and just needs some rest. I know I'd be pissed if you kept it from me for my well-being," I scold them.

"I'll go. There's nothing I can do here anyway," Tirrian offers. "I'll let Caspian know we're back as well. What should I tell the Adams brothers if I see them?"

"There's no hiding this, so maybe just tell them we're back and let them see for themselves. They won't believe we failed if they don't see it for themselves." I heave out a heavy sigh as Tirrian gives me a kiss on the cheek.

"You failed?" Saxon sounds confused as he looks at the figure on the other bed. Zeydan is still holding her hand and hovering over her, and that stab of jealousy has me flinching again.

*Jesus, Lila, get a grip. You're jealous of an unconscious woman. Maybe wait until she wakes up and see if she makes a play at your god before you can be jealous.*

"Who is that then?" Link lifts Maxsim, careful not to pull out his transfusion. Saxon grabs the pole that holds it, and they both move over to a clean bed away from Lilessa. Link lays him down gently and pulls up a sheet to cover him, while Saxon situates the blood bag close by.

"Should I let Broderick know we're ready to leave, Lila?" Silac asks, and when I turn to face him, he's wringing his hands in front of his body in agitation.

We achieved what we set out to do, so he must be anxious to return to Fluxx now. I can't wait for the day when I can complain of boredom.

"Yes, Silac. Have him set a course for Fluxx and not to stop for any reason. Let's rescue your father." In this form, I feel his wave of gratitude. Celestians must pick up emotions similar to warlocks.

"Thank you." He places his hands together and bows before he and Tirrian both leave.

"I'm just going to wash up. This black gunk is stuck in my fur, and it smells." Ghosie plucks at the Madovian blood splattered across his face and arms, staining his bright fur. "Let me know if I can help with anything." He waves and starts to depart.

"Ghosie," I call, stopping him. He turns back with raised eyebrows. "You need to decide what you want to do now that the job is finished. Do you want to return to your planet?"

His eyebrows drop, and his fur seems to droop ever so slightly. "Ah, yeah. Okay, I'll think about it." He hurries out without waiting for a response.

Xavier groans. "Jesus, Lila." He runs his hand through his hair, yanking at the strands falling out of the ponytail.

"What?" I snap.

"Are you really that clueless?"

"Look, Xavier, spit it out. I don't have time for games. I'm tired and hungry and can't decide if I want to fuck you or rip out your throat," I growl, and my wings flutter behind me.

He shakes his head, glaring at me. "Never mind, we can talk about it when you're more rational. I'm going to make sure he doesn't decide to drown himself in the shower." Xavier disappears in a flash, leaving me speechless.

"What is his problem?" I growl, looking around and hoping someone will clue me in.

"I'm going to go and do the same thing." Brannock steps into my line of sight, and I blink. He leans in and kisses my cheek. "Let me know if you need me."

He starts to depart, and I grab his hand, stopping him. "There's a room in our suite for you if you want it. Can you tell Tirrian the same thing? I would love to have both of you there if you want." Even though we aren't officially mated yet, I want him around because I know it's just a matter of time.

His smile is almost blinding. "I'd love to, and I'll let the dragon know."

"Once we deal with Silac's parents and his problem, I promise we will head back to Earth and handle Agent Smith once and for all," I promise him, and he leans in and kisses me again.

"I can't wait for you to meet her." He leaves, and my mouth drops open. Meet his daughter? Shit, I just became a stepmom. You know what? That's another future Lila problem. Future Lila is fucked.

A chuckle has me spinning around. All that's left are Link, Saxon, a sleeping Maxsim, and the god, but it's Saxon who's laughing. Link is busy doing something to the goddess. My Vilaxian husband approaches me slowly, like I'm a rabid animal he has to be wary of.

"Babe, I can practically feel your mind imploding. Forget about everything else for now. Your grandpas are going to be here soon, and they need you present instead of spiraling. We will get you something to eat and drink shortly, so just hold on for a few more minutes." He carefully grabs my arm and leads me over to the bed.

Link placed a sensor in the middle of Lilessa's chest, lowering the neckline of the dress she's wearing to do it. He reads the results on his arm, and his eyes widen as his skin loses its shine.

"Holy fuck," he mutters very unprofessionally.

"What's wrong?" Zeydan asks, and I can hear the concern in his voice.

"Well, I can confirm she is in a form of stasis, but I hope she can't feel any pain, because these readouts indicate just about every bone in her body is broken."

My eyes widen, and my stomach roils with nausea as I take a closer look at the pale female. "What are all these lines on her body?" I ask, tracing the silver streaks with my eyes. She has them all over her, and it looks like they continue under the long dress she wears. I lift the hem, and sure enough, her ankle and calves have the same kind of lines.

Link is quiet, and when I look up, his eyes are shimmering with tears. "I think they are scars. I am absolutely certain that this woman has been tortured repeatedly. I need you to heal her, Lila, and maybe once her pain is gone, she may wake up on her own."

# CHAPTER TWO

### Lila

"Tortured?" The voice has me whirling around to find all three of my grandpas standing at the entrance of the med bay. John is as pale as a ghost, and he wavers slightly, while William puts out a hand to steady him.

"Did you say tortured?" Eric is beet red, and he's a hairbreadth away from exploding. I hold my hands up.

"Whoa. Wait before you explode. This woman isn't your wife." I hope that stops the impending explosion. "Zeydan says her name is Lilessa, and she's the goddess of life. She was in there, not Grandma Liliana."

"Zeydan?" That distracts Eric, his gaze moving to the god. His mouth rounds in a silent O.

"Not Liliana?" William tugs John into the room

by his arm, both of them approaching the bed with distraught looks on their faces, but when they study the woman, their expressions are replaced by relief and love.

"What are you talking about? This is our Lili. Her hair's a different color, and she's a lot paler, but this is definitely our wife," William says as John picks up her hand, tears streaming down his face.

Eric hurries around to the other side and pushes Zeydan out of the way, taking her other hand as he cries. "Lili. Thank God. I can't believe you found her for us."

I exchange a confused look with Link. "This is your wife?" I ask as William leans in and presses a kiss to her forehead.

John nods enthusiastically. "Yes, and your grandma."

"And you say this is Lilessa, the goddess of life." I point at Zeydan, who stepped out of the way to give my grandpas room. He has a thoughtful look on his face.

"Yes," he confirms.

"So how can they be the same person?" I ask, but Link shakes his head.

"We have plenty of time to have questions answered later. The most urgent thing is healing her. Please, can you all step back so Lila can do her thing? It's downright barbaric to leave her in the state she's in." He gestures for me to come forward.

The grandpas don't argue, but I can see their reluctance to move away. I give John a side hug and a kiss on the cheek. "Not much longer now. You've waited this long, so just be patient for a little bit more," I tell him, and he nods.

"Fix her, Lila. I hate that she might be in pain." He steps back to give me room, and I take his place. I hold out my hands and allow the Celestian power to manifest in them, unable to stop the sob of despair from escaping my lips. Link is right, just about every bone in her body is broken, and I can feel her pain. It's indescribable. I have no words. How can anyone cause this kind of suffering to any kind of being? Whoever did this truly has no goodness left in them.

The power expands as I place my hands over the middle of her stomach, sending it out to encompass her whole body. Tears stream down my face. She's so broken, I'm not sure she is strong enough to come back from this. I am so confused about how this can be both my grandma and the goddess of life. Hopefully once we heal her, she can help us find some answers.

My Celestian magic does its thing. I feel the magic drain out of me as it heals all the damage to her body. Each bone knits back together, and all the internal damage—which Link didn't mention to save everyone heartbreak—heals. Even the silvery scars seem to fade before our very eyes. As I take a deep breath and cut off the flow, I slump over, exhausted and drained. Saxon flashes to my side and wraps an arm around my shoulders, securing me to his side so I don't topple over.

"She's healed," I tell everyone, breathless and unsteady on my feet.

They all stare at her with hope, but deep down, I know the truth. Despite her beating heart, there doesn't seem to be any response to my healing.

"I've done everything I can. Her body is healed, let's just hope her mind can heal too. Give it time. She has been through something none of us would probably survive, except maybe Zeydan." I look at him, and he nods.

"Yes, we are resilient and can withstand much, but this—" He waves his hand at the goddess's still form. "She should have died from this, but they held her in stasis instead, trapped inside a broken body. I would be surprised if her mind wasn't as broken."

It may have been kinder to let her pass and reincarnate once more if she really is the goddess of life, but I'm not sure what that would do to my grandpas if she is also their wife, so I need to pray that she comes through this mentally intact.

John's sob is loud in the silent room, and it looks like William and Eric are only holding on by a thread.

"Gods can die?" Link asks. I guess Saxon must have filled him in on everything when they returned.

"Yes, we can if enough damage is sustained to our physical form, but we do reincarnate, and all of our powers and memories return as we mature."

"Someone wanted her to suffer." Eric's fists are clenched, and equipment starts to rattle around the room.

"Easy." William puts a hand on his brother's shoulder, giving it a squeeze, and the equipment stops rattling.

"No wonder she gave up the location of the orb." John's despair floats in the air like it's a tangible thing. "No one would have been able to withstand that. What about the flower, the one that saved me didn't we save a petal?"

"We did, but it's not going to be enough to fix this," I explain and he sobs.

"If only I hadn't need so much we could have used it on Lili."

A siren suddenly sounds, and Bubby's voice comes through the loudspeaker. "We need to make the jump to hyperspeed. Please strap in so we can do this. This is a five minute warning."

Link moves over to a console and presses a button, then straps come up and over both Maxsim and the woman on the table, securing them. I'm going to call her Grandma until we get to the bottom of things. I don't want to upset my grandpas more than they already are.

The rest of us head out into the hallway. "Come on," I call to Zeydan, who stands by the bed.

He looks reluctant to move but does so, and I show him how to strap in so no one gets hurt on the jump before taking a seat next to him. After strapping in, I remember my can of tuna in the pool below.

"What about Nikos? Is he going to be alright?" I

ask, wondering if I can change into my warlock form and teleport down there.

"The pool's forcefield, which keeps all the water in, actually makes it the safest place for him to be. The water doesn't move no matter what the ship does," Saxon explains, and I sag with relief. At least one less person I have to worry about. "Poor Cas has to wrangle the babies into the chairs. Hopefully one of the others is helping him."

"I'm surprised that Echo isn't here yet," Link says, pulling on the strap to make sure it's secure.

"I'm certain he will be shortly after we jump," I murmur, watching my grandpas carefully to make sure they don't neglect their own safety in their grief. The five minutes passes quietly, all of us lost in our own thoughts. The jump to hyperspace goes smoothly, and we all unbuckle before the seats retreat into the walls.

"Why don't you all go get some rest? I'll stay here and watch over her, and I'll let you know the moment something changes," Link suggests, and I decide not to argue. I'm so tired, I can barely stand. In fact. I feel my Celestian form fade away, and I wobble again. Saxon swoops in and scoops me up before I collapse to the ground in a heap. Thankfully I'm so depleted of magic, the dress doesn't disappear in the change.

"Whoa, you need blood and rest," Saxon says, and I see him and Link exchange a glance. I need something else as well. I feel my cheeks pinken, but thank goodness they didn't mention it in front of my grandpas.

"I'm not leaving." Eric stubbornly crosses his arms,

and I can tell from the look on his face there is going to be no changing his mind. Link must see the same determination, because he sighs.

"Why don't we start a roster? You can stay while the other two rest."

William and John splutter their arguments, but Link shakes his head.

"No, John, you have barely recovered from your own ordeal, and there's no point in either of you staying. You can't do anything. The best you can do is keep yourself healthy. If she wakes up, she's going to need a lot of support to recover from what she went through. Get a hot meal and a solid eight hours of sleep and then another meal before I allow one of you to return. You can take eight hour shifts, then she won't be left alone." He turns to look at Zeydan, arching one of his perfect eyebrows in question. "Do you want in on this too?"

Zeydan studies my grandpas intently, and I kind of wonder if he's reading their minds. I try to reach out with my warlock powers, but I'm empty, and there's a small moment of panic that maybe I overdid it. Can I burn my powers out?

Zeydan's gaze slides to me. "No, little mimic, you can't burn your powers out, but you will need to rest and..." He pauses and looks at my grandpas before continuing. "Recharge."

I release the little breath I was holding, grateful he didn't mention fucking in front of my grandpas either

—not that I think they would notice, since they are so caught up in their worry.

Zeydan gives me a slow wink. "No, I will leave these men to care for my sister. There seems to be some validity to their story, and I have no doubt they have her best interest at heart."

"Sister?" William eyes Zeydan suspiciously. "Who are you? Liliana didn't have a brother, only her sister, Vivian."

Zeydan's eyes narrow in contemplation.

"Yeah, she's a real peach," Saxon mutters under his breath, and I have to clamp my lips shut to stop a snort from escaping.

"There's a lot we need to fill you in on, but can we do it once I get a nap? I can barely keep my eyes open." I try unsuccessfully to smother a yawn, and my grandpas are quick to assure me I can catch them up when I wake. They shoo me off, and I worry about leaving Link to deal with the three of them on their own, but he waves me away.

"Come on then," Saxon says to Zeydan, and then he leads the way to the elevators for us to return to our rooms.

The rocking movement as I lie in Saxon's arms is soothing, and I find myself dozing on the way to our rooms. I vaguely hear them talking, but I'm so tired, I can't force myself to listen, so instead, I allow the calming sounds of their voices to wash over me.

"Lila." Caspian's voice has me cracking my eyes

open, and I smile when I see my beautiful blue kraken peering at me as he takes me from Saxon's arms.

"Hey," I mutter, trying to keep my eyes open. He looks down at me with that beautiful smile that makes me want to sigh like a Disney princess.

"Hi, gorgeous. Let's get you some rest," he says softly, but I struggle in his arms and look around.

"The babies?" I ask him, and he shakes his head.

"They are fine. They are sleeping. I took them down to swim with Nikos while you were all doing your thing. I think we wore the poor guy out. He was practically asleep when we left, but they all had fun. Xavier helped me put them to bed." Oh good, at least I know my warlock husband is around. I still need to get to the bottom of his crabby mood, but that can wait until the morning.

"Okay, good. Did someone tell Echo about Maxsim?" I ask, and he nods as we move farther into our suite.

"Yes, you just missed him. He left to go sit with him. He's fine too, but I'm sure Link will give him a workup while he is down there," he reassures me, and I relax in his arms.

"Oh, Zeydan..." I try to look back the way we came to see if I can find the god, but Caspian squeezes my thigh.

"He will be fine. Saxon will get him settled. Both Tirrian and Brannock are in the process of moving into one of the spare rooms in here, and I'm sure he can have one of their rooms."

Everything has happened so quickly, and I don't know how I feel about the god. He claims I'm his mate, but I don't know whether to believe him or not. Can a god really have a mate, and just one at that? I mean, he's fucking gorgeous, and I am super attracted to him, I felt an attraction mark form on my body, but maybe it was a mistake. Maybe he's disappointed he's mates with a lower being.

"Lila, stop overthinking things," Caspian scolds me, and I pout.

"Are you like Xavier now, picking up on my emotions?" I grumble, and he chuckles.

"No, but I know you. You need to rest and recharge, and we can worry about everything else tomorrow. We have a long trip back to Fluxx before we'll face our next problem. Let's just conquer one thing at a time." He reaches my room, and instead of putting me on the bed, he passes it and heads into the bathroom. "Let's wash some of this gunk off you." He places my feet on the floor, and I look down my body.

I'm wearing the dress Xavier conjured for me, but the rest of me is filthy. I'm not quite sure how I ended up so dirty. I also hadn't realized the dirt stayed when changing forms. Black Madovian blood is splattered up and down my arms, and I can't even begin to consider what my face looks like.

I wince. "Yeah, that's probably a good idea. I can't believe Brannock even looked at me twice like this."

"From what I hear, you were wearing your Aaz'axian form. There is no way he could have resisted that, and we all find you attractive no matter what form you're in or if you're covered in blood." He turns the shower on before stripping the dress up and over my head. I lean against the wall as he removes his shirt before peeling his sweats down his legs. He wraps his arms around me and walks us both under the stream. I moan loudly as the hot water washes over my tired, aching body.

"They don't have any mating rituals that I need to know about, right?" I ask him, knowing he and Link have discussed all of my possible mates' needs.

He shakes his head. "Nope, you can mate him the Skarrian way, but before their women started dying, they were a very fertile bunch, so keep up with the birth control unless you want to carry his baby."

I shudder. "Nope, no thanks. Maybe one day, but I think seven is plenty for now."

He pumps some soap into his hands before rubbing them together then gliding them over my body. I close my eyes and lean against the wall, letting him take care of me. "Actually, it's eight."

"Eight what?" I mutter, loving how his hands feel on my skin.

"Well, Brannock's daughter makes eight." My eyes pop open, and I stare down at my kraken who is kneeling as he washes my legs.

"Fuck. I'm going to be a stepmom. What if she hates me?" I bite my lip as nerves prickle in my belly.

He presses a kiss to my thigh before standing up. I feel a slight moment of disappointment that he didn't kiss anything else while he was down there, but I'm too fucking tired right now to be really upset.

"How could she? You're amazing. She never knew her mother, remember? She's probably desperate for some female attention."

"I wonder if they age at the same rate as shifter babies. She's supposed to be like four or something, right?" I ask, and he shrugs unhelpfully.

"I think so, but I don't know. We'll have to ask Brannock."

"Ugh." I bang my head against the wall. There's so much I don't know, and I hate the thought of her being trapped with Smith. Thankfully he thinks Brannock is still on his side, so he should be treating her well for now.

"Hey, we've got this. We're a team, you aren't in this alone." He cups my cheek and presses his forehead against mine, and I sag into his arms as they wrap around me. "Everything won't look so big after you get some rest."

He quickly finishes washing me, leaving me to my thoughts, then shuts off the water. He wraps me in a giant towel before drying himself off. Cas scoops me up, and we return to my bedroom. It's dark, and when he places me on the bed, I'm disappointed that no one else is here. I know Link, Maxsim, and Echo wouldn't be and that Tirrian and Brannock are busy and Nikos is unavailable to snuggle, but I thought maybe Saxon and Xavier would be here. Xavier did leave the med bay pretty upset at me, though, and I still don't know why.

Cas rolls me out of my towel and tosses it to the side before climbing into bed next to me. He pulls the covers over us, and I feel his body shift, and then his tentacles wrap around me in a way that I love, and I let my worries drift away as my eyelids flutter shut.

He presses a kiss to my cheek and whispers, "Sleep well, baby."

# CHAPTER THREE

## Xavier

### Earlier

I huff in frustration as I hurry after the bear. I could feel how hurt he was by Lila's comment, and I'm super annoyed at her for not realizing that all he wants is to be part of a family—our family. She's either too dense to figure that out or too distracted by everything else that's going on. It's more likely, however, that it hasn't even occurred to her that he may want that, because nobody has wanted her for most of her life—or not permanently anyway. She's come so far since she discovered her heritage, but every now and then, her past rears its ugly head, making her act stupid.

"Ghosie, wait up," I call. Even though I could just appear in front of him, I don't want to startle him.

He's lost in his own misery. I don't usually care so much about people who aren't in my family, but if things go right, then he's going to be a part of it eventually, so I need to make an effort.

The bear stops and looks over his shoulder, and I see tears glistening in his eyes. He quickly looks down, and I watch him wipe his face, so I pretend not to see them. "Hey..." I go to touch his shoulder but hesitate, knowing what will happen to me if I do. I drop my hand and sigh. "Fuck, man, I want to give you a big hug, but then I'll probably end up humping your leg."

Ghosie snorts, the sound a mix of amusement and misery. "That's the story of my life."

"Come on, I'll walk with you. Look, Lila has a lot on her plate, and quite frankly, it probably hasn't even occurred to her that you would want to stay."

"But the attraction mark appeared on her body as well as mine," Ghosie argues. "She knows this isn't a one-way thing."

I sigh heavily. "Yes, but you need to remember this is all still very new to Lila. Heck, it's only been a little over a couple of months since she's known about any of it. Someone who grew up Skarrian would recognize the attraction as what it is, but Lila has had so many that she thinks it will happen with everyone she finds attractive, and unfortunately, up until now, it has, but once she interacts with more people, she will realize it's not like that."

"I never thought it would ever happen to me. I've never known if someone was attracted to me or if it was a byproduct of my fur. I'm worried it's the same for Lila," he tells me as we step into the elevator, and I shake my head.

"If it was because of your fur, it would have worn off. The marks would fade if the attraction waned, and they cannot be circumvented by magic. Yours was still on Lila's back when she was naked earlier," I assure him, and he nods.

"Yes, hers is still on my back too."

"Look, you're just going to have to woo her. The little darling is delightfully unaware of how attractive and refreshing she is, so I suggest you inform her that you would like to stay on, request for her to find a job for you in the circus, and then seduce her. Prove to her that you want her not just for her ability to give you little ones, which will be one of her biggest fears."

He looks at me with horror as the elevator comes to a stop on our floor. I gesture for him to follow me. I know he has his own room, but I don't want him to hide and wallow in his misery so I'm going to tempt him with our rug rats. I saw the way he looked at them with longing.

"But, ah, er..." He sputters, and I shush him with a hand.

"You and I both know that's not what you see in her." I try to put his mind at ease, because I know that is not the reason he is attracted to her.

"No, I wouldn't care if she never changed into her bear form again. I just want to be part of her life, and I would be perfectly content raising her children as my own if she would let me." I want to smile at the declaration, but I don't want him to think I'm laughing at him. I just love the fact that my wife has so many men who want to make her happy.

"It's been hectic, and I don't think that's going to change anytime soon, so it's going to be up to you to put yourself in her path. Now, I had an idea about how you can help her if you're game," I tell him as we get to our suite—the only one on this level after the ship refurbishment. I wave my hand in front of the sensor, and it reads my aura and opens to allow me in. I hear the chatter of little voices, and love washes over me as I take in the sight of Caspian and Echo sitting at the table with our babies. They seem to be having a meal, and when I look at the clock on the wall, I realize it's definitely dinnertime.

"Daddy X." Jack claps his hands and holds them up. "Fly," he demands, but I shake my head.

"No, you need to finish your dinner first, and then I'll fly you to your bed," I promise him.

They love it when I use telekinesis to zoom them around the room. He turns back and starts shoveling food into his mouth, and Caspian mouths, "Thank you." Both he and Echo look exhausted. I feel a little guilty that both of them keep ending up on children duty. We definitely need to make sure we spread it out a little better.

"Grab a seat," I tell the bear and point to the table before going into the kitchen and getting us both drinks. I could conjure them, but I'd be as big as that slug of a merman king if I never did anything manually.

"You're back!" Echo sounds relieved. "Where are the others?" He looks over our shoulders like he's waiting for the rest of them to come in.

I wince, but my back is to them, so he can't see my reaction. I don't want to upset him, but Lila is right, I need to tell him about Maxsim.

"Teddy, so soft," Cally says as I return to the table with a drink in each hand.

I slide one over to Ghosie, who sat down between the two girls. We leave a seat between each of the children, otherwise chaos will ensue if they can reach each other. Cally and Cordy are both running a hand through Ghosie's fur on his arms, even though he needs a bath to wash the Madovian blood off him. Thankfully that's farther up, and they can only reach his wrists, but he does gently pull away from them. He has this look of pure awe, and I can see by the way he clenches his hands into fists that he's trying to stop himself from reaching for them.

"Here." I hand him a drink, and he takes it.

"Girls, you need to finish your dinner if you want me to fly you to bed," I tell them, and they reluctantly turn their attention back to their plates and keep eating. They are still trying to get the hang of the baby spoons, and more ends up on them than in their mouths, but they refuse our help. They are so independent already.

I sit down next to Echo and take a sip of my drink

before putting my other hand on his nape, knowing he's not going to like what I have to say.

"Shit," Caspian mutters, and their anxiety spikes.

"Maxsim was injured. We were ambushed by Madovians who also had some Nelecs on their payroll."

Echo pushes back from the table, and his tail and ears twitch in agitation. "Where is he? I need to see him." His panic is bitter, and I have to force myself not to gag. It's such a visceral reaction. I hate my wife's mates' negative emotions.

I leap to my feet and stop him by pulling him into my body and wrapping my arms around him. "Easy," I murmur, stroking my hands over his back and sending him calming vibes. He sags in my hold. "He's fine. Lila healed him as soon as she returned, and he is resting in the med bay. Link said you can go sit with him, but you need to be calm. Your alpha is fine. You need to remember stress is not good for your babies."

His breathing, which was ragged, eases, and I feel his heartbeat calm as he takes a couple of deep breaths in and out.

"Is everyone else okay?" Caspian asks.

I look over Echo's shoulder and nod at the kraken. "Yes, everyone is fine, though there was a complication with rescuing Lila's grandma."

"A complication?" he asks as Echo pushes away from me.

"I'm okay," he assures me when I eye him to make sure. "I promise. I'm going to go sit with him, but tell us about the complication first." He goes to the kitchen and pulls out one of the washcloths that we keep in the drawers for the kids. He rinses it under the faucet and then goes to Jack and cleans his face and mouth before removing the bib that was protecting his clothes. Once I'm reassured he's calm, Ghosie and I explain what we found on the planet.

"So they didn't find Lila's grandma?" Caspian starts to gather the children's plates as Echo cleans the girls.

"Lila's new god informed us the being we rescued is Lilessa, the goddess of life, but I'm not convinced that Lilessa and Liliana Adams are not the same person," I tell them, and Ghosie purses his lips and narrows his eyes thoughtfully. This is new information for him too.

"Actually, that would make sense," he remarks. "Otherwise, why would the seer tell Lila that was where her grandma was? Tirrian assured us that the seer is never wrong."

"But the Adams brothers hadn't arrived at the med bay, so I'm not sure if my suspicions are correct or not." I shrug. I'm sure we will find out once the others return to the room.

"But how is that possible? I thought they all grew up together." Caspian puts the plates in the dishwasher before wiping the table.

"I'm not sure. It could be a number of things—implanted memories, reincarnation, or illusion. We won't know anything until she wakes up."

"Are you all okay if I leave now?" Echo asks. He was listening while cleaning up the kids, but I can feel how impatient he is.

"Go," I tell him. "I'll help Cas get the children to bed. I just want to talk to Ghosie about something first."

Echo hurries out of the suite. I wave my hand, and the three little kraken babies lift into the air before I send them over to their playpen. "You can play with the blocks for a little bit while I speak to your teddy, and then if you're good and quiet while we do that, he can help tuck you into bed," I tell the children, and they clap and cheer. When I set them down in their playpen, they follow instructions.

I look at the bear, who is still covered in Madovian blood, and then at myself. I'm still sticky from the Nelec web residue. I wave a hand, cleaning both of us instantly. It shows how upset and distracted I was that I didn't think to do that earlier.

"Come sit," I say, waving at our lounge area. "You too, Caspian."

I tell the kraken about how Lila inadvertently hurt Ghosie, and he rolls his eyes and shakes his head.

"She really is hopeless," he agrees affectionately. "She doesn't realize how appealing she is to all of us, not just her looks, but her soul."

"Now this is my idea. We originally put off the basilisks by telling them we were doing auditions in this quadrant of space, because we didn't want to advertise our real reason for being here."

"Someone obviously found out though, because the presence of the Madovians was not coincidental," the bear points out, and I nod.

"Yes, someone possibly overheard us talking and decided to make some money off us or we have a mole. I don't think it's anyone on this ship, but any number of us have spoken to family members, and I know Rick has been fielding inquiries from performers. If whoever stuck her there found out we were in this area, then it wouldn't be too hard to guess we knew she was there."

"That's true." Cas slides one of his arms along the back of the couch and winds a strand of my hair around his finger. Poor guy is probably a little touch starved or missing Lila and doesn't even notice. He seems to be the one left behind all the time, but he never makes a fuss about it, so of course I don't mention he's playing with my hair. Plus, it feels nice.

"Anyway, we obviously didn't do auditions, but with us being close to wrapping up everything we need to do, we need to look at restarting the circus, and we are down at least one act, probably two."

"No Aquilians, but which other one?" Cas frowns and slides a little closer to me. He's in humanoid form at the moment, and his thigh presses against mine.

"Well, the Vilaxians are a problem too. We've been summoned to appear before the queen and a tribunal, since those damn females won't allow Saxon to dissolve their clan despite meeting his blood rose causing an automatic dissolution."

"Crap, I forgot about them. What about Saxon's brothers' clan? Were they interested in staying on?" he asks, and I shake my head.

"I'm pretty sure they won't be. They considered it beneath them to be circus performers. They were only here because the queen commanded it while Saxon was incapacitated, so that means we need to replace a couple of acts."

"Don't forget the lightning cats. We aren't sure if they are returning or not. Echo won't be able to perform anymore either," Caspian reminds me, and my heart sinks.

"Damn it, that's three big draw acts that aren't guaranteed, which is where I suggest you come in, Ghosie. Lila is going to be too busy with all our personal stuff to even worry about the show. I suggest you approach the Adams brothers and take this off her shoulders. They have a list of applicants, acts that have expressed an interest in being a part of the circus, and while we are on Fluxx, you should arrange for them to audition."

"Actually, Lila already has the list. It's on her tablet in her room. I'll grab it for you." Cas pushes off the couch and leaves the lounge area, and I focus my attention on the bear. I can feel his excitement at my suggestion.

"I would be happy to do that for Lila, and it means I can spend more time with her during the auditions."

I nod, resting my elbows on my knees. "Yes, and afterwards, you can sit down and discuss them and help her make a decision on whom we should employ. You've seen a lot of the galaxy and should know what is and isn't popular, but whatever you decide, it needs to be Earth appropriate, and she can help with that."

Caspian returns and swipes across Lila's tablet. He presses a few buttons and then holds it out. "Put your paw on this," he tells the bear, who quickly follows his instructions. The tablet scans it, and Caspian allows him access before handing it over.

"Now you don't need to find one of us to open it for you. All the information is on there under an icon labeled auditions. Have a chat with Rick about when we'll arrive at Fluxx, and maybe organize them for a week after we arrive. That should give us plenty of time to sort out Silac's problems." I'm so glad that Caspian is instantly on board without me having to explain anything, but then again, he also knows our wife the best by now.

"I don't know how to thank you," Ghosie says to us, taking the tablet from the kraken.

"Pfft, don't even worry about it. We both know how stubborn and unaware our wife is. Don't worry, we will work on her from our end as well, I promise," I assure the bear.

He takes his leave, telling us he wants to get started on looking over all the acts, leaving the two of us alone.

"Let's get these children to bed, and you can tell me more about this god," he suggests.

"I'll try, but Lila probably isn't too far behind, so I can start, but she's going to need you when she returns. She's exhausted," I tell him and wave a hand, picking up our babies who laugh and put their arms out like they are Earth planes.

"Well then, you better cut to the good stuff." He chuckles, following behind as the babies make silly noises as we fly to the bedrooms. Hopefully it won't take them too long to get settled, and I can tell the kraken about his wife's new mate.

# CHAPTER FOUR

## Lila

I wake the next morning with the wet, hot slide of someone's tongue between my legs. I moan and reach for the covers, lifting them so I can look down at whoever is between my legs. I see a flash of purple hair before my chin is grabbed and my head is turned. I look into the glowing red eyes of my Vilaxian husband and feel my fangs click into place. My throat is parched, and my hunger explodes in my stomach. Shoving Caspian away, I roll and pounce on Saxon, burying my fangs in his neck before he can react. He grunts and wraps his arms around me as I take big, gulping draws of his blood, rubbing my pussy against his hard cock as I writhe against this naked body.

I hear chuckles behind me, and I recognize my

warlock's dry tone. "I guess Saxon was right. Her hunger does trump her horniness."

Saxon reaches down and notches his cock at my entrance before slamming home. I moan and feel a small amount of blood trickle out of my mouth. This is going to be messy, but I don't care. He fucks me hard as I feed. I was on empty when I returned last night, and the bloodlust is riding me harder than it ever has before. I hope the other two are ready to offer up a vein as well, because I'm going to need all of them.

Caspian crawls up the bed and wraps his lips around one of my nipples, the pressure making my toes curl with the added stimulation while Xavier slips a hand between Saxon and me and flicks my clit. I swallow a mouthful of blood and groan before flicking out my tongue and sealing the holes on Saxon's throat. He leans in and kisses me roughly. Our tongues battle, and I slice it across one of his fangs. My blood fills our mouths, and he groans and picks up the pace, pulling away and nuzzling into my neck. He slides his fangs into the thick vein there and injects his venom. My body spasms as he takes the first long draw, and my orgasm detonates. Moaning, I wrap my legs around him and hold him in place as my cunt chokes his cock, pulling his seed into my body. He grinds his pelvis against mine, prolonging the pleasure for both of us. I can't believe he held on as long as he did with my venom in his system. Caspian strokes my hair, and Xavier continues to flick my clit lightly, even though his hand is mostly just pinned between us. Saxon groans again as Xavier fondles his balls, and Xavier chuckles. He is such a tease. Finally, he stops drinking and pulls away.

"Did you take what you need?" I ask him and study my mate carefully. He looks good. His eyes and skin are bright, and he smiles at me.

"Yes, my beautiful blood rose. I feel amazing. Thank you for sharing your life force." He gives me a gentle kiss as he pulls from my body.

"Thanks for sharing your huge cock," I tease, and he rolls his eyes.

"I think you need to juice up some more, right? I can tell from the taste of your blood you are very much depleted."

"I could go again," I say, not looking at any of the others. "Sex with Brannock was off the fucking charts, but I didn't seem to take much energy from him," I admit as Saxon sits back on his heels and Cas and Xavier join him, all three of them watching me carefully.

"I'm going to guess it's because you're not officially mated to him. You need your Skarrian mark permanently on him to be able to draw energy from sex," Xavier says carefully. "You do want that, right?"

"Yes I do," I admit quietly, feeling ashamed. I'm never going to get used to this need or stop feeling guilty about it.

"Then you're going to have to wring a few more mutual orgasms out of the man. I'm sure it won't be a hardship."

"It's certainly different, that's for sure," I mutter, and Xavier arches an interested eyebrow.

"How so?" he asks as I lie here, feeling Saxon's cum drip out of me. He must notice too, because he sneakily slides his fingers up and tries to push it back into my body. I'm not sure how he thinks none of us wouldn't notice that.

"You know, I can think of better ways of keeping your cum inside our mate." Xavier smirks at Saxon. "Cas, get your cock in her and help her husband out, will you? Lila is going to tell us about what fucking her Aaz'axian was like."

Cas doesn't even hesitate. He slides between my legs, stroking his large cock with one hand. "Oh, it will be my pleasure." He leans in to give me a kiss as he notches it at my opening and smoothly slides inside. My mouth drops open at the stretch. All of my husbands are big, and my pussy forms around them like a glove—perks of being me, I guess. I try to wrap my legs around his body, but Saxon quickly jumps to hold them in place, his large hands circling my thighs and holding me open like a butterfly.

Cas sits back and brings my lower half up off the bed, and then Xavier leans in and flicks his tongue across my clit. My eyes roll back in my head at the sensations, and I grab a handful of his long hair to hang on to.

"Talk, Lila, or we'll stop," he orders, and I groan. How am I supposed to form coherent sentences when they are wringing delicious pleasure out of my body? "Did you take his spikes? Did he shred your pussy?"

"Yes," I answer. "His cock completely shredded my pussy. It was painful and pleasurable all at once."

"So he filled your pussy with his cum? I bet there was a lot of it. Was he dripping out of you as well?"

"Blood and cum, sounds like my idea of fun," Saxon murmurs, and when I pry my eyes open, he's smirking.

Caspian lazily slides in and out, plucking at my nipples while Xavier teases my clit, and I feel my orgasm start to build again.

"One of my harem members had a spiky cock. It certainly was a unique experience. I wouldn't mind trying it again. I wonder if Brannock is open to men," Xavier murmurs, curiosity in his eyes.

I growl, not liking to hear about his former lovers. "I don't know, you'll have to ask him yourself," I snarl, although I wouldn't mind seeing Brannock fuck Xavier. The warlock prince does like his kink, and I'm sure he's not afraid of a little pain.

"If we add Ghosie to the mix, his aphrodisiac fur may make it so the pain is negligible," he says conversationally, and I've had enough. Although I'm intrigued, I want his attention on me. My inner mimic is pissed at him.

"Hey, instead of pimping yourself out to all the other men, how about you get in here and give your wife some attention?" I growl, and he chuckles. The asshole is deliberately riling me up. I don't know if he meant any of what he said, but I don't hate the idea. I just want them to focus on me for now.

"How do you want me, my love? Shall I ride our kraken while he takes care of you?" he suggests, and I know he wants me to tell him what I want, even though talking about what I want makes me blush.

"No, I want you in my ass," I snap, sick of being teased.

"Of course, how could I deny such a request?" He's grinning, and I have the urge to smack him, but before I can, Saxon lifts me slightly so Xavier can slide beneath me. He snaps his fingers, and a bottle of lube appears on the bed. Cas takes over holding me and continues to slide in and out of my pussy, sucking on my nipples as I writhe in his grasp. We watch as Saxon pours some lube into his hand, and I turn my head to watch him stroke the lube over Xavier's cock. They kiss, and my pussy clenches.

Caspian murmurs to me, "You like watching them, don't you? I don't blame you. It's sexy as fuck."

Saxon pulls away and squirts more lube on his fingers, and then I feel him probe my back entrance, sliding a finger in and stretching me out, and my pussy clenches again. I love being filled in both holes. He pulls out and pushes back in, adding more fingers until I'm stretched enough to take Xavier. I appreciate the effort, but my body doesn't need it. It's designed to take many cocks in all holes. I also kind of like the burn. It makes the pleasure so much better when it does come.

Cas lies me back over Xavier, and he wraps his arms around me as Saxon helps him feed his cock into my ass. I'm well stretched, so the burn is slight, and soon I'm filled with both men.

I moan in delight. "Yes, now fuck me hard," I demand, greedy for more orgasms.

"Not yet, my sweet. You have one more hole to fill, and Saxon has the cock to do it." Xavier pins me to his body and angles my head so it's hanging over his shoulder. Saxon sits behind him and feeds his cock into my mouth.

Now I am well and truly trapped between the three of them and can't move. All I can do is take what they give me as they use my body for their pleasure. The three of them start to move, and I sink into the pleasure, my mind blanking of everything but the three of them sliding in and out. Saxon's cock leaks precum, and I swallow it down eagerly, using my tongue to lash his length. His flavor is delicious, but I want more, so I use a fang to nick his skin, and blood joins the taste. I suck hard, wanting it all, but Cas and Xavier pick up the pace, and I can no longer concentrate on Sax's cock. Now all I can do is feel pleasure pulsing through me.

"Such a good girl, taking your husbands—a fuck toy for our pleasure." Xavier has such a dirty mouth. "We're going to fill you with our cum, and you're going to say thank you," he tells me, his thrusts getting harder.

Caspian matches his pace. My kraken purrs at her

mate then projects, *Breed me, please*, into their heads, my warlock powers being driven by my kraken.

Cas freezes, and his body shudders.

"Cas," Xavier growls in warning. I can't look at them, but he must get himself under control. "You know she doesn't mean it. It's her kraken speaking, even I can tell that."

"Yup, I'm good. I can't implant eggs in this form anyway," he rasps between thrusts.

"Such a naughty girl, trying to drive your mates wild," Xavier murmurs in my ear. "You know all of us would like nothing more than to keep you constantly round with our babies, but we know you don't really want that—not at the moment anyway."

*I do want your babies, but not now. I do want you to fill me with your cum please. I want it*, I beg, and this time they hear my voice in their heads. *I want to drip with it.*

I know exactly how to trigger my mates, and they don't disappoint. All three of them pick up the pace, and I don't know if they are communicating, but as my own orgasm rips me apart, they fill me with their seed. I swallow Saxon's as quickly as I can, the blood and cum mix making me insatiable. He groans and pulls out of my mouth before leaning over and kissing me as my pussy and ass strangle Xavier and Cas, milking them for all their cum.

When they pull away, I'm an exhausted, dripping mess, and I couldn't be happier.

The three of them collapse around me, kissing me

all over and stroking my body, and I float like I'm in the clouds. I'm completely recharged after so many delicious orgasms and all that cum. I'm almost certain their cum helps recharge my body, and that's why I'm so greedy for it all the time. It's something I'm going to have to talk to the old mimic about. He did say sex was the key to our powers, but I'm wondering if cum is the icing on the cake.

# CHAPTER FIVE

## Lila

Cuddling with my babies is high on my agenda today. When I exit the bedroom after showering, leaving Cas, Saxon, and Xavier to nap, and head in the direction of the living area, squeals of delight can be heard coming down the hallway, and I can't stop the smile from spreading across my lips.

I feel like I'm probably letting the team down with how much I have on my plate, but I'm lucky to have such an amazing group of men to pick up the slack. I did have a moment of worry when I woke and all three of my original guys were in bed with me, knowing both Maxsim and Echo are in the med bay, but then I quickly let it go. I have more mates now, and it's their turn to take up daddy duty. The others are getting a trial by fire at their new status. Brannock already knows what he's doing, and Tirrian, well, he will either quickly get with the program or suffer in silence if he knows what's good for him.

I'm pleasantly surprised, though, when I stop in the doorway. Tirrian is sitting on the floor, surrounded by blocks and toys and cardboard books, entertaining my three troublemakers. Cordy, Cally, and Jack are thoroughly enthralled by little smoke dragons that swoop and dive and fly around their heads. The smile on his face is kind of blinding, and I get a little starstruck. He's usually so surly and grumpy, and seeing the joy he feels from playing with my children is nothing short of intoxicating.

When Jack stands up to reach for one of the dragons, he's quick to snatch him up and sit him in his lap, quietly warning him that the dragons are hot. I have no idea how he's doing it, but my inner dragon purrs with delight and coos something about being a good daddy and giving him his own hatchling. My kraken pokes her head up and murmurs her agreement. The horny bitch doesn't care who knocks us up as long as we get a good dicking when it happens.

*Settle down, there will be no more babies coming out of my hoo-ha anytime soon. You have four more coming shortly, so that's going to have to keep you happy.*

They both sulk, and I roll my eyes.

*Doesn't mean we won't be practicing*, I assure them, which seems to mollify them for now.

I push off the frame and head toward the kitchen to get a cup of coffee, but I freeze when I catch sight of a strange human in my kitchen. My heart starts to race, and I can't decide what to do. The man's back is broad, and he has tousled black hair. He wears jeans and a shirt that stretches deliciously across the expanse of his back, hugging his golden biceps like a lover. My eyes drop to his ass cheeks, which are perfectly cupped by the jeans he's wearing. My gaze stops on his bare feet as my brain tries to make sense of what I'm seeing.

"Brannock, I think you are freaking out my mate with your appearance," Tirrian grumbles.

I blink in surprise as the human man turns around and smiles at me. His green eyes sparkle with mirth, and I just about swallow my tongue. He pushes a hand through his hair and holds out a cup of coffee as I study his face. He has black stubble across his jawline, but it doesn't hide his pouty lips that sit below an aristocratic nose and sharp cheekbones. He looks like he could be modeling some expensive fragrance in some high fashion magazine. The look on his face is so completely different from the sneer and aggression that I originally saw when he wore this glamour, he's practically a different person.

"Brannock?" I ask, a little unsure as I take the offered cup. I mean, who else could it be? I recognize his glamour from the prison, but I'm not sure why he's wearing it.

"Hi, I guess you're probably wondering why I'm wearing this," he says as the kids notice me and shout their hellos.

"Mama, look, dragons," Jack calls and points at the

smoke entertaining them. "Roar!" he growls adorably and hisses like he's trying to blow fire. I'm not sure how he knows that's what dragons do, but I'm sure his new father has something to do with it.

"They are great, baby," I call, still slightly distracted by Brannock. I'm pleased that he's here and moved in, but we still haven't done the mate thing, aka fucked five times, and I'm kind of nervous that maybe he's going to change his mind or that life with me isn't what he thought it would be. It's going to be a real trial by fire. He's either going to run screaming or possibly throw me over his shoulder and drag me off to his bedroom so we can finish mating. I'm secretly hoping for the latter of course.

"Why don't you come and sit down. I'm making scrambled eggs for the kids. It's one of Chloe's favorites, and I'm pretty damn good at it." He points to the eggs on the counter in front of him.

"You're making them?" I take a seat. The children's chatter in the background provides a soothing balm to my soul. None of them seem upset about my lack of attention. "I didn't even know we could do that. I thought the replicator did everything for us."

I lift my cup to my mouth, swallow a large mouthful of coffee, and sigh, feeling some of the tension easing out of my body. There's nothing better than starting my day with a mug of coffee. I think it's because it's familiar and reminds me of my life before everything that's happened. It's reassuring and comforting that despite all the changes, I'm still me.

"Yeah, you can still get things to make from the kitchen if you feel like cooking, but with no staff or deliveries at the moment, the stores are pretty bare except for a lot of stuff in the deep freeze. Eggs come from the chickens on the bio zone level. No one else is eating them, so they are going to waste. The automatons collect them every day, and I've been going up and moving them to the cold storage. I've been cracking them into containers and freezing them. I figured we can use them for baking or just get rid of them later."

My eyes widen, and I look at this man with a whole new perspective. It hadn't occurred to me that he would be the most like a human male. How domesticated is that? I'm not even sure Mark would have known you can freeze eggs if you crack them.

"Why this look?" I ask him. "You know I'm just as attracted to you in your other form, right?" I want him to know this. He had to hide himself for so long while he was on Earth, and I don't want him to feel like he needs to hide here as well.

"Yeah, I know, but it's kind of comfortable to be back in this one. I wore it for so long that it became natural. Also, I was thinking it wouldn't hurt for people not to know you have an Aaz'axian in your pocket. The Madovians were certainly surprised by the two of us. Plus, I don't have to worry about the children getting hurt by my spikes."

"But I thought they didn't hurt. They haven't hurt me." I think about touching him all over when he was naked. I also hugged him previously, didn't I?

"No, because I'm attracted to you, but anyone else probably would have been damaged," he explains. "I'm almost certain the children would be fine, since they aren't perceived as dangerous, but I don't want to risk it. I wore a glamour all through Chloe's childhood, and I can do it for these children too."

I narrow my eyes, thinking there is more to this than just that. He was happy walking around in his natural form previous to us fucking. I hope I didn't make him feel inadequate or something.

He sighs and looks at Tirrian. I follow his gaze, and Tirrian nods encouragingly at him. What is going on? Are these two suddenly besties?

Brannock stops cracking eggs for a moment and looks me dead in the eye. "I don't want you to feel like I'm with you because you are the only female of my species that I have come across. I like you for you and couldn't care less if you never change into that form again," he announces, and I blink, kind of shocked and not sure what to say. That's certainly a declaration, but I hadn't been worried about it, though it must be nice for him to be able to have sex without worrying about destroying a woman's vagina.

"But you can't orgasm in this form," I remind him, and he winces.

"Actually, I can. The glamour doesn't stop the barbs on my cock. It just means your insides will be ripped to shreds. I never let myself get that far with my wife. Remember, I got very good at faking it."

I grimace at the thought. I wonder if I can change

just a part of me. I know Oshan said it wasn't possible, but I've been able to use some of my powers in this form, so I think it is worth investigating.

He returns to cracking eggs into a bowl. He has ten in there already with ten more waiting to be cracked. I guess he's feeding himself, a dragon, and three hungry kraken shifters as well as me. The others can feed themselves when they eventually surface.

I get up and move around to him, wrapping my arms around him from behind and leaning my cheek against his broad back. Oh, this is nice. I sigh and close my eyes.

"Well, just so you know, I like you either way, and I don't think you're with me just to procreate. You've heard me complain enough to know there aren't any babies being pushed out of this body for the time being."

His body shakes with his laughter, and he stops what he's doing and spins around so I'm pressed against his chest. Hmmm, his chesticles feel wonderful. This man is ripped in this form. I can't actually feel any of his original form underneath him. Maybe he actually changes forms completely, so it's not a glamour but a full change. I think about his cock—well, almost a full change. I wonder if Chloe is the same and has two forms because she's part human. I'm nervous about meeting his daughter, but also desperate to get her out of Agent Smith's clutches, and that is weighing on me. We need to get all of this other crap wrapped up so we can do that.

He presses a kiss to the top of my head. I'm not short, but all of these guys are so much taller than I am. They make me feel dainty, which is nice. "Oh, I am very aware of that. Now grab a seat unless you want to put some of that bread in the toaster." I pull back and notice a loaf of bread on the counter. It has a label on it I recognize from Earth.

"What the heck?" I release him reluctantly, and he returns to crack the last couple of eggs before adding a splash of cream into the bowl.

"There are all sorts of things in the cold storage in the kitchen. There is lots of Earth ice cream too. I guess the boss men must have stocked up while we were there."

"The cold storage must be huge for a ship this big," I mutter as I remove the plastic tie from the loaf of bread and pop some into the toaster sitting on the counter. This all feels so normal, and for the first time since I left my apartment I shared with Susie, I feel like I'm at home. Who would have thought that it would take an alien man making me breakfast while wearing his Earth glamour to make me feel settled? Don't get me wrong, I love all of my mates, and I feel like I have a place here, but the normal, mundane exercise of making toast just really drives home the fact that Earth is no longer where I belong.

I watch as Brannock whisks the eggs and cream before adding a shake of salt and pepper. I didn't even know we had any of these things in our cupboards. Tirrian wrangles the children over to the table. Their chubby little legs are adorable as they all race to get there first. I pop the toast down and help Cordelia into her chair. She gives me a kiss and wraps her chubby little arms around my neck, and I just breathe in her scent. Much like Caspian, she smells of sun and sea, as well as having that delicious baby scent.

My heart melts as she claps her hands to my cheeks to purse my lips and plant a sloppy kiss on them. "Love you, Mama," she says before I place her in her chair.

"Love you too, baby," I tell her, brushing a hand across her mop of purple hair exactly like her father's.

"Mama, can you watch fish movie with us today?" Cally asks as she tugs on the leg of my sweatpants. I bend down and pick her up before swinging her around and placing kisses all over her onesie-covered belly. She giggles with laughter and grabs my hair with her hands. I extract her and place her in her seat.

"Of course I can watch the fish movie with you." I don't really want to watch *Finding Nemo* for the billionth time, but it's better than *The Little Mermaid*.

"Daddy Dragon and Daddy Bran are going to watch them with us too," Jack tells me from Tirrian's arms as he places him in his seat before sitting down next to him. "They haven't seen them before." He sounds like he can't believe they've never seen such cinematic masterpieces. I stifle a laugh. I bet the others are relieved that there are two more men to watch movies with now. My kids are slightly OCD when it comes to what they like to watch.

"Well, they are in for a real treat then," I reply, returning to the toast and buttering it now that it has popped up. Brannock heats a large pan on the stove before pouring the egg mixture in.

Before long, we are all sitting at the table, enjoying a nice, uneventful family meal. For a small moment in time, I forget all of our worries and enjoy just being with the ones I love. Future Lila is probably going to be annoyed at me, but I need this.

# CHAPTER SIX

## Lila

I'm in absolute bliss being surrounded by my babies as we watch Marlin, Nemo's father not Nikos', try to find his way to Sydney to rescue Nemo. The kids think the turtle is awesome, and they asked if they can have a pet Bruce to put into the Aquilian tank. I quickly shut that idea down, telling them that Sweetpea would be sad if we let another large animal swim in her tank when she isn't there.

Zeydan appeared briefly to inform me he was going to sit with Liliana and give Link a break. I still don't know where I stand with the god. He's become slightly standoffish since we found the woman, and I wonder if he thinks he was wrong about me being his mate. He seems to have other things on his mind now, which probably isn't such a bad thing. I just mated with Tirrian and still want to take things further with Brannock, as well as keep all my other mates happy. It's a juggling job, and I'm not sure I'm up for the task.

He leaves, and I watch him go, his brightly colored tails waving behind him. He hasn't let them free yet, and I wonder if they have their own consciousness or if they are an extension of him.

"He looks a little lost," Tirrian murmurs to me. The children have rotated between the three adults throughout the movie, and both men are completely smitten with their new family. My children are expert manipulators. I wonder if that is Xavier's doing.

"Yes, he does," I agree.

"It must be a huge shock for him to see the goddess of life after her being gone for so many years. He said the six of them were a family." Tirrian sounds as curious as I am. We're all desperate for her to wake up and shed some light on the whole Lilessa-Liliana drama.

"Yes, he mentioned she disappeared just before the Una's war with the Aaz'axians. Not being able to ask her where she's been must be driving him crazy," Brannock chimes in as Cally climbs across the couch and into his lap. He looks shocked for a moment but quickly cuddles her against his chest as she closes her eyes and sticks her thumb into her mouth.

My mind isn't on the movie anymore, and I'm trying to make sense of what happened. My grandpas insist she is my grandma, yet Zeydan claims she's his nonblood-related sister. How can she be both? She supposedly went missing over six hundred years ago, and I know Skarrians age slowly, but my grandpas are not that old, and they claim she and her sister Vivian grew up with them. Her body is healed, we just need to wait for her mind to catch up. I wonder if the flamegem flower which healed John could help, but that would mean returning to Rilu and my cave, and we can't do that until the spring equinox.

I don't want to wait that long to get to the bottom of this. We just need to hope she wakes up soon.

The door to the suite opens, and Maxsim bursts in, snarling and looking around the room like he's spoiling for a fight. Tirrian jumps to his feet.

"Whoa, alpha, easy. Your mate is fine," he says in a tone that confuses me.

Brannock stands up, keeping one hand on Cally's back before scooping Cordelia up from my embrace. "I'll take the kids to their room for a nap," he tells me before calling to Jack, "Come on, buddy. How about you show me where you all sleep?" He gives Jack a task, which quickly distracts him from the snarling kitty.

He puffs up his chest, slides off the sofa, and hurries in the direction of the rooms. "Come on, I'll show you," he calls, their speech getting better every day.

Now that the kids are safely out of the line of fire, I can pay attention to what is going on in the doorway. Echo has his hands against Maxim's chest and is talking quietly to him. Link slides past both of them. His eyes are bloodshot, his skin has lost its sheen, and his hair is tousled, like he's been running his hand through it constantly. I forget about the posturing cat for a moment, confident that Echo can manage him while I talk to my cyborg husband.

"God, you look exhausted. Is everything okay?" I ask him, concern coloring my tone.

He walks up to me, gathers me in his arms, and holds me. I feel some of the tension drain out of him, and I'm pleased I can do this for him.

"Yeah. I'm fine. I haven't slept for a few days, and it's catching up with me. I'll grab a nap while Zeydan is sitting with your grandma. Eric is in there as well, and the two of them seem to be fine, so I don't feel like I need to run interference. I set alarms, and my monitor will alert me if anything changes."

"Maybe we do need to get you another nurse," I suggest, but then I remember that Mark and Susie made a comment about wanting to join us. Maybe I should offer Mark a job as the second doctor now that Link has a family, but they probably want to stay with Aura and their family.

"I just need a few hours, and I'll be good again, but Maxsim woke in a mood. I think he was worried because he never saw what happened to you once he was injured, and he doesn't remember you healing him in the med bay. Soothe his ruffled fur for a little bit, and he should calm down." He gives me an absent kiss on the lips and stumbles in the direction of the bedrooms.

"Can you see that he gets to bed okay? Put him

with the others in mine," I ask Tirrian, and he looks between me and the raging alpha behind me.

"You got this?" he asks, double-checking, which I appreciate. I let my lightning cat form wash over me, my clothes disappearing as I perfume the air with the scent of my omega.

"Yup, I'm going to let him fuck me into submission. A good time for everybody." I grin, and he chuckles, wearing a rueful grin on his face.

"Yes it is. I will have to get pissy with you more often if that's the kind of response it gets." He winks and follows Link down to the bedroom, and I'm relieved that he will be looked after.

I turn my attention back to the cats to find them both looking at me with hunger in their eyes. I want them to chase me, but there isn't enough room in the suite to get the full effect. Thankfully their former quarters are ready and waiting for Minx and her streak to return to, so if I can get past the two of them, then I can create a chase they are going to have to work for. Shit, but Echo and the babies. Will this be too much for them? He's starting to show now, but not a huge amount.

Maxsim growls, and I switch my attention back to him. He stalks forward, but there is still a decent amount of furniture between us. I edge around it and reach out to Echo's mind. Now's as good a time as any to try my other powers.

*Can you hear me?* I ask him, tapping into my warlock powers. I see his eyes widen and know that he did. He's still trying to calm Maxsim and is murmuring to him.

"Max, you're going to scare her," Echo says, but it's actually the opposite. My nipples pebble, and I feel slick drip down my legs in excitement. I am ready to be chased and forced into submission, but not too quickly.

*Can you distract him so I can run for your former quarters? Are you okay playing these games? Are the babies safe?*

*Yes and yes, this is going to be fun.* He's practically panting, and I can feel how excited he is by the idea.

Echo puts himself in front of Maxsim again and murmurs more words of reassurance. "Look, you can see your pretty omega. She's fine. She even got herself a new mate during the attack," he tells him, and Maxsim's snarling revs up a notch. "Okay, shit, maybe I shouldn't have said that." Echo is doing a good job of distracting him as I slowly make my way around the furniture in the opposite direction of Maxsim. He's tracking my every move, his gaze remaining on me despite Echo getting all up in his face.

I was successful in using mind speak in this form, so I wonder if I can also teleport. I stop moving and concentrate on how it feels to use the teleporting power. I haven't gone very far, and I'm not as skilled as Xavier, but I bet I can at least land in the hallway. That will get me out of the room and allow me to run. Maxsim can then track me down using his nose. It will be good for him to have to work for it for a change.

He's used to his omegas presenting themselves for his entertainment, and let's face it, snarly, aggressive Maxsim is intoxicating. I can't wait for him to angry fuck me.

I grasp the power and marvel that it's as easy as when I'm in my warlock form. It washes over me, and I see both Maxsim's and Echo's eyes widen in shock before Maxsim expresses his anger with a loud roar just as I dissolve into particles.

I reform in front of the elevator and push the button. Another loud roar echoes down the corridor from our suite. It doesn't sound like he's made it outside yet. I hope for his sake he didn't wake the children, otherwise Tirrian's going to cook his behind. The elevator doors open, and I quickly enter, allowing them to close just as I hear footsteps running toward me. It sounds like more than just two feet, so I'm wondering if he changed forms when he got out of the room. The sound of lightning crackling makes me smile. He's mad.

"Maxsim, be careful, you haven't been healed all that long," I hear Echo call to him. He obviously stayed in humanoid form. Hopefully he changes so he can frolic in the snow with us. I haven't actually tried my cat form yet, but now is as good a time as any. I'll wait until I get to their old quarters before I change. I need to be able to open the door.

The elevator opens on the right floor, and my pulse pounds in my veins as I hurry toward their old rooms. I'm breathing heavily when I get there and consider slowing so he will catch me, but my inner cat wants him to work for it, so I keep up the pace. At their door, I swipe a furry hand over the sensor, and it opens, a blast of frigid air and a flurry of snow coming out. Grinning, I step into the arctic tundra and allow the door to close behind me. It's cold, but in this form, I don't really feel it. Instead, I feel a wave of energy and allow the change to wash over me, but like changing into dragon form, it fucking hurts.

I clamp my lips shut, holding in the scream of pain as my body reshapes itself. I find myself on four paws while my eyesight, hearing, and sense of smell increase exponentially. I take a careful step forward and stumble slightly, but I allow my lightning cat to push forward, sending Lila to the back, and our gait straightens out as we pick our way carefully across the uneven surface. The presence is familiar, the one that insisted the cats were hers, and she easily adapts to the conditions, her strides lengthening until she's running and leaping through the deep snow. There are large banks that would have stopped human Lila in her tracks, but in this form, we easily manage them.

She arrives at the entrance to the den as another roar echoes loudly through the habitat. Maxsim has arrived, and with his size and experience, it won't take him long to find us. She shivers with delight and considers hiding inside the dens, but instead, she leaps up the rock wall, jumping from surface to surface until she's high up, then she enters a small cutout at the very top of the rock face. I didn't even know this was here. You certainly can't see it from the ground.

She belly crawls down a tight tunnel, but it eventually opens into a cave. It's a large, open space slightly taller than head height, and there is a pile of furs and nothing else. Our nose itches, and we sneeze a couple of times as Echo's and Maxsim's scents tickle my senses. She pads over to the furs and stretches out on them, rolling around and spreading our scent. Theirs is old and faded, and they obviously haven't been here in a while, but I can smell that when they were here, they fucked. Maybe this was where they came to be safe from Natalia.

We start to purr and place our chin on our paws as we wait. My cat wants to fuck in this form, and I don't need to be here for that. Instead, I close my eyes and allow myself to shut off like I do when my kraken takes charge.

# CHAPTER SEVEN

## Maxsim

A snarl escapes my mouth as I bolt upright in bed. The smell of antiseptic and sadness bombard my senses, causing unease to coil in my stomach as I look around. It is quickly replaced with Echo's frost and crisp apple scent, and some of the panic wanes.

"Hey, easy. You're safe and healed. You're back on the ship." My pregnant omega runs a hand through the fur on my arm, and his touch settles me a little more, but I'm missing my other omega, and when I lost consciousness, she was missing while we were battling a hoard of Madovian reptile bitches. I won't feel completely secure until I see her with my own eyes.

"Lila?" I shove back the sheet covering me and swing my legs to the side. My vision wavers slightly, and I close my eyes, but it soon settles, and I peel them open to look around the med bay. Link is standing over another patient in a bed, and my heart starts to race as a growl rumbles in my chest. I go to push off, but Echo shoves me back firmly. I blink in surprise at the aggression from my omega.

"Calm yourself," he snaps. "That is not Lila. She is fine. She went to our suite to get some rest. She was exhausted after switching forms a few times and healing you." My usually unshakeable omega looks flustered, and I feel slightly guilty, but it doesn't calm me down.

"I need to see her," I tell him, unable to control the snarl that follows. He has the audacity to roll his eyes at me, and I growl at him.

"Of course you do, but are you just going to wander through the hallways naked?" He waves a hand at me, and I look down. I shifted, so of course I'm naked.

"Yes," I reply, not caring about my naked state. There is no one else on the ship to look apart from family anyway. I'm a shifter, so being naked is natural. He chuckles and steps back. I push off the bed, pausing as my paws touch the ground, but unlike my dizzy spell before, this time, I'm fine.

Before I get any farther, Link approaches me.

"Good, you're awake. I've monitored you all night, and all you needed to do was rest. Lila healed everything else." He looks me up and down like he's marveling at Lila's healing abilities, and I only just stop myself from preening under his admiring gaze. What the hell?

He pauses on the side I was attacked, puts out a hand, and brushes it over the healed injury. I almost jump when my body reacts to his touch. It doesn't recoil but leans into it. I frown, confused by my reaction. I inhale and smell my mate all over the cyborg. Maybe that's why I'm having such an intense reaction to him. I hadn't noticed before how much he smells like Lila now that they are mated. We've been so busy, I don't think we've been around each other without everyone else's scents muddling the air. I feel my cock twitch, and my eyes widen with surprise. Am I attracted to the cyborg? I know he and Lila's other mates play with one another occasionally, but I haven't been interested in that before. I'm happy with both my omegas, and I don't need anyone else —not to mention other races aren't necessarily compatible with alpha lightning cats because of our knots. They will do damage to someone not designed to take them.

Before I can speak, he continues. "You can head back to our suite now if you want. No need to hang around here."

"You should go get some rest too, Link."

I startle and snarl in the direction of the voice. I hadn't even noticed Eric Adams sitting in a chair on the other side of the form on the bed. That must be his wife. Why is she still asleep, and why is he so sad? I would have thought it would be an occasion for celebration.

Echo must see my confused look, because he leans forward and whispers, "I'll explain later." I give him an almost imperceivable nod.

"I think I might. Liliana has been stable all night, and there is no sign of change. I haven't slept in days, and I'm starting to worry I'll make a mistake with my fatigue."

Before anyone can respond to him, the doors open and the god of earth appears in the doorway. I freeze for a moment. Lightning cats still worship the old gods, but Tito, the god of water, is our deity. Although he hasn't been seen for hundreds of years, we still give thanks to him during special occasions and ritual holidays. Seeing evidence that he may still be alive was shocking to say the least. For Zeydan to announce that our mate is his as well is something I still need to adjust to. Despite him claiming to be diminished of power, if he ever gets them back, what's to stop him from getting rid of the rest of us so he would have Lila to himself? The gods are known for being ruthless. Look at what they did to both the Aaz'axians and the Carevasta bears—cursed them to face extinction and persecution.

He looks around the room, his gaze stopping on me, and he studies me like I'm an experiment he doesn't know what to do with.

"Contrary to your thoughts, I would not dispose of you if I got my full powers back. Lila loves you all, and losing you would destroy her. I want my mate's happiness more than I want to keep her to myself. I am not that selfish, and I am perfectly capable and content to share. If my true powers ever return to me, and I reunite with my fellow gods, then we will need to decide if we wish to retake our control of the galaxy, but to be honest, I'm not interested. The council has things well in hand. I don't need to be worshiped."

I snarl, annoyed that he read my mind, or maybe I was just projecting loudly. Either way, at least I know where he stands, and I feel my muscles relax ever so slightly.

"Poor alpha. You're not having the best of times since you woke up, are you?" My omega murmurs behind me, and I can't miss the amusement in his voice. Did he smell my reaction to the cyborg?

"I will watch over Lilessa... Liliana, so that you may get some rest. I will summon you if her condition changes." Zeydan takes the seat next to Eric, giving him a nod in greeting. "You should go too. You will be no good to her if you make yourself sick with worry. She's going to need her mates when she wakes."

Lilessa and Liliana? The goddess of life and Lila's grandma. I look to my omega for help. I must have missed something while I was injured.

"I'll explain it on our way to the suite. Come on," he tells me, tugging my hand, and we don't wait for Eric's response to the god. I feel Link follow us out, my body very much attuned to his presence.

Between the two of them, they tell me what they know about what happened after I lost consciousness and Saxon returned to the ship with me.

"So Brannock and Lila are mated now?" I ask, trying to get everything straight. Apparently they both went into berserker mode and made quick work of the rest of the Madovians then fucked in the aftermath of the carnage. How very primal. I approve.

"Aaz'axians don't have fated mates." Link sounds more tired than I've ever seen him. "So Lila will need to mate him in the Skarrian way."

"Lots of sex and mutual orgasms," Echo announces happily, and I can scent his arousal in the air. Just like Lila during her pregnancy, he is also easily aroused. I growl at the thought of my other omega having an orgasm with another man, and both of them look at me in surprise.

I'm not normally territorial with Lila, but after being injured and not seeing her when I awoke is messing with my mind. I'm sure once I am close to her again, and I can reassure myself she is fine, I will calm down. I stalk down the corridor to our suite as soon as the elevator doors open, hearing Echo and Link following in a hurry.

"Max," Echo calls, but I ignore him. I just need to see Lila, hold her in my arms, and make sure every single hair on her head is unharmed. There's a low, possessive growl rumbling from my chest that I can't stop. I think the fact that she mated the dragon and then was intimate with the Aaz'axian is urging my inner cat to stamp our own mark on her. All I want to do is fuck her and fill her with my seed so she'll smell like me again. I know I have to share, and usually I'm okay, but my inner animal likes to rear his head occasionally and force the issue.

The door to our suite slides open after I swipe my paw across the sensor, and I step into the room. A snarl leaves my mouth when I catch sight of her on the couch. I stop as the sound of the babies' favorite movie reaches my ears, but not even the vision of them snuggling with her can ease my worry.

The dragon jumps up, putting his hands out and warning me to be calm. He must sense how on edge I am. I'm sure he was feeling that way too, but he spent the morning with her reassuring himself of her safety and well-being. It's my turn now. I know he's just being protective, but I ignore him and focus on the strange man sitting next to Lila. If I couldn't smell that it's Brannock in a different form, I would be tempted to rip his heart out of his chest. I need to reclaim my omega, and I need to do it now, and nobody is going to stop me.

I watch on as Brannock scoops up the girls and Jack hurries off to their bedroom for a nap. Lila has a conversation with Link, and he and Tirrian disappear in the same direction, leaving the three of us alone. Echo has been muttering soothing words to me and rubbing my back, but none of it is calming me like it usually does. Lila turns her attention back to me and smirks.

I snarl and stalk forward, moving around the furniture between us.

"Max, you're going to scare her," Echo cautions,

but I'm too far gone. I don't take my eyes off Lila as her cat form appears. My cock starts to harden as I scent her, and I pick up my pace, but all of a sudden she shimmers and disappears. I stop, and my mouth drops open.

"Did she just teleport in cat form?" Echo asks.

I roar loudly, furious my prey got away from me as a thrill of excitement rushes through my body. Now I'm going to chase her, and when I get her, I'm going to pin her down and fuck her full of my seed.

I rush back to the door, not caring about pushing any of the furniture over. Echo steps out of my way, but I hear him follow behind me. Good. When I'm done with Lila, I'll pin him down and fuck him full of my seed too. Both of my omegas will be begging for my bite before I'm through.

I track Lila's scent to the elevators. I can smell how excited and turned on she is, and I grin with anticipation.

"You know that smile on your face is half crazy, right?" Echo points out as the doors close and I stare at the buttons, trying to figure out where Lila would have gone. "You're going to scare her off if she sees you like that."

I snarl and grab hold of my omega, pinning him against the wall with my throbbing cock jammed between the two of us.

I kiss him hard, and he relaxes into me, moaning softly. Although I couldn't hear them, I could feel that Echo and Lila were having a telepathic conversation before. I have no idea how, but Echo knows where our mate is, and I'm not opposed to using dirty tactics to get that information out of him.

I reach under his loin cloth and stroke his rapidly hardening cock. He groans a little louder into my mouth, and I pull away, sliding my other hand into his mane and grabbing it so I can look him in the eye.

"Where is our omega?" I demand, and his eyes widen in shock. "Tell me, and I will fuck you with my knot once I've dealt with Lila."

His perfume fills the air, and my eyes drift closed, the heady scent of both my omegas making me unsteady and slightly scent drunk.

"Tell me, Echo." I use my alpha bark that a bonded omega can't resist. He just looks at me with his big doe eyes.

"She's in our old habitat."

I reward him with another kiss.

"Good boy," I praise him, and he preens as I press the button for the correct level. It's but a matter of moments before I'm stalking through the corridors to our old room with Echo still firmly in my grasp. I can smell Lila, although it's fading, but it definitely leads to the door to our old room. I pause and release my omega.

"You can have a head start, but you better run, because if I catch you before I find Lila, I will punish you," I promise him.

His pupils dilate, and he breathes heavily as he absently strokes his cock through his loin cloth.

I bark again to get his attention. "Run, Echo."

The door slides open, and cold air seeps out. We have the charms Xavier gave us to regulate our temperature, but the cold still doesn't affect me. I feel invigorated and ready to stalk my intended prey.

Echo doesn't wait, my bark having the desired effect, and he hurries through the snow while I pace back and forth and give him a fighting chance. When I can't wait any longer, I let out an ear-splitting roar, a bolt of lightning bursting from my tail, then I shift and stalk my prey.

# CHAPTER EIGHT

### Echo

My fur prickles with excitement as I race through the snow and ice, following Lila's scent which sits heavily on the cold surface. I can tell by the paw prints in the snow that she's in her cat form, which almost had me stopping with surprise, but I know Maxsim is impatient and won't give me any leeway, so I keep running. I don't think Lila has taken cat form before, and I'm slightly disappointed she didn't wait for Maxsim to help her through the shift. An alpha's pheromones make the shift slightly less painful, but Lila is tough. She's shifted into both dragon and kraken form now as well as Aquilian, so I'm sure she managed just fine.

I track her through the icy landscape until we get

to our former den. When they did the rebuild, they changed the layout to one large den for Minx and the others when they return, but they left one den for Max and me to retreat to if we ever need a break from family life, as well as a small cave at the top of the structure. Max and I found it when we were exploring the renovations recently, and it's to that small cave that I follow Lila's trail. She seemed to have no trouble climbing the structure in her cat form, and I feel a warm wave of pride. Our mate has adapted so well to everything thrown in her path. It's not as easy for me, but I unsheathe my claws and drag myself up and over the rocks. My body isn't quite as agile now that the babies are starting to grow. I won't be able to attempt this further in my pregnancy, but I don't care. I wouldn't change anything for the world.

I hear Maxsim roar behind me, and my spine tingles and my cock gets harder. I can't wait to watch him dominate Lila. Hopefully he'll allow me to help, and then the two of them will make me feel good. My body is constantly in a state of arousal. Lila wasn't wrong when she said being pregnant made you continually horny. I wake up wanting to be fucked any way I can get it. Scenting Maxsim's interest in Link earlier almost made me moan out loud, but I clamped my lips shut so not to advertise it to everyone else.

The cyborg has been on my radar since I watched him knot Lila before she mated with the two of us. I would like to know what it would feel like to be with him too. I didn't think there was any chance because Maxsim is such a possessive alpha, but much like Caspian, now that I am pregnant, he seems more amenable to sharing the love.

I reach the entrance to the cave, and the tunnel isn't tall enough for me to walk down, so I shift and crawl through the narrow hall leading to a cozy nest area. Maxsim and I spent a couple of delightful hours using this cave. It gave us a moment of reprieve from all the hustle and bustle of our family. It's taken a little adjustment, and as much as we both love being part of such a large family, it was just the two of us for so long that sometimes, we crave our solitude. Lila and her mates don't mind in the least. In fact, Xavier suggested it might not be a bad idea to create a space like that for all of the others to use—just a room to escape to when we need a moment of quiet. We have three kids with two more who will join us very soon, and then my two in a few months. A moment of quiet is not going to be a possibility in our family suite.

Lila's scent gets stronger and stronger as the tunnel opens up, and I find her lying calmly, facing the entrance. Although I changed forms, I am still in the driver's seat. I haven't let my more primal side take over yet. I get down on my belly and crawl across the ground, hoping Lila will let me into the nest while I take in the sight of her magnificent cat. Unlike most lightning cats that come in various shades of blue and white, Lila's cat is the same color as her hair—a beautiful, shimmery pearlescent white with streaks of pink, orange, and blue running through it. She's stunning. When I look into her beautiful green eyes, which are exactly the same color in any form, I can see that her cat is in charge. Her tail lazily flicks back and forth as she licks her paws, grooming herself. She seems relaxed, but I can feel the tension in the air, her lightning barely being held in check.

She doesn't snarl at me, so I continue crawling over to her, lying down next to her and butting my head against hers. She drops the paw she was licking, grabs my head, and starts licking my ears. We both freeze as we hear Maxsim roar once more, and the air fills with her perfume. She is waiting for him and is excited. I bet she has slick dripping down her back legs. Max is going to fuck her in cat form. He's so primal and aggressive in this form. I hope she's prepared for a lot of biting and scratching.

I purr and arch into her as her rough tongue rearranges the fur on my head, but my attention is completely on the tunnel. Max will be here any moment, but I bet he's in stealth mode and creeping down the tunnel so he can pounce on us. It's dark in here, and only our excellent eyesight allows us to see in the dark. There's only a soft phosphorescent glow to the ice on the rocks overhead, but it's not enough to see for normal beings.

I hear a slight scuff, like he dragged a claw against the ground, and my whole body becomes taut with anticipation. Lila catches on and drops her paws, staring at the opening like I do. Her body practically vibrates and sparks with small arcs of lightning.

Like a god appearing out of the darkness, Maxsim's huge body pushes through the tunnel. It's a tight fit for him, and his eyes lock onto the two of us waiting patiently. He leaps, pouncing on Lila, but the good girl doesn't give in immediately though. She yowls, and they roll across the cave floor, fur flying and fangs snapping. She tries to dislodge him, and he tries to overpower her to pin her to the ground and mount her. I shuffle out of the way, happy to watch, knowing I will get my turn when he's established his dominance. Normally an omega would comply and present themselves to their alpha, or I would anyway, but because she's dual omega and alpha, I believe she's struggling with allowing him to dominate her without proving he's stronger. That's how multiple alphas behave in a streak. One has to prove they are more dominant to be on top, and while Lila is a strong alpha, she's also an omega, and Maxsim is the ultimate alpha. It won't take long for him to subdue her.

Lightning flashes, illuminating the cave, and I squeeze my eyes shut so it doesn't destroy my vision. I'm not worried about it hitting me. Now that all three of us are mated, their lightning can't hurt me, nor can they hurt each other. The hissing and snarling gets louder, and I huff with amusement as Lila momentarily gets the upper hand. I'm not sure if Maxsim has ever been dominated. I wonder if he would submit for Lila. She can take both male and female forms, though she tends to stick to female ones. I'd like to see her rail our alpha into submission. I squirm at the thought, and they both lift their heads and look at me for a split second as my perfume fills the air. That's all Maxsim needs to regain the upper hand. He quickly flips Lila and pins her to the ground, his teeth buried deep in the nape of her neck. I see the moment Lila submits, and his cat mounts her. It's time to let my own cat out to play, since he doesn't want to be left out of the fun. I allow him to surge forward and take a small nap until it's time for the two-legged people to have a turn.

My cat nudges me awake, and I allow the shift to wash over me. When I reform into my two-legged form, I find myself lying on the pile of furs, facing the ceiling. My eyes take a moment to adjust, but I look around and find Maxsim and Lila have both shifted as well, and like their cats, Maxsim has Lila pinned to the ground, his large body holding her down. I watch with a smirk as she struggles and spits curses at him.

"Let me up, you fucker," she yells, and my eyes widen.

She's going to get a spanking for that. Sure enough, Maxsim's big hand comes up and slashes through the air, landing a swipe on her ass. She yelps, but I can tell she's turned on. The whole cave is saturated with the scent of sex and slick. Maxsim leans forward and sinks his fangs into the space where Lila's neck and shoulder join. I reach down and stroke my cock, wishing he was sinking them into me, but I know I'll get my turn, I just have to be patient.

He slams his cock into her pussy at the same time. She yelps and continues to fight halfheartedly as he fucks her hard. I crawl over to join them, distracting the spitting hellcat with a kiss before sliding under her body so I can lick her clit while Maxsim fucks her. I gasp when I feel her wrap her lips around my cock and can't help but thrust up. I hear her choke a little, but she soon recovers and slides her mouth up and down my cock, her nose brushing against my pelvis. Lila can give head like no other person I know. Her body is just designed to take it all with no gag reflex.

Her body softens, and her fight dies as she succumbs to the pleasure we are wringing from her body. I use my tongue on her clit and Maxsim's cock, and as his knot starts to inflate, I lick over that too. Finally, he slams his knot home, and Lila's mouth leaves my cock as she screams as her orgasm detonates. A little cum and slick leak out despite Max's knot plugging her, and I lap at it, delighting in the taste of my two mates combined.

Maxsim doesn't let me take too much though. He rolls onto his back, taking Lila with him. She's splayed out across his chest like an offering, her eyes closed and her body twitching with aftershocks every time he grinds his knot into her pussy. He looks at me and nods at her body. He wants me to fuck her now, and I don't wait for another invitation. I scramble to my feet, stroking my cock. It's nice and slick from Lila's spit. I kneel between his splayed legs and feed it into her body, pushing past his knot. I wasn't even sure if it would be possible, but Lila's body is an amazing thing. It stretches and lets me in, and soon, I'm lodged alongside Max's knot.

"Holy fuck," I growl as he grinds it into both of us.

Her eyes widen at the pressure of having both his knot and my cock deep inside her, and I feel her pussy ripple as another orgasm washes over her. I can barely move, so I just rock back and forth, needing the pressure. Being pregnant has made me an even needier, whiny omega, and I'm soon begging for release. I feel Max's knot deflate, and he pulls out, all the fluid inside Lila flowing around my cock. The hot, thick coating feels incredible, and I moan as I start to thrust in and out a little harder now that there is more room. Max's knot may have deflated, but his cock is still rock hard, and I feel him swipe up some of the mess and rub it against my asshole, and then he feeds his cock into my ass.

I groan and cling onto Lila, still squeezed between the two of us. She murmurs praise and strokes my hair, knowing exactly the kinds of things that turn me on. The ring of muscle inside her pussy that is for me and me alone starts to tighten. She locks me in as Maxsim pounds into my ass, my lower half held in place by them. It's not long before my own orgasm races through my body and I'm spilling my seed into Lila, triggering another orgasm for her. She and I growl together, while Maxsim roars out his pleasure, his knot inflating, and I close my eyes, happy to be pinned between my mates.

# CHAPTER NINE

### Lila

Maxsim, Echo, and I snuggle for a little while, but eventually, we have to return to our room. I want to check on my grandpas, and I might take the kids with me. They've been cooped up for so long, it would be good for them to run around the ship, especially since there is no one around to bother. We will have to work on a playground for them sooner rather than later with the circus resuming as soon as we sort out all of our problems.

I spent the night with the cats. Maxsim was reluctant to let me or Echo leave his sight, which I completely understand, but his protective alpha instincts have been eased, and he is once again happy to let me out of his sight. I can't deny I didn't enjoy his more primal side, but I need to go check on everyone else.

When we arrive back to our suite, it is in chaos. Everyone must have decided this was the place to congregate. Apart from Bubby, Nikos, my grandpas, and Zeydan, everyone else who is on this ship is in our living area. I'm not sure they made it big enough when they did the refit. I know there is more space on this level we can expand into, and I think it will have to happen sooner rather than later—probably while we are on Fluxx sorting out Silac's parents.

Speaking of Silac, both he and Ghosie are drinking what I hope is coffee with the rest of my mates while the children play with their toys on the floor. Only one of my mates is missing, Nikos, and I hope our babies come soon, because I miss him so much.

The noise gets even louder when the children spot the three of us. There were some spare clothes in the cavern for Max and me, so neither of us are naked. Echo must have stored them there previously for us— he's thoughtful like that. When the kids see the three of us, me still in my cat form, their eyes widen with surprise. I don't think they've seen me like this before.

"Mama?" Cordy asks, slightly confused, and I hurry over and get down on my knees and hold out my arms.

"Hi, babies." They recognize my voice, and all three of them tumble into my arms for snuggles, chattering excitedly and stroking their hands over my fur.

"Mama's a pretty pussy." Cally pokes at my ears as Jack runs his hands over my tail.

"She sure does have a pretty—oof." Caspian elbows Xavier, cutting off what was sure to be a rude comment.

"Can I go for a ride on your back, Mama?" Jack asks, throwing his arms around my neck and trying to haul himself up.

"How about we go for a picnic instead? We can go to the bio level and run around in the big open space there. There is even a pond with some fish. Maybe we can feed them," I suggest, which does the trick of distracting the children. They jump up and down on the spot, cheering even though I'm pretty sure they don't even know what a picnic is.

"What's a picnic?" Ghosie asks, and I turn my attention to him.

There is just something about the man that makes him seem so sad and lonely. I want to gather him into my arms and pet him and tell him he's pretty. My hands involuntarily make grabby motions, and I have to shove them between my knees so nobody sees them.

I also can't touch him without wanting to hump his leg like a dog. I would totally be fine with that. He's dad bod sex on legs, and I am so here for it, but he did what he set out to do, helped us with grandma, and I guess he probably wants to return to his life instead of being shanghaied into becoming one of my mates. Let's face it, if I get my hands on his fur again, I'm going to let it do its thing and ride that train all the way to the station. We'll be five mutual orgasms in before you can say, "Lila's a whore," and Ghosie will be sealed and mated to me permanently.

"Lila?" I blink away my fantasies and return my attention to his previous question. I hear Xavier chuckling. The damn man can feel my emotions and knows how turned on I am by the bear. I'm sure my shifter mates can also smell the same thing. I don't dare look at any of them.

"Oh, ah... um, a picnic. It's when you take food, usually in a basket but we may have to be creative, and a blanket to sit on, and you find a nice spot to eat outdoors and enjoy the sunshine and fresh air while you have your meal."

I can see him thinking it over. "That sounds like fun. Would it be alright if I came along too?"

I push off the ground and swipe my hands over my dress to smooth it out. "Of course, everyone is invited. We need to get out of this room and take a moment to relax. We've been on the go nonstop for weeks now with more to come."

"It's a great idea, Lila." Link stands up and stretches, his shirt lifting and exposing his shiny six pack. I feel drool gather in my mouth. He winks at me before tugging it back down. "I'm going to stick my head in and check on Liliana, but I don't anticipate any change, otherwise I would have heard about it. I'm going to send Zeydan up to join in the fun. He needs to get the full idea of what he's in for, and herding three rambunctious krakens at the park should be a crash course in being a daddy."

The others all chuckle evilly, but I just roll my eyes. "I'm sure he will be fine. He's a god, so in his very long life, I'm certain he's had some interaction with children." I figuratively cross my fingers.

"Then I'm going to go check on Nikos. I worry he's lonely."

Shit, the guilt I feel is real, and my smile drops.

"Don't feel guilty, Lila." Xavier stands, shaking his head at me. Damn warlock emotion thief. "He knows you have a lot going on. Maybe after you've spent some time with the children, you can have a swim with him. It might relax you too," he suggests.

"That's a good idea. We will take the children. They love swimming with him and are excited about their new siblings," Caspian agrees.

"That's if they aren't too worn out by the picnic," Saxon cautions. "You know how they get when they are overstimulated and tired." Echo and Max shudder, and I bite down so I don't laugh at their misfortune. Echo especially watches the children more than most of the others. Although I know he loves it, it is hard when the three of them are on a rampage together. We need to look at hiring some help. I'll add it to the to-do list.

"I'll let Nikos know that he will have visitors this afternoon. Maybe they can have a nap before," Link suggests, "and then I'll join you on the bio level."

"I'm going to see if Broderick needs a break," Silac

says, not meeting my eyes. Damn it. It's like we take one step forward and two steps back. I know he wants to sort out the situation with his fiancée before we start anything, but I need him to stop running away.

"Oh no you don't." Tirrian clamps a hand onto the naga's shoulder, not letting him move. "You are going to forget about your drama for a moment and enjoy the bio level. There's enough room for you to shift and sunbake if you feel like it. I know it's been a while since you felt the sun on your body, and snakes enjoy that kind of thing. I'm going to shift and fly, and I may even join the others for a swim too." He turns his attention to me, his eyes heated. "And maybe Lila can see if she can shift into the water dragon form as well."

"Do you think it's possible?" I ask, feeling excited. Although I really don't need another voice in my head, it's almost become normal. Hell, you might as well call me Kevin. I almost have as many voices as that character from that movie.

"We won't know until you try," he answers, but he's excited at the prospect, so I will give it a go for him. I can always mimic his form if it doesn't work... or I think I can. I haven't mimicked an animal before, only a sentient being.

"Come on, kids, let's change into something that can get dirty." Brannock kneels down and gestures for Jack to get on his back. Jack quickly does what he tried to do to me, and squeals with delight when Brannock stands up. He holds out his hands for Cally and Cordy who both eagerly take them. Together, they wander off to the children's room to change them out of their pj's.

"That's going well." I nod in their direction, and Caspian chuckles.

"They love both of their new daddies. They already have him and the dragon wrapped around their little fingers."

Tirrian snorts, smoke drifting out of his nose, but he doesn't deny it as a small smile creeps across his lips.

"I'm not going to come for the picnic. I need a nap," Echo says, rubbing his small belly. "You two kept me up all night," he complains halfheartedly, and Maxsim smirks smugly, proud of our achievements. We really did spend most of the night fucking, and it was awesome. My body is fully recharged, but I could use a drink. I can wait until after the picnic though.

"I think I'll stay with Echo. Although we have the charms from Xavier, I still prefer the cold, plus I'm kind of tired too." Maxsim yawns and stretches, his eyes drooping with fatigue.

The poor alpha was worn out by his omegas. Can't say I'm not preening at that. We did, however, talk about Link maybe playing with us one day. He has the ability to create a knot at the base of his cock, which could help us through our future heats.

"Shall we all meet back here in half an hour?" Xavier suggests. "Saxon and I can organize some food while you take a shower." He looks at me when he says this. "While we all enjoy you smelling like sex, I think it's going to be more distracting than anything else, and with children around, an orgy in nature is not on the cards."

I stand up quickly and feel myself blush. Of course I smell like sex and debauchery. Thank goodness the children don't know what that is yet. "Ah, yup, okay, and someone grab some blankets to sit on as well please," I call over my shoulder as I hurry toward our shared bathroom. I stop in my closet to grab some clothes and strip off my dress, which I throw in the laundry basket. I prefer not to lose clothes when I shift.

The claws on my toes clack on the bathroom floor as I look from the shower to the bath. I know it would be quicker to shower, but I really feel like floating around in the tub, so I change back to OG Lila and put my clothes and towel on a nearby bench before stepping down into the tub. This bath is one of the best things about my suite. It's large enough to fit all of my mates if we wanted to. I duck down, allowing the water to wash over me.

Unlike the small pool we now have in the suite for my aquatic family members, this one is not deep. I can stand, and the water is chest level. It's also hot, unlike the other pool. Bathing products sit on a little shelf at the side, including salts, oils, bath bombs, and bubble bath choice which have multiplied since the children enjoy them so much, as well as various body and hair products. The bath is self-cleaning, much like a swimming pool but without the chlorine. As far as I'm concerned, it's magic. I don't need to know how it works, just that it does. The water will filter out when

I'm done, get scrubbed of the dirt, and then refill automatically. It only takes a few moments, and it's amazing.

I decide to test out my abilities while I'm underwater, just to make sure teleporting in cat form wasn't a fluke. I picture my mer form and the gills that appear in my neck. I focus on that and let the magic of the mimic activate. Lashes of pain tear through my neck, but as soon as the pain stops, I take a deep breath of air, and instead of choking on water, I can breathe normally. Holy crap. I just confirmed what we suspected—I can partially shift and use other forms' powers without needing to be in that form. I situate myself on the bottom of the pool and close my eyes, pondering this discovery. Oshan had informed me that I shouldn't attempt it because I could get stuck or splice myself, but that was as easy as breathing apart from the slash of pain. It's a small discomfort in the grand scheme of things, and it felt like it took a lot less power than to change forms. It could come in handy when I'm down on the old sexual juices. I wrinkle my nose. Okay, maybe I won't use that turn of phrase, but when power is limited, then a partial shift works. I'll have to do some more experimentation, but I might keep this to myself for now. I don't want to stress my mates out if I don't have to.

I spend a good ten minutes at the bottom of the pool, just letting the quiet wash over me. Silence will be in short supply for the immediate future, so I need to take it where I can get it. That's why Echo and

Maxsim have that little cave in the lightning cat quarters. It's somewhere to escape to if they need a moment. I fully support that, and I need to come up with something for the others. Caspian and Nikos have the pool, but with five out of our seven children having water shifting capabilities, that's just not going to be the escape they think it is. With the other two being able to cope with the frigid temperature in the lightning cat quarters, it won't be long until that is out as well. I'm going to ask for a small suite on the other levels with a few rooms, just so that my mates have someplace to go in the future. Even Link's library was moved to our newly renovated suite, so he no longer has that to escape to. As soundproof as the rooms are, it doesn't stop the children from barging in, and he loves to encourage their love of books. I've found the four of them in there a few times, reading fairy tales and snuggling by the fire.

I push off the bottom of the tub and stand up, letting the gills recede, then I quickly wash my body and hair, feeling rejuvenated and ready for our picnic. I hope we have some balls or a frisbee or something we can throw around as well. I also hope the orchard has some fruit hanging on the trees. It would be fun to teach the kids to pick them. Even if they are not tall enough to reach the branches, I'm sure the daddies will help.

Using the steps, I exit the bath, dry myself, and get dressed, ready to take a break from our worries to spend some quality time with our family.

# CHAPTER TEN

## Link

While the rest of the family gets ready for our day out, I make my way to the med bay. I want to ask Zeydan to come with us, since it's time to get to know him better, and I want to encourage the grandpas to either rest or join us too. They are looking more and more broken the longer Liliana stays unconscious. It was different before, because they weren't sure if she was still alive, so they had gotten on with their lives as much as they could in the aftermath of her disappearance and their son and his wife's deaths. Now, though, knowing she's alive and was tortured repeatedly, it's weighing them down. If she doesn't wake up from the coma she's in, I'm not sure the three of them will survive it. They will probably lose the will to live and pass over so they can be with her.

I'm pretty sure that would destroy Lila. Physically, we could keep her alive, but she has such a big heart, it would break if she lost her grandpas, and I'm not sure anything could fill that void. Sure, Xavier's and Cas's parents love her, and Tirrian's parents will as well. My mother will see her as a commodity to exploit, so I plan to keep her far away from them. Saxon's parents were killed in battle many years ago, but his aunt, the queen, will dote on her, as will his female cousins. Actually, scratch that, we may need to keep them far away from Lila too. They are known for being mischievous, and I don't want them leading her astray. Echo's and Maxsim's families conspired to force a mating, so they are very happy having Lila as their daughter-in-law. Nikos's dad is a non-issue, but I'm not so sure about his mom. She's supposed to be benevolent, but there's only so much tyranny a person can be subjected to before they turn cold and bitter. Her position as Queen of Aquilia bears watching, and I don't really want Lila to have anything to do with her until she proves what kind of ruler she is going to be.

I know nothing about Ghosie's or Brannock's backgrounds, and Silac's parents are a wildcard too. He's going to renege on the arranged marriage, which is going to cause some issues, but Lila will be responsible for rescuing them from the basilisks, and she can also assure the naga line will continue, so we will have to wait and see what happens there as well. In all, there's no shortage of family, but it's not the same as your own blood.

When I get to the med bay, Zeydan is there with his seat pulled up on one side of Liliana's bed, and John is on the other side. He still hasn't completely recovered from his ordeal, but there's a strength in the set of his shoulders that wasn't there before. Maybe I was wrong, and they will get through the loss of their wife if the worst were to happen.

"Good morning," I call to them as I step up to the monitors to see if anything changed overnight. My alarms didn't alert me to anything major, but I purse my lips and hold back my exclamation of surprise. Her brain activity has increased, almost doubled overnight. I release a rush of breath as relief washes over me. This is a good sign. It means she is healing. It's not enough for her to wake up anytime soon, but it's a step in the right direction.

I move over to her and pick up my light pen, opening first one eye and looking for pupil reactivity, and then the second, pleased at what I'm seeing. When Lila first healed her body, I had done the same test and had no reaction. I worried that she was brain dead, but before I left last night, I did the same test again, and there was a slight reaction, which gave me hope. Today's reaction is even more significant.

I move to the base of her bed and do a reflex test, running a tool over the soles of her feet, and unlike before when there was no reaction, there is a very visible flinch this time. Both Zeydan and John stand up and look between me and the woman they both love. I'm hoping that Zeydan's love is platonic and that of a sibling, because killing a god won't be easy.

"Link?" John sounds hopeful, but he is holding himself back.

I return the tool and penlight to the tray on the cart nearby, and then I turn back to face them. "I'll be honest, when Lila first healed her, I really didn't have much hope that Liliana was going to come back to us at all, let alone in one piece." John's mouth falls open in surprise, but Zeydan just nods like he knew all along. I guess he may have. He is a god, so I'm sure he can read minds. "But I am now very hopeful she will wake up. Whether her mind is intact when she does will be anyone's guess. You need to be prepared that she may not be the same person she was before she went missing. Her mind may have fractured, and she may not know you, remember what happened, or even be able to communicate."

Tears well in John's eyes, but he nods. "Yes, my brothers and I have discussed the possibility, but it doesn't matter. She is our wife, and we will care for her in whatever capacity she needs."

"I sense she is still in there," Zeydan announces calmly, picking up Liliana's hand and closing his eyes. A green glow encompasses him and Liliana, and both John and I wait for him to finish whatever he is doing. I doubt it's hurting her, since he has had plenty of opportunities to try in the past. It's a tense few moments, but the glow fades away and he opens his eyes and nods.

"She is still in there. I can hear her. She is fighting to return to us. I tried to help her by giving her something to focus on and move toward. Hopefully it will be enough, but it's something she has to do on her own. It seems like her mind retreated to protect her from the torture, but it built such impenetrable walls, she's having trouble tearing them down."

"Why didn't you tell us this earlier?" John doesn't sound mad, just curious.

"I got no response earlier, and like the doctor, I did not want you to lose hope." Zeydan delivers the news without emotion. I hope that's not what he's going to be like with Lila, because that is not going to fly. Saxon told me he had been alone for a long time, since the goddesses of life and death disappeared. The four elemental gods went their own ways. Hopefully we can coax this unemotional man out of his shell. Spending time with the family will help.

"But you feel differently now?" John pushes.

"Yes. For the first time since she went missing, I believe I will be able to talk to my sister and find out why."

"But not blood sister, right?" John picks up Liliana's hand and gently strokes a finger over the back of it. "Because I heard that you believe our granddaughter is your mate, and I know gods probably have a different concept of incest, as do one or two other species, but Skarrians frown on that sort of thing..." He trails off, but I can see he's waiting for a response.

Zeydan's mouth kicks up on one side. "There is no blood tying Lilessa and me together. We weren't born so much as willed into existence. Lila is not going to be mating with a blood relative if she and I seal our mating bond."

"How do you do that?" I ask, not wanting to miss the opportunity to gather more knowledge so Lila can be properly informed.

"She and I will complete the bond while I am in my godly form," Zeydan replies, and I arch an eyebrow.

"And what form would that be?" I ask him, and before my very eyes, he grows taller and wider, and his face elongates, shifting to a fox-like countenance with his body remaining mostly the same. He looks very much like an Egyptian god from Earth's history. I wonder if they ever messed around on Earth in the past.

Something starts to writhe beneath his skirt, and long, frond-like tendrils sprout out of his back and fan out much like a peacock's tail.

I scan the length of him. He has to be close to eight feet tall now, and the green glow from before has returned. "Is there anything special that happens that she needs to know about?" I ask, wanting to make sure I have all the information for Lila.

"Only my true mate would survive copulating with me in this form. The fronds at my back will sprinkle her with my godly essence, thus allowing her to be able to take my seed and survive, transforming her to have a small sliver of godly essence herself."

"And that's it?" I push, not trusting the fact that something under his skirt is moving independently.

He grimaces and looks down his front. "My cock is probably slightly different from what she is used to. The dust will help her take that as well."

John looks green and has reached his limit with this conversation. He turns his back to Zeydan, tuning out everything about his granddaughter's sex life.

"You need to elaborate. I won't have her being surprised anymore. She's had too many shocks and had the decision to mate with someone taken out of her hands too many times. She needs a little bit of control." I cross my arms. Even though he claims his power is diminished in this form, my jaw throbs as his energy pulses menacingly.

"You are a good mate of my mate." Zeydan inclines his head in appreciation. "I have three appendages. When it is time to penetrate our partner, they twirl around each other, combining into one member, but it is ridged and curved like a corkscrew. I need to make sure she has been covered in my dust before I can penetrate her body. The dust will allow her body to change to accept my member. It will swell inside her, filling her with my seed. I cannot tell you if having a child is possible. None of my brethren have found their true mates." His gaze slides slightly to John and the woman on the bed. "Or none that have been confirmed, so I am not certain conception is possible."

"You are very big, so I'm assuming that is big too." I nod to his writhing crotch. "Will Lila be able to take you?"

"Yes, my dust will make her body relax so she can take my member."

"Well, I'm almost certain she will enjoy the challenge," I mutter under my breath, but I think the god hears me, his eyes sparkling with amusement. He starts to shrink again, and the green glow disappears, as do the frond appendages, and his head returns to normal. I don't know if they are wings or are simply for procreation. I don't need to know. "Make sure you let her know everything you told me, or I will. I don't want to kill you because you accidentally mated her against her will," I tell him sternly, and he drops his amusement and nods his head.

"I would not take her choice away from her. I will make it very clear. Also, having sex in this form will not seal the mate bond." He gestures to his body now that it has returned to the form we are familiar with.

"Good, I'm holding you responsible. Lila's mimic powers push her to mate and keep her permanently horny, and she sometimes forgets herself. It's up to us to be responsible while she adjusts to her new destiny. Now, I think it would be best if you all took a break from your vigil. Liliana is perfectly safe here. I will lock the med bay down despite there being no one else on the ship. Lila is planning a family day, and both of you, as well as Eric and William, should show your faces," I insist firmly, not willing to hear any arguments.

Zeydan doesn't protest. He seems happy for the invitation, but John drags his feet, reluctant to leave his wife's side. I sigh and pick up a nearby tablet and activate a screen. It shows a live feed on the camera facing her bed. I turn it so he can see it.

"Look, you can keep an eye on her, but if you don't look after yourself, how are you going to be able to look after her when she wakes up?" I try a different tactic, and it seems to work. He sighs loudly but stands up and places a kiss on her cheek, quietly murmuring that he will be back later. He takes the tablet from me, and the three of us leave the med bay. I activate the locking mechanism once we are clear of the door.

"Now, how about you go retrieve your brothers? We are having a family picnic on the bio level. The kids are going to run around, and we are going to enjoy some down time. If you don't arrive there in the next half hour, I will send Xavier for you, and he won't give you a choice, he will just teleport you there without your permission."

"No need. It's fine, you're right," John says as we make it to the elevator. "This will be good for us. I'll make sure we are all there, I promise."

We let him off at his level, which is below our suite, and instead of going to ours, I hit the right button for the Aquilian level. I wanted to stick my head in and check on Nikos, so that still needs to happen.

The silence is awkward, and the god fidgets, his tails bristling with agitation behind him. "Are you okay?" I ask him, and he bites his lip before sighing.

"I've never been on a picnic. Are you sure Lila wants me there?" Holy shit, he's nervous. "I haven't spent a lot of time around people for a while, only the halla harvesters, and I was not invested in them or their feelings. It's why I didn't care if they followed my instructions or not, and if they died, that was their own fault. I'm afraid I don't have the capability to feel any of the right emotions needed to be someone's mate or father or friend."

Wow. I'm kind of shocked that he admitted all that. I assumed he'd be an arrogant asshole, but that's not turning out to be the case.

"Don't be nervous. Our family is a lot, but I'm sure you will fit in. Just be friendly and patient. Ask as many questions as you want, and don't be afraid to speak your mind. We are a bunch of strong-willed creatures and will steamroll over you if you are timid. They are probably more afraid of you than you are of them. You're a god, and that comes with big expectations and incorrect assumptions."

The doors open, and we step out onto the entrance platform. I frown as I notice the weather program is set to stormy. The waves wash up and over before draining back into the pool. I don't think I've ever seen it like this before. I hope Nikos is okay.

I'm not sure I'm going to be able to engage the bridge I need to get to his house. I know he's unable to travel very far, so I can't expect him to appear in front of me. I'm not sure what to do. I don't know how to change the weather program, and I don't want to worry Lila by asking Silac. He's familiarized himself with all the ship's workings, so he would be the one to know.

# CHAPTER ELEVEN

## Zeydan

Watching the water churn like it's being driven by an angry water god, I feel the cyborg's worry like a palpable thing as I try not to let the water soak the bottom of my skirt. I am not a fan of the ocean—that was my brother's domain.

"Where are we?" I ask him, shocked that there is such a large body of water on this ship. It really is an engineering marvel.

"This is the Aquilian living quarters. We had a pod that used to perform in the circus, but most of them opted to stay on Aquilia for the birth of their first child. Only one remains, and he is also expecting. He is Lila's Aquilian mate, Nikos."

I feel my eyebrows jump in surprise. Pregnant? I had no idea Lila's family was expanding so rapidly. I could hear the extra heartbeats in the omega lightning cat, but I hadn't heard anyone mention that's why the merman wasn't able to leave his pool. I assumed it was because he was an arrogant ass, like so many of them are. They really are the closest race in temperament to my brother, who is more of an asshole than anything else.

"Are his emotions driving the ocean? Is he unhappy?" I ask, and Link looks at me in shock.

"They can do that?" he asks me. I hear his heart rate increase with his anxiety.

"Yes. The more powerful ones can control the water, and it's often driven by their mood."

"Crap, I need to get across there. I'm worried he's in pain or labor, but I can't put the bridges out with the water like that," he replies.

"Come here," I order him, and without waiting for him to respond, I grab his arm and teleport us the short distance to the dwelling he had been eyeing.

When we reach our destination, he hurries away from me, tossing a, "Thank you," over his shoulder. I move after him and descend a set of stairs into a cavern at the bottom of the dwelling. There's a small pool of water, allowing for an easy transition in and out for the Aquilian. The water isn't much calmer in that pool, splashing up the sides of the rock wall and drenching the small platform area. There's no sign of any Aquilian, but I can just make out some gold and green at the bottom of the pool.

"Nik," Link calls, seeing the same flash of color I

do. "Nikos," he calls louder, but I doubt the merman can hear him.

"Would you like me to bring him to the surface?" I offer, and he nods.

"Yes please. I want to make sure he isn't in trouble."

I hold out my hands and use my telekinesis, latching onto the Aquilian with a little difficulty. I struggle with all my powers that came so easily before, but I try not to let anyone know. That's a surefire way to end up dead or as someone's prisoner.

I draw him to the surface, and he starts to fight when he feels himself moving, but it's a halfhearted effort, and I can see why when he gets to the surface. His belly is huge, but the two heartbeats inside are strong.

There are dark bags under his eyes, but he brightens once he sees Link. "Nik, are you okay?" The cyborg toes off his shoes and socks and drags off his shorts then steps onto the water filled platform. It's up to his knees, but he doesn't seem to care. I deposit the merman on the platform, and Link strokes his hand through the merman's shiny gold hair. He leans into it and practically purrs, before his eyes alight on me, and they widen with interest.

"I am so tired. I can't get comfortable without my anemone, and I'm so fat," he wails, and I have to smother a smile. The cyborg is very good and doesn't so much as change a face muscle, keeping his concern front and center.

"I know this must be difficult for you, but if you go back to the anemone and go into labor, I can't help you with it. Only Cas and Lila will be able to reach you." He keeps stroking the merman's hair in a soothing way, and I watch with interest as his whole body relaxes, and the water around us calms.

"I'm lonely and so grumpy. I miss my sister, I miss Sweetpea, and I especially miss my mate." Now I feel sorry for the poor man. I know Aquilians can't shift during their pregnancy like some other creatures, and he would be surrounded by family and friends if he was back on his home planet.

"Can we get your sister to come stay with you until you give birth?" I ask, and they both frown.

"No. Unfortunately she is back on Aquilia and unable to be here at the moment," Link explains, and I can tell by the tears that well in Nikos's eyes that there's more to the story, so I let it drop.

"Lila, Cas, Tirrian, and the children are going to visit you after the babies have their afternoon nap," Link promises Nikos, which seems to have his mood brightening even more.

"They are? That will be lovely. I feel like I'm missing so much. Like who is that?" He points to me and looks me up and down, angling his body so he can see me better.

"Nikos, this is Zeydan. Zeydan, meet Nikos, Lila's Aquilian mate." Link does the introduction, and the Aquilian smiles at me, but when he does, his mouth is full of sharp teeth.

"Who are you and what do you want?" he demands fiercely, a trident appearing in his hand. Link stumbles backward but then rolls his eyes. He and I both know Nikos probably couldn't hurt a fly at the moment. I can appreciate him being protective of his family and friends though.

"Zeydan is the god of earth and Lila's new mate," Link answers, and Nikos frowns.

"God of earth? Is that like our god of water, Tito? The old gods are fables, they don't exist. They are just stories parents use to get their children to behave," he argues, shaking his head. "There is a statute in the middle of the palace grounds, which my mother told me was Tito, but that he was just a legend because if he was real, surely he would still look after his people."

"Oh, I can assure you that Tito is very real, but he's a real asshole and cares for nothing but himself. It is the nature of gods," I tell them offhandedly. "We are long lived and get bored easily. Back when we were creating life and planets and new races, it was a bit of a competition, and we really didn't pay too much attention to them after we finished and moved on to the next one. It's why the council was able to grab control. It started as a very small movement just before the Una's and Aaz'axian war, but now it encompasses the whole galaxy."

Both Link and Nikos frown as I get slightly off topic. "It's nice to meet you. Would you like me to check on your babies?" I offer, hoping it will earn me some favor.

"You can do that?" Link asks, sounding surprised, and I feel slightly disgruntled.

"Yes, I am a god. My power may be diminished, but I can still do things most people can't," I reply, hiking my skirt up and securing it with the long sash before stepping into the water with them. I lean down and hold out my hands, examining the merman much like I did Lilessa. My hands glow green with my power, and I wait for the merman to give me a small nod before it sinks into his body. I close my eyes as it spreads out and can't stop the smile from crossing my lips as it reaches their babies. Both of them are perfectly formed, and I can already touch their minds and feel their personalities. They are going to be a handful. I feel joy and laughter and endless energy, as well as a great potential for power and compassion. There's also impatience. These babies are ready to meet the world. I can't imagine it's going to be long before we meet them in person.

"Are they okay?" Nikos asks in a small voice, and when I retract my power and open my eyes, there's a wrinkle of concern between his eyebrows.

"Be at ease, my mate's mate. They are perfect, but impatient to come out and meet their family. You really should get some rest. It won't be long now, and from what I remember, labor can be intense."

He and Link both sigh with relief, but the merman grumbles, "My back aches so much I can't get comfortable. I need some kind of support, so I don't sleep. The anemone was perfect because it molded around my body but gave me some support as well."

"Anemones have a movable foot, don't they?" I ask, stepping out of the water and frowning down at my wet legs. Water is really not my favorite element.

"Yes. I've tried to coax it up here, but it is really happy at the bottom of the pool." Nikos pouts with his annoyance, and Link climbs out of the pool and grabs towels from a nearby shelf, handing one to me before drying himself off and putting his shorts and shoes back on.

I rub over my legs and release my skirt before placing the towel to the side. "I can bring it here for you," I offer. "But I don't want to upset it. Would you be opposed to me encouraging another one to grow up here?" I offer. "I can take a piece of the other one and place it in the bottom of this pool, and then use my growing powers to accelerate its growth."

Link looks thoughtful. "Your idea of diminished powers and mine must vary greatly."

"That would be wonderful. It won't hurt the other one, will it?" Nikos asks, his frown turning into a small look of hope.

"No, not at all." I close my eyes and let go of my powers, feeling my god form take shape once more. I have more control in this form, and this is going to require a little more finesse. I shake out my body and hear an intake of surprised breath from the merman. Link has already seen this form when he quizzed me about my intentions for Lila. Although I would have been annoyed at anyone else for questioning me like that, I accepted that as Lila's mate, he and any of the others that wish to may ask questions, as is their right. I approve of him looking out for her.

When I open my eyes, Nikos is looking at me with wide-eyed amazement, and I can't help but give him a playful wink. He startles, almost falling off the small platform he is settled on. I chuckle as he recovers and scowls at me before allowing my power freedom to sink below the surface in search of the anemone growing deep in the pool. My power is attracted to live plants and animals, and I'm surprised to see an abundance of both below. I was expecting an empty pool, but I can sense a large coral reef with thousands of living organisms, both the coral and sea life. I don't slow my search to explore, instead searching for the anemone which should contain a resonance of Nikos's life force if he spent much time there. That's how I am able to zero in on it and direct my power to slice a small section off.

Happy with what I've done, I allow my power to return back to me, drawing the small section of the anemone with it until it's at the bottom of this cavern. I place it into a small crevice and then pump my growth power into it. My heart rate increases, and I feel my breath start to labor and curse my diminished powers. Something that should be a breeze is taking a huge amount of effort. Finally, it reaches a size capable of holding the large merman, and I release the power, drawing it back to me. A feeling of lightheadedness plagues me, and I stumble slightly to one side. Link is quick to grab my arm and steady me.

"Are you okay?" he asks, and I nod, feeling sweat pearl on my brow.

"Yes," I grumble. "This is what I mean about diminished power. That should have been as easy as blinking, yet I'm exhausted afterwards."

"How can you recharge?" Link's concern makes me feel something that I haven't felt in a long time— cared for.

"The bio level should help if there are plants up there," I tell him, regaining my balance, but he keeps his hand on me a moment more to be sure. I pat it in gratitude.

"I'm fine now, you can let go, but thank you." I turn my attention to the merman. "It is done. I hope you sleep well, and it was lovely meeting you and your babies," I say politely.

His eyes light up, and he beams at me, the mouthful of sharp teeth replaced by blinding white teeth. "Thank you so much. Welcome to the family. I look forward to getting to know you better when we can leave this pool." He doesn't wait around. He gives us both a wave and awkwardly slides into the water and disappears.

Link chuckles. "You made yourself a lifetime friend, I think." He slaps me on the shoulder. "Thank you. Now let's get you recharged. I'm sure the bio level will have you back to normal in no time."

He leads the way up the stairs, and I follow behind

him slowly, cursing myself the whole way. When I get up there, he is out on the deck and pressing a button, which has a bridge sliding out across the now calm water.

"I didn't want you to tire yourself even more by teleporting us," he explains, and we both walk back to the entrance and the elevator door.

It closes behind us, and he presses a button on the wall. I make note of which one it is, because being able to spend time in nature despite being on a ship in the middle of space may be a game changer. The small ship I used to travel had a little conservatory, but it wasn't as affective as being on a planet.

"Everyone should be up there by the time we get there. This is going to be fun. We need to blow off some steam, and what better way than a family picnic? I'll be honest, I've never been on one either. My family is definitely not the picnicking type, more the five-star restaurant where you need to be dressed in fancy clothes. I'm looking forward to there being no pressure to perform or impress anyone," Link explains.

There is so much I need to learn about the family I will be mating into. "What does your family do that requires that kind of dining?"

He grimaces. "We are the owners of Pleasure Bot Industries."

Huh, well that was not what I was expecting. I don't socialize very much anymore, but I do keep abreast of everything that goes on through the galaxy, and I know the company he is speaking of. "And you're a doctor? With your family's fortune, you don't need to work."

He sighs. "No, but I never wanted to be a part of the business. My mother is an unpleasant woman, and I never wanted to become like her. My father is much more understanding and pushed for me to do whatever I wanted. Luckily for me, it's his company, and she is only chairman of the board. He can replace her at any time, and it's how he keeps her in line."

"Being a doctor suits you. I think you made the right choice. I've never met your parents, but rumors of your mother's beauty expand the galaxy, as do the rumors of how her beauty cannot outshine her devious and cunning nature."

His face stays blank, but I see the corner of his eye twitch. "The rumors are not unfounded. Count yourself lucky. She would have tried to seduce you into her pocket. Having a god at her beck and call would suit her needs."

"She would have overestimated her appeal. While I admire deviousness and cunning, I cannot abide cruelty," I reply just as the doors of the elevator open, and we step out. I look around and breathe deeply. The sight before me is one I had not expected. Looking up, I notice clouds floating across a blue sky with a sun that is so realistic, I can feel the warmth soaking into my skin, a slight breeze making it so it's pleasant instead of stifling.

My skin prickles with the presence of all the plants, and I feel a smile creep across my lips as I take notice of a large clearing beyond rows and rows of crops. The family is gathered there, and I itch to join them. The sounds of shouts and laughter and joy make my ears prickle and my tails shiver with the desire to be released. I allow them to take form, and they scamper down the rows of crops and join the family, circling the children who laugh with delight and pounce on them to give them cuddles. I soak in the love they lavish on my creatures, and the exhaustion starts to drain away.

"Come on." Link slaps my shoulder again. "Let's join the chaos." He starts down a path, and I follow behind, taking in the massive area. It is going to be one of my favorite places on the ship.

# CHAPTER TWELVE

## Lila

There's an intense feeling of love in my heart as I watch my family get some quality one-on-one time in the bio level. Although the cats aren't here with us, I understand their decision not to join us. I'm sure there will be plenty of more times like this to come.

Saxon and Xavier out did themselves with the food. There was all sorts of tasty treats, and as I stretch out on the blanket, my head in Tirrian's lap, I smile as I watch the grandpas teach the children to feed the fish that are swimming in the pond. At one stage, Jack shifts and tries to climb in with them, and I laugh as William wrestles him to keep him out of it. All three of them look exhausted, and my worry was high, but in the last two hours, some of that worry has eased as they've taken a moment to enjoy time with our family. Even Bubby came for the meal, putting the ship on autopilot. Brannock promised he would give him a break in a few hours. The man certainly deserves a raise. He has gone above and beyond for us over the last few weeks. Usually it takes two of them to captain the ship, but Captain Lester never warmed up to me, and I always had an uneasy feeling about him. It's why I voted not to bring him. The others agreed with me.

Tirrian's hand brushes through my hair, and I feel his body tense beneath me. When I look up, I see him watching Cas, Link, Saxon, Brannock, Silac, and Xavier. They have a weird looking ball thing that is hexagonal in shape. It isn't a solid object, but it flies through the air almost like a frisbee. They are divided into two teams and are throwing it back and forth and talking smack to one another.

"Go join them," I encourage him, and he drags his attention away from them.

"Are you sure?" he asks, and I nod, looking at the two men who have remained on the blanket with me. Ghosie and Zeydan both declined to throw the ball around. Ghosie claimed it was way too much exercise for him. Zeydan didn't say why, but I think he is still wary about all of this, not that I blame him.

"Yes, of course. I'm sure Zeydan would like to be my cushion." I lift my head and raise a challenging eyebrow at him. Let's see him turn me down.

He surprises me and quickly agrees. Tirrian gets up and waves an absent hand as he hurries over to join the rest of them, and Zeydan slides into his spot. He gathers my hair out of the way so it doesn't get caught in his skirt as I lower my head into his lap. His tails are all snoozing under one of the trees. When Eric asked about them, Zeydan explained they were soaking in much needed energy from the surrounding nature, which they stored for him.

I asked why it wasn't killing the plants like I did on Husadavia, and he explained it was a much slower process, and he only took small amounts from each plant. He said I would learn that in time, but that form was starved, which was why I killed everything. Our picnic blanket is actually sitting over the patch of grass I killed before we went to Husadavia. Some patches of green are returning, so I'm hoping it will make a comeback.

"This is really nice," I murmur as he continues to stroke a hand through my hair. The artificial sun is shining, and the sounds of my family enjoying themselves soothes a part of me that was feeling jagged.

"Tell me about these automatons," Zeydan requests, and when I crack my eyes open, he's looking at a machine that is moving down one of the rows of plants. It's not one I recognize, and I'm as clueless about the automatons as he is, so I can't help him with that, but thankfully Ghosie has some mechanical knowledge.

"I think they are a subsidiary of Pleasure Bot Industries. They can be programed for certain tasks. I know there are some that can be programed for general household duties as well. My father has one in his household."

"Tell me about yourself, Ghosie," I say, wanting to learn more about the gorgeous bear, even if it means I grow more attached despite being unsure of where we stand. The attraction marks are still on both our bodies.

"What do you want to know?" he asks somewhat hesitantly.

"You grew up with your father? Was your mother in the picture?"

"The colony my father lives in is one of the few colonies that does have females. They are females of other species, but they have decided to make a life with a bear that asked them to be the mother of their children. They are all there willingly and have relationships with the male or sometimes groups of males."

"How do they get around the fur thing?" I ask, hoping there might be a way for me to touch this obviously touch starved bear. He always looks so desperate every time he sees the rest of them show affection for one another.

"They only touch when they want to have sex. It's not ideal, but neither is capturing and keeping women while they are pregnant and then disposing of them and their female children. Most of the residents of that colony are happy. My mother lives with my father and three other males. I have half-siblings, but I am my father's only child."

"Your species was cursed, is that correct?" Zeydan

asks, also sounding curious, his hand pausing in my hair.

"Yes, just before the war. All of our females became males, and instead of our fur being an aphrodisiac on command like it used to be, we can't be touched without it sending our partners into a lust craze. We have no females and rely on other species to bear our young. Any female children are born of the other species. In their desperation to see our species survive, our men became more and more inclined not to ask permission, because their fur had the effect it does. We became the pariahs of the galaxy, a whole species punished for one asshole's mistake. No one would trade with us or employ us because our fur is problematic, and so we became space pirates to support ourselves."

"You say it was a goddess that did the punishing?" I ask and shift my focus from the colorful bear to the god whose lap my head is in. He's breathtakingly beautiful, and I can't help but stare at his perfect features. "Can you help him or reverse the curse on the species?"

"A goddess cursed you?" Zeydan sounds confused.

"Yes. An old chieftain offered her a chance to warm his bed, and she laughed in his face and told him she was waiting to find her mate and wouldn't lower herself, so he used his fur to manipulate her. When her mind cleared, she was furious and cursed our race... or that is the story I know."

Zeydan purses his lips. "Well, that could have been

any one of them, but my guess it was either Vivax or Sanshia. Both of them had tempers and could be vicious. Lilessa was a lot more benevolent."

"Can you help him?" I ask again.

"A curse is usually placed on a single being. Once that being dies, the curse should end with them. I take it the chieftain is still alive?"

Ghosie shakes his head vigorously. "No, that was the first thing they tried. Somehow, the curse is linked to our DNA. Even medical intervention wasn't able to help us have female children. They always change to male."

"That is unusual. I can take a look, but I would guess the original goddess would need to lift it. Come here." Zeydan gestures next to us, and Ghosie moves closer. I struggle to move out of his lap and give him room to work, but he places a hand on my breastbone.

"Stay. I don't need you to move. I like you there." I shiver at his commanding tone and instantly do as he asks, my inner animals practically purring at his dominance. Zeydan holds out one of his hands and gestures for Ghosie to take it.

Ghosie hesitates. "Will my fur affect you?"

Zeydan shrugs. "I guess we will find out."

Ghosie doesn't look convinced, but he does as he's asked and clasps his hand. I hold my breath, waiting to see if and how the god reacts.

Zeydan's eyes widen in surprise, and he grunts, his body shaking as it starts to glow green. His cock hardens beneath my head, but that is the only outward sign that he is affected. Unlike me, he doesn't rub himself all over Ghosie. His eyes drift closed, and I feel him reach out with his power, but then he frowns, and his eyes pop open, and he releases Ghosie's hand.

"I'm sorry, I can't see anything. My power is too diminished in this form." Ghosie's hopeful look drops, replaced with one of disappointment. The breath I'd been holding heaves out as I mimic his feelings.

"Never mind. It was silly getting my hopes up." He goes to move back to where he was sitting, but Zeydan holds out a hand, stopping him in his tracks.

"Hang on, let me change to my god form. I may be able to tell more in that." He looks down at me and runs a nervous hand through his hair. "Can you get up please? I'm going to change, and I don't want you to be frightened, but promise me you won't run away no matter what you think," he pleads, which surprises me. What about his god form makes him so worried I'm going to be scared?

I purse my lips and roll over to the side before getting up onto my knees. I take his hand and give it a squeeze. "I turn into various creatures, including a dragon and a kraken, so you aren't going to frighten me no matter what you look like," I assure him, but then I curse under my breath. If he looks like the Barcoa, it might be a hard pass for me, but I hold my ground. I said it now, and I won't take it back. We can deal.

Zeydan whistles, and his tails abandon their nap and stream back toward him, flowing onto his body and reforming as tails behind him. His whole frame starts to glow green, and his body grows, expanding up and outward until he's close to eight feet tall. His face changes, growing a muzzle, and velvet-like fur covers it, making him look like a true fox. The fur is the same red as his ears and tails. The rest of his body stays smooth, but growing up out if his back are a pair of extra appendages. Green fern fronds extend like extra limbs. I'm not sure what their function is, but they wave elegantly. Shifting beneath his skirt draws my attention to his crotch area. Something is moving under there, and my curiosity increases.

Both Ghosie and I look up at him with wide-eyed amazement. He's like the living, breathing embodiment of Anubis from Egyptian mythology, and I am so here for it. I want to release my inner slave girl to see to his every need and press my thighs together and hope that nobody can smell how turned on I am. This is not the time or the place. Well, it might be the place, but it is so not the time.

I shove down my musings as I notice that all the sound from the game, as well as the sounds of the children, die off, leaving the bio level in anxious silence.

Zeydan in his god form is stunning, awe-inspiring but gorgeous, and not anything I want to run away from.

My kraken purrs and whispers inside my mind. *Look at the size of him. I bet his cock is huge.*

*Shut up, you silly bitch. That cock would split us in half,* I remind her, and I feel her laugh at my expense.

*Your body will adjust. You are made for him. You are his mate. You need to take a ride on that very soon.*

How did I end up as a mate to a god? He deserves a goddess as a mate, not a boring, slutty Skarrian.

I can feel her amusement at my thoughts, and I get the feeling she knows more than she's saying, but she keeps the rest of her opinions to herself.

Zeydan holds his hands out to Ghosie once more. Ghosie hesitates for a moment before standing up and grasping the god's hands. His body is enveloped in the green glow, and he lifts slightly into the air, his back arching and his mouth dropping open like he's in pain. He moans loudly, and I jump to help him, my fangs clicking into place. Zeydan should have warned us it was going to hurt him, but I slam up against a barrier and can go no farther.

"Easy, mate." Zeydan's voice has deepened, and it feels like a caress against my skin. "I am not hurting him. In fact, my power probably feels good to him, sort of like what his fur does to everyone else."

I ease back, my eyes zeroing in on his face. His eyes are squeezed shut, and what I thought was pain is actually exquisite pleasure. My gaze drops to where his cock sheath is, and my eyes widen when I find it. The sheath has contracted back, and his cock is exposed. It's the same color as his fur and not smooth like a human cock. It has various different ridges and lumps and bumps along the length of it. I bet it hits all the magic spots on the inside. Sitting at the base of it is a nub very much like a woman's clitoris, and I would love to know what the function of it is.

"Teddy!" Cally screams, and my head wrenches in their direction. Shit, they probably don't need to see what is going on. I'm hoping they are far enough away that they can't see his cock. Eric is quick to grab her and hold her close, whispering words of comfort to her.

"He's okay. Zeydan is just trying to see if he can make him feel better." I guess that's as good an explanation as he can give. None of the others really know what we're doing, just that Zeydan's god has appeared.

"Zeydan is trying to see if he can do anything about the curse on the Carevasta bears," I announce loudly for everyone, and I can see the rest of my family visibly relax. They were all on high alert at the appearance of Zeydan's godly form, which I don't blame them.

The men return to their game, and I hear John suggest to the children that they go see if the orchard has any fruit on the trees. That is enough to distract them.

I turn my attention back to the god and bear and find both of them floating slightly off the ground. Zeydan's power creates a jaw throbbing pulse in the air, and I grit my teeth and hold my ground. Eventually, it seeps into my skin, changing from terror inducing waves into something more sensual and pleasant. I sigh and allow it to flow over me, but it doesn't last long. The frown on his face tells me that whatever he was attempting isn't working.

They both lower to the ground. Ghosie's frozen muscles relax as Zeydan draws his power back into himself. He shakes his head, looking frustrated as he holds out a hand to steady the bear.

"I'm sorry. Much like the block on Liliana's mind, I can't force your DNA to rewrite itself. It will take the goddess who laid the curse or the god who is responsible for their creation to do that."

Ghosie seems to sink in on himself, but he nods, even though his disappointment is visible. "I understand. Thank you for trying. I think I'm going to call it a day. I'll see you all later," he says, cupping his hand across his still erect cock. Without waiting for a reply, he departs.

I watch him retreat and take a step to follow him, but Zeydan puts a hand out to stop me.

"Give him a moment. He was so hopeful." He sounds disappointed that he couldn't help him.

I whirl to face him. "So were you able to tell who laid the curse?" I ask, my hands on my hips. "Who was the Carevasta bears' creator? Obviously it wasn't you."

He shakes his head, and I watch as he allows his god form to recede. "No, it wasn't me. Market is responsible for the Carevasta bears' existence. If we ever find him, he may be able to help him, but with all our powers diminished, it just may not be possible, unless we can figure out why they are. I could tell it was

Vivax who cursed them, but if she's as diminished as the rest of us, it may not be possible either."

"Would killing her fix the problem?" I ask, feeling slightly bloodthirsty. I hate seeing Ghosie so miserable. He's such a gentle, loving soul, and he doesn't need any of this.

He grimaces. "Probably not. She would have to use her power to undo the curse, and it is not easy to kill a god."

My heart sinks, and I bite my lip. "Damn it. Well, I guess we need to add find Vivax to our list." My eyes slide to Brannock as he leaps into the air to grab the frisbee thing they are playing with. "What about the Aaz'axian curse? The one where all their women died too? That sounds like a very similar curse. Brannock has a daughter. She is part human, so he's hoping the curse won't work on her, but ideally, we shouldn't rely on that to save her either. Which god or goddess cursed them?"

He shakes his head and follows my gaze as Link tackles Brannock to the ground. The cheers and groans from the opposing team bring a smile to my lips. "No one knows. Hopefully Liliana may be able to shed some light on it."

I turn my attention back to the god. "So you think it's possible my grandma and your goddess is the same person? My grandpas sure seem to think so."

He shrugs as childish shouts draw our attention to the orchard.

I stand up and hold my hand out to Zeydan. "Come on, let's go see if they found some fruit."

He doesn't hesitate to take my hand, and I feel all warm and gooey. "It seems like the most probable thing. How that happened, I don't know. Lilessa often spent more time with her creations than the rest of us, inserting herself into the societies she created so she could pretend to be normal. Vivax was the exact opposite, holding herself aloof. Being the goddess of death comes with the stigma of being intimidating and scary, and she did nothing to expel that reputation. Us elementals were a little different. We tried to be involved in our creations' lives, but not to the extent where we inserted ourselves into them. We were happy to appear at religious services or holidays and bestow blessings when prayed too."

"Sounds lonely," I muse as the children notice our arrival and descend on us. There are hugs and kisses for both me and Zeydan, which startles him, and I can't help but grin as he bends down and awkwardly returns the affection.

He looks up at me with slightly bewildered eyes and nods. "It was, but I have a feeling that is all about to change." The smile that spreads across his lips as he manages to pick up all three children is blinding. He walks over to a tree that has fruit too high for them to reach and helps them each take a piece.

Eric sidles up next to me and mutters, "You're fucked." He grins wickedly and walks over to join them, holding out the basket for the fruit.

"You're not freaking kidding," I mutter to his retreating back. "So fucked."

# 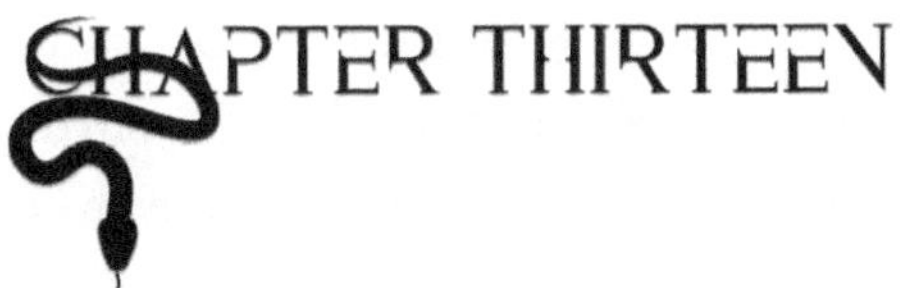CHAPTER THIRTEEN

**Lila**

We return to our suite once the children start to get clingy and cranky. They may be growing quickly, but they are still only a couple of months old, and they need plenty of sleep. In fact, they probably need it more because they are growing so fast. They don't put up any protest when we get them into their beds, and the rest of us collapse in the living area to chill for a while. Xavier makes coffee, and Cas turns on the television, the volume muted with some galactic movie playing in the background.

My grandpas headed to the med bay with Link to check on my grandma, and Echo and Maxsim have appeared from their rooms, looking much more refreshed than they were earlier.

"Hey, babe, how are you feeling?" Echo throws himself onto the couch next to me and snuggles into my side, giving me a soft kiss on the lips.

I smile at him. "Weary, but that was just what I needed." I pause, thinking about Ghosie who must have headed to his own room, because he wasn't here when we returned. Zeydan and Silac both promised they would go check on him when they went to their rooms, but I kind of want them all here too. My greedy mimic keeps whispering words of want in my ear, insisting they are ours too, but I barely know them, and my psyche, which is still struggling with my Earth upbringing, keeps telling me that it's wrong to want them as well. Silac is keeping firm boundaries despite his overt display a few nights ago. He's an honorable man, and at the moment, he wants everything to be sorted with his fiancée before anything goes further between us. I think avoiding being in my company is helping with that—out of sight, out of mind kind of thing.

"Good. You need to take every scrap of downtime you can get," he replies as Xavier hands me a coffee. When I take a sip, I'm surprised to find it laced with blood. Caspian's blood, by the taste of it—all ocean breezes and passionfruit. It's the best coffee I've ever had. I think maybe all my drinks should be laced like this in future. I wiggle with happiness, and my mates chuckle around me.

"We've all had Link draw some of our blood so we

can supplement your drinks during busy times. Saxon insists you aren't taking enough from the vein, and it's going to make you more volatile," Xavier explains.

"Don't want you gnawing on some random stranger's neck," Maxsim grumbles adorably as he stretches and heads to the kitchen, looking in the fridge for something to eat. He finds the leftovers from the picnic and pulls them out, making himself and Echo a plate, which he brings over and deposits in our pregnant omega's lap before taking a seat on the floor at his feet.

Echo purrs and tackles the food like he hasn't eaten in weeks. He is eating for three now, and I remember very well what that feels like.

My gaze swings to my Vilaxian mate, and I think about what Maxsim just said. Shit, I am the worst blood rose ever.

I drain my cup and place it on a nearby coffee table before going over to Saxon and climbing into his lap. "I'm sorry you ended up with such a neglectful blood rose." I put my arms around him and turn my neck to the side. "Please take what you need," I say to him, but he chuckles, and instead of sinking his fangs in, he places a kiss on the side.

"It's okay. The guys are supplementing my diet. We all know how much you've had on your plate, and they are happy to help. You didn't notice, but when Tirrian shifted before, he offered his vein to me after he stretched his wings. Let me tell you, that dragon is delicious, and I drank my fill. I'll be good for a day or two. Plus, if I drink from you now, that's not going to be all it is."

I squirm, remembering exactly how good Tirrian tastes, and mouth, "Thank you," to him. He just winks, and I stare for a moment, stunned at the complete one eighty from grumpy asshole to sexy, all-in bond mate. Saxon must enjoy my wiggling, because I feel his cock harden beneath me. I'm about to suggest we take this to my room, but before I can suggest it, Link appears in the entry of our suite. His silvery locks stick out in all directions, and he looks more panicked than I've ever seen him before.

"Lila," he shouts when he sees me. "Nikos is in labor. You need to hurry, he needs you." His panicked gaze shifts to Cas. "Can you go too since I can't be in the water?" Cas doesn't even hesitate as he gets to his feet, but I'm still frozen with shock on Saxon's lap.

Holy crap, it's time. I'm about to become a mom again, but because I wasn't the one actually carrying the babies, I don't know if I'm prepared for it. We haven't even really had a chance to stock the nursery with everything they might need. I have been meaning to read up on Aquilian babies, but with everything else that has happened, it's one of those things that hasn't happened. What if they don't like me? What if I can't bond with them? I haven't spent nearly enough time in my own Aquilian form. Hell, I've practically neglected my mate during his pregnancy. He's been very understanding, but how can he not be hurt by it?

I tried to call Nixie to see if she could give me some information, but she didn't accept my call. I was hurt but didn't let it stop me. I also put in a meeting request through the official Aquilian royal family secretary, hoping maybe she was too busy with her new responsibilities to take a moment of personal time, but that was also denied. I haven't shared that with any of my mates. I didn't want to upset them. I'm upset that Nikos's sister wasn't willing to help, but also because I thought Nixie and I formed a friendship. I guess I was more invested than she was.

"Lila," Xavier calls my name, and when I look up, everyone is staring at me impatiently. "Nik needs you." I feel him push a wave of encouragement and confidence at me, even though he's frowning. He must be able to feel all my doubt and anxiety.

"Yes, okay, yes, let's do this." Everyone stands up at the same time, and I freeze again and look at them with confusion. "Are you coming?" I ask, and it's Echo who answers.

"Of course we are. We may not be able to be in the water, but we want to be there to greet the new members of our family as soon as they arrive."

My heart melts, and my worry seeps away. This is my family, and we can do anything together. Hell, if we can wrangle three kraken shifter babies, two more aren't going to be that much harder.

"Okay, cool. Let's go. We're having babies." Okay, maybe my panic hasn't completely left the building, but at least it's died down to a slow simmer.

"I'm going to stay, and I'll call Silac or Ghosie to come sit with the babies, then I'll join you." Maxsim places a kiss on Echo's lips, followed quickly by one on mine.

"Thank you." I brush my hand down his furry arm and hurry to the door, not willing to wait around any longer, but as I pass Xavier, he reaches out and grabs me.

"We will meet you there," he tells the others, and in a flash, we materialize in the cavern at the bottom of the pool. I strip off my shirt as Xavier drops to my feet and slides my shorts and panties down my legs, tapping them so I step out.

My heart races as I look at the crystal blue water, which is churning like a washing machine. I can't see Nikos, but he has to be down there somewhere. "Should I wait for the others?" I ask him, doubting myself once more. "Link might have instructions."

He shakes his head and chuckles. "Did you need instruction?" he asks me, and I feel a little silly. "It should all be instinctual, at least for Nik. You just need to be there for moral support. Go, Cas will catch up."

I nod and give him an absent kiss then dive into the pool, my shift happening the moment my head touches the water. By the time my feet enter, they've already merged into a tail. The special film slides across my eyeballs, and the hazy water clears so I can see perfectly. I hear a sound that has my stomach roiling with sympathy, and I glance around for the source.

Nikos is moaning, and it's not the heady sounds of pleasure that I know he's capable of. This sound is filled with pain.

Instinct has me swimming downward, searching for the place inside me that is all his in the hope it will guide me in the right direction. The sight of an anemone much like the one in our special cave has me pausing with surprise. Where did that come from? Another pain-filled groan has me flicking my tail hard, giving me a burst of speed toward my mate. I push through the long, flowing tendrils of the sea creature and find my mate curled up as much as he can with such a huge belly. His tail is tight against his body, and his arms are wrapped around his baby bump. Agony is etched into the strained muscles and lines on his face, but his eyes brighten when he sees me.

*You're here.* His relief has me moving to his side. I slide my hands into his hair, stroking through the golden mass as I reply to him.

*Of course I am. I wouldn't want to be anywhere else.* I lean in and press a kiss to his lush mouth, which is pressed into a grimace. *I'm sorry I haven't been here more often. I'm a terrible mate.*

He shakes his head and relaxes slightly under my touch. *No, you're not, but I'm glad you're here now.* He gasps and then rolls away from me, his body twitching, and I watch on, helpless to do anything to make it better. I run my eyes over his body. He told me his sexual slit is where the babies will come out, but so far, it hasn't opened up, although his belly is way lower than it was the last time I saw him. It's like it sunk slightly into his groin.

*What can I do to help?* I ask him as he opens his mouth and bubbles stream out as he starts to pant through what I'm assuming is a contraction.

He can't answer me, the pain obviously too great, but a hand on my shoulder has me jumping and turning to find Cas has joined us, his tentacles stroking down my back in a soothing manner.

*Link said if you rub your tail against his, it should ease some of the ache. He should be swimming too, so lets get him up and in the water.* He moves to the side and wraps two tentacles around Nikos, carefully lifting him before swimming backwards through the anemone, wincing as the tendrils sting him but being ever so careful with our panting merman.

I follow after them, feeling a little helpless, but I can hear Caspian whisper to Nikos to unfurl his tail and move it back and forth. It takes a little coaxing, but he listens, and see the instant relief wash over his tight features as he sighs. I dart forward, wrapping my hands around him, his belly pressing against mine as I rub our tails together. He moans, and more tension drains out of him.

*That's good,* Cas encourages. I'm surprised I can hear his voice in my head, and I can tell that Nik can too. *Now, your tails rubbing together should help Nikos create a secretion to allow the birthing channel to open. Once it does, Lila, you need to let him swim on his own for a little bit. The movement should encourage the babies to move through the birthing channel. Then, when it opens even more, Nik needs to start, and I quote the good doctor, humping the water on the spot. The back and forth movement should help ease the babies out.*

I flick my tail again, and we start swimming in slow circles. Cas stays with us, his own tentacles propelling him to keep pace. His encouraging words and tone ease some of my panic as I feel a secretion start to build between our tails. It's thick, and I think it's actually leaking from my sexual slit, but we are pressed too close together for me to be able to look down and see for sure. Nik sort of sighs and goes lax in our embrace.

*Feels nice,* he murmurs as I lift a hand to push back his hair, wishing I had thought to grab hair ties to keep our locks off our faces. Our hair floats and tangles together, but I barely notice, my focus completely on my pregnant mate as I monitor his pain levels.

We swim for about ten minutes in slow circles at the bottom of the cave before his body goes taut in my arms again, and his breathing picks up once more.

*Little faster now, Lila. The more we move through the contractions, the better,* Cas advises us.

*How do you know all this?* I ask him, and he taps a finger to his temple.

*Xavier has Link in my head, and I'm just repeating all his instructions.* He grins. *It's really helpful. Apparently when a mer gives birth on Aquilia, there's usually a whole maternity team with the expectant parent.*

I can't stop the growl that rumbles up and out into

the water, the bubbles big and explosive. As much as I'm hurt that Nixie ignored my attempt to contact her, I'm more angry now. Nikos has basically been abandoned and has done nothing to deserve it. Maybe his mother is no better than his father was. It wouldn't surprise me, since enduring horrible treatment can make people change—sometimes for the better, but more often than not for the worse. I hope she isn't making her people suffer as much as she is hurting her son. Otherwise, I may have to have a discussion with my father-in-law and Saxon's aunt about the Vilaxians and warlocks overthrowing the current Aquilian royal family. That crown is my mate's birthright, and through him, the first baby we're about to welcome into this world.

Another groan from Nikos has all of that leaving my brain for now as I focus on his well-being. We do as Link and Cas instruct, and I move us swifter, my tail beating faster. The slick slide between us gets thicker, and I feel his slit open beneath me. I pull back and look down to judge how far it's opened. It's a long line, much longer than when his cock pokes out, but the edges are still close together. Cas releases his grip and swims around to have a look. He must be relaying the information to Link, because I see him nod, and then he returns to his place at Nik's back, rubbing his lower back.

*That's good. The contractions should start coming faster now as the babies move through the channel, but you need to keep rubbing together. It needs to open wide* enough to see a baby's head and allow the tail to pass through, which will be wider than the head. He keeps his voice low and soothing, but I feel my own muscles tighten at the thought. Fuck, poor Nik. That's going to tear him badly if it doesn't open farther. I rub harder and faster, my nipples pebbling at the friction as it presses against my clit inside my own sexual slit.

Link suggests you suck on his nipples. It should stimulate the sexual slit open, and they will swell with milk, ready to feed the babies, Cas says. His eyes are heated with lust, and one of his tentacles floats forward and strokes over my tail, sending spikes of pleasure through my body. I lean forward and wrap my lips around Nik's pebbled nipple, his fingers sliding into my hair as I suck hard before flicking my tongue over the nub. He groans, and his fingers tighten. I swap back and forth between the two, biting and sucking and rolling it around in my mouth, my hands massaging the flesh around it, Caspian holding the two of us together. I pull back and watch in amazement as they start to swell slightly.

Keep massaging them, Cas says huskily in my head as one of his tentacles drifts up to help. Nik throws his head back, leaning it on Cas's shoulder as I watch his suckers suction onto his nipple. I quiver, remembering how good that feels.

Things should start moving quickly now, he explains as I lean down, alternating licks and sucks when a gush of fluid flows into my mouth, and I just about choke on it in surprise. It's milky and musky but doesn't taste bad at all, and I swallow it down.

*The more you suck, the more that will develop for both babies,* Cas says as fluid gushes out of the nipple he's attending. Nik writhes between us, and I feel a roll of movement along my stomach. It won't be long now until we greet our babies.

# CHAPTER FOURTEEN

### Nikos

My body shudders under the dual sensations of Lila and Cas attending my nipples and the rolling waves of contractions. Alternating bursts of pain and pleasure cause me to moan and thrash in their hold, but they hold on tight, not letting me go. I feel my slit start to stretch and moan in pain as another contraction just about has me curling into the fetal position again, but Lila's tail and Cas's tentacles hold me in place. My pecs ache as they fill with milk and stretch, allowing more room for it to gather so I can feed my babies.

I learned all about pregnancy for both males and females in school but didn't pay too much attention. I wasn't looking for a mate back then and had many males and females begging to take my cock. Not once was I tempted to mate any of them, so I assumed I wouldn't be the one bearing our children. I was going to be king, after all, and kings don't show weakness, nor do they lower themselves to bearing children—or that's what my father drilled into me. That all changed when I met Lila, but the pain is worse than anything I've ever felt. It's like someone took a trident and shoved it directly into my stomach. Red-hot waves claw at my insides over and over again, so intense I can barely catch my breath. The contractions are so close together now that I barely have time to recover before another crashes into me, stealing my breath. I'm exhausted and miserable.

*You're doing so well,* Lila coos to me as Caspian strokes his fingers through my hair. *You're the best Papa these babies are going to have, working so hard to bring them safely into our lives.* I want to preen at her praise, but I'm too tired, so I give her a weak smile before gritting my teeth as another wave of pain crashes over me.

Lila pulls away slightly and looks down at my stomach, and her eyes widen with surprise. I tense up, worried something has gone wrong, but she recovers quickly, blanking her face.

*Cas, Nik's slit has opened wide, and I think I can see a head,* I hear her tell Caspian. Somehow, we've all been able to connect telepathically. The wave of pain eases, and I flop my head back on the kraken man's shoulder, unable to hold it up anymore. His tentacles caress my body in a gentle massaging way that has me sighing as he soothes my tired muscles.

He doesn't respond right away, and I assume he's communicating with Link. Thankfully, one of us had the forethought to learn about Aquilian births. It's not like I could do much from the bottom of the pool. He did share some of it with me during my checkups, but I'm embarrassed to admit I was too nervous to really pay attention.

My mind was firmly fixated on what kind of father I was going to be. I had a terrible role model growing up, and I refuse to be anything like him. When he wasn't ignoring us, he was berating us over what he perceived as our flaws. The way he treated my mother was worse. She was such a loving, caring woman when I was small, but over the years, his treatment of her and us made her a fragile, bitter thing. It didn't help that he paraded numerous women through his harem and sired other children with them. The crown of Aquilia was hers through her family bloodline, but once he married her, he usurped the power through cruelty and subjugation, and once he had hold of it, he didn't let it go.

I watched my mother's soul wither and die, and I swore I would never forgive him and that I would never become like him. I'm ashamed to admit the minute we were offered a chance to leave with the circus, both Nixie and I jumped without any other thought. That only allowed him to spread his foulness to the rest of Aquilia. I had let my people down, and now I'm not sure there is any chance of forgiveness. Even with his death, I fear my mother's rule will be no better, her nature as corroded and unforgiving as my father's from her own bad treatment.

I should have challenged him and taken his crown from him, but having been torn down for so long, I couldn't see my way past the apathy I felt toward being the crown prince of Aquilia. Now, being mated to Lila, there is no chance for me to be the king my people need so desperately, and I can only hope that Nixie can be queen sooner rather than later. Hopefully my mother will see the potential in her favorite child. When she looks at me, she just sees my father and feels disdain.

Now all of that is in the past, though, I have to focus on being the best mate and parent I can be. With the next wave of contractions, I grunt as Caspian's tentacles release me and Lila swims backward.

*Nikos, you need to swim on the spot, and your tail needs to beat forward and backward in a rocking motion, this will help push your first merling out.* Caspian's tone is urgent, and I feel the loss of their touch greatly, but I steal my spine and grit my teeth, determined to do right by my family. Another huge contraction hits, this one bigger than any of the previous ones, and I open my mouth and shout, unable to keep quiet.

*Flap that tail, Nikos, now,* Lila growls, her eyes focused on the gaping hole in my tail. *I can see their head, and this one has your gorgeous golden hair with beautiful green streaks like your scales. Wow, so much hair.* She holds her hands out as I do my best to pump my tail back and forth, my whole body twitching and shuddering like it's covered in sea mites.

*You're doing well, keep moving.* Cas has moved to the side of me, and he splits his attention between my face and my tail. *That's it, their shoulders are out now. Keep going, the next part should be easier, but the tail is going to be the hardest bit. Even though it's curled up, it's still a lot wider than the head. It's going to hurt the most, but you have to bear down.*

Fuck, it's going to hurt more? I don't think I have the strength for this. The contraction wave eases, and I pant, my chest heaving, and I struggle to catch my breath.

*Look down, Nik,* Caspian encourages, and my eyes go to Lila and then my tail, and I gasp in shock. Half in and half out is one of my babies, and my exhaustion just seems to float away as I stare in amazement. Lila is right, it does have my coloring, and a tingle of excitement flutters in my belly. I can do this. I want to hold them in my arms and shower them with kisses. When the next contraction starts, I grit my teeth and pump my tail back and forth, jerking around like an electrified jellyfish, but I feel the body slide out, and Lila reaches forward.

*No, don't touch them,* Caspian shouts. *They need to be born into the water for their tails to uncurl, and then their swimming instincts kick in. If you touch them before the first breath and stroke of their tail, you'll interfere with the natural urge to do any of that.*

Lila's eyes widen with panic, and she swims backward out of the way. I'd laugh at her panic if I wasn't in so much pain.

*Move, Nik, they are just about here*, she says, unable to take her eyes off what's happening.

I feel one of Cas's tentacles grip my shoulder and give it a squeeze, even though the rest of him is staying clear of my thrashing body.

*Just a little more, my friend, and your merling will be here. What do you think it will be, boy or girl?* he asks, and I know he's trying to distract me from the pain. The pain eases once more, and I still, trying to catch my breath, but the water feels like it's syrup as it flows in and out of my gills, and my lungs struggle to expand, but the next contraction rushes through my body, and I grit my teeth and pound my tail, determined for this one to be the one that brings my baby into the world.

Pain like nothing else tears through my body, and I scream loudly, the water around us shuddering with the shock wave. Both Lila and Caspian are thrust backward, but they watch on with sheer wonder in their eyes as my baby shoots into the water, their beautiful tail unfurling as they take their first breath. Their eyes open, and their tail starts to beat in tiny motions mirroring mine. I heave out a rush of relief as my eyes rake over their form. I instinctively know it's a boy, and he has my coloring. His hair is golden with green streaks, and the scales on his tale are a beautiful golden color, with interspersed green scales, making it shimmer like a hologram. He looks around, dazed and confused, but his eyes alight on Lila, and he darts toward her, slamming into her body and snuggling his head against her breasts, nudging at her nipples to feed.

Her mouth drops open in shock, and I can't help the blast of laughter that flows from my mouth. Caspian echoes it as we watch her try to wrangle the slippery creature. When he doesn't get what he wants, he screws his face up and starts to cry. Yup, that's my boy.

*Ah, help!* Lila gathers him into her arms and rocks him back and forth and sings to him, but she looks at us with panic in her eyes.

*He's hungry*, I tell her, and she looks down at him in wonder.

*He's a boy?*

I smile at the love in her eyes and nod my head.

*Link says you need to hang onto him for now. It won't be long until the contractions start again. Nik can feed them both when labor is over*, Caspian tells us as he rubs a soothing hand over my back.

Lila swims closer, and I run a finger over his little cheek. His tears fade away, and he looks up at me, his beautiful glowing green eyes wide with awe and wonder. I feel love pulse through my mind. His brain is unable to form words yet, but he can still share feelings telepathically. I can tell he's very hungry, but he loves both Lila and me.

*Did you feel that?* she asks me, her voice filled with reverence. I nod as a smile lights up my mate's face. *He loves us.* She sounds as awed as I am, and she swims a little closer so we can both snuggle our baby between us. A tentacle creeps up and brushes the little boy's tail. He makes a squeaking sound and looks around for the source. Caspian appears, and the two of them study each other. I can feel Caspian's nerves and his worry that he's going to scare our new boy, but after a moment, a small smile appears on his lips, and he coos inside our heads, his love spreading to our kraken. I watch as Caspian's body visibly loosens, and he smiles back.

*He's beautiful. You've done so well, you two,* he tells us, running a finger over the baby's nose and bopping him on the end. The little one squirms, but Lila holds him tight.

*Hang on, you have plenty of time to play. We need to wait for your sibling,* she tells him gently.

Just as she says that, I feel the muscles in my back start to tighten, followed by the ones in my stomach, and the pain that eased to a dull throb comes back with a vengeance. I screw up my face and clamp my lips together, determined not to cry out and frighten our little one, but the pain proves to be too great. Instead of screaming like before, I just groan as my eyes roll back in my head, and I release my hold on our boy. Lila keeps her grip and swims backward, worry written all over her features.

*Okay, Nik, you've got this. Just a few more flaps, and you'll be able to hold both babies in your arms and nurse. I know it's painful, but you've got this. You're the prince of Aquilia and a warrior, so pain is irrelevant. Cas's* tone hardens. *Now pump that tail*, he commands, and I take a huge breath, water rushing through my gills, giving me a burst of energy as I wave my tail back and forth.

*I can see another head*, Lila tells me, keeping her distance. *Oh, they have my hair. I'm not sure how, since it wasn't that color when they were conceived. It must be magic.* She sounds awed and mystified, and I can't help but smile despite the pain. This is so worth it, and I would take ten times the amount of agony to see the look of love and wonder on her face.

The contractions come and go four more times, and finally, another baby pushes into the water, their tale unfurling, and I know we have a daughter. She's a gorgeous girl with hair and a tail just like her mother's. Her fins are longer and more delicate than her brother's, whose are thick and solid and designed to cut through the water. Her eyes open wide, and she has the same glowing green irises as her brother. Her little lips purse, and I expect to hear a wail of discontent, but she just yawns sleepily, swims toward me, and nuzzles against my chest.

My heart just about explodes as I gather the little girl in my arms, projecting love and warmth and safety to my little girl. I feel her own emotions inside my chest and sigh with contentment as Lila swims over with our son in her arms. The four of us snuggle together, nuzzling our heads against our babies and whispering words to them. Caspian extends a tentacle toward our daughter, stroking it gently over her long, delicate tail fins, and her eyes widen in shock, but she soon giggles, and Caspian practically melts.

*That's Daddy Cas*, I tell my children, wanting them to know that he's their father as well. They both push out of our arms and zip toward the startled kraken. Lila and I laugh, wrapping our arms around each other as he struggles to catch the little merlings, who are darting in and out of his tentacles, almost like they are playing a game of chase.

Lila wraps her arms around me and presses a kiss to my lips. *You made beautiful babies. I love you so much,* she tells me, and I smile as a wave of utter exhaustion drags me down. She holds me tighter as her tongue delves into my mouth, but all I can do is hang on as she praises me and lavishes me with affection.

I preen, but it's halfhearted. I need a nap, but first, I need to feed our babies. My pecs are heavy and full of milk, and the urge to nurse is a dull ache deep inside me.

Caspian manages to catch the two babies and cradle them in his tentacles. He rocks them back and forth, soothing them. *You need to nurse. Link says this first burst of energy is going to wear off. It's designed to be able to escape predators, but it soon runs out. He suggests we settle in the anemone and Nik feeds them and then you all nap. Feeding will cause the slit to close and return to its former use. You also need to feed them often over the next twenty-four hours.*

He starts in the direction of the anemone, and Lila and I follow, her arm wrapped around my waist to support me. We push through the long, flowing tentacles of the anemone, and I settle myself into its cushioned heart. Caspian passes me both children, and I cradle one in each arm, holding them each to a nipple. I watch as they both latch on immediately and start suckling. A rush of pride fills me as I nourish my babies. I feel my eyes drift closed and struggle to keep them open. A small ache continues in my tail where my slit is, but I also feel the muscles and flesh start to move back together, healing the birthing channel.

*Sleep, my prince*, Lila whispers, brushing a hand through my hair as Cas strokes my tail flukes gently. *You need time to recover. We will be here when you wake up, and we will decide on names and introduce our babies to our family.*

I feel my eyes drift closed, knowing I did good and delivered our babies safely into the world. Now I need to get fit and strong again so I can keep them that way.

# CHAPTER FIFTEEN

### Caspian

I watch as my mate and her mate sleep with their children snuggled between them. I know there is nothing down here that can hurt them, but I want to be here in case they need anything. I also need to leave them and go back to the surface to give everyone else an update. I told Link I was going radio silent, and we still haven't announced the babies' sexes to the others yet. I think if I make them wait any longer, they may try to swim to the bottom of the pool themselves. I'm sure the warlock is already trying to plot how he can spell the others to breathe underwater.

After I place a kiss on each of their foreheads, I make my way to the surface. I find most of Lila's mates there in various states of impatience. Echo and Maxsim are both in feline form, their eyes closed as they wait patiently. Link is making notes on the tablet built into his arm. I'm sure he's recording everything that happened in case Nikos ever has another pregnancy, though I doubt he wants to go through that again anytime soon—it was brutal. Lila's egg laying was practically a walk in the park compared to that. I could tell by the horrified look on her face whenever Nik wasn't looking.

My gaze slides to the pregnant omega, and I pray that his isn't anything like that, because Maxsim will lose his shit.

Saxon and Xavier are the most agitated. They pace back and forth, growls of annoyance rumbling from their chests. They are the ones that sound like shifters at the moment, and I stifle the laughter that gathers in my chest. They both look like they would dive in and tackle me, and I know Saxon hates water.

My gaze slides to the grandpas. They have made themselves comfortable, bringing down a little table and chairs from the upper levels. They have coffee and are playing a game of cards with Silac and Tirrian. I hear muttering as the pot grows and cards are exchanged. I grimace. I've played cards with the Adams brothers in the past and have been lucky not to lose my shirt. They are card sharks.

Brannock and Zeydan have also brought down chairs from the upper levels, and they are sitting in a far corner, murmuring quietly to each other. I know Zeydan felt guilty about not being able to help Ghosie, so I wonder if he's trying to work out the root of the

Aaz'axian curse. Zeydan is still an unknown entity, but I genuinely believe he doesn't mean any of us any harm. He helped Lila defeat the Madovians and get to the middle of the death forest. He claims she's his mate, and who am I to argue with a god? The only people missing are Ghosie, whom I'm assuming is watching the other children, and Broderick, who is either manning the ship or resting.

Maxsim is the first to notice my head poking above the water, and he rumbles a purr, then everyone's eyes swing to me.

"Well?" Xavier demands, putting his hands on his hips and glaring down at me.

"I'd like to announce the arrival of two new members of the family. Nikos gave birth to a beautiful baby boy first, followed by a gorgeous baby girl who looks just like her mama. Congratulations, Daddies and Grandpas."

Shouting and cheering echo through the cavern as everyone celebrates the arrival of our new ones. Hugs are exchanged, and everyone is beaming like they were the ones who gave birth themselves.

"Is Nik okay?" Link asks, and the worry on his face makes my already mushy feelings for the cyborg even mushier.

"It was a long, hard labor, and the pain was great, but he is fine—exhausted but fine. When I left them, they were sleeping. Nik nursed them, and his body is recovering like you predicted," I assure the cyborg, and he nods, relief finally gleaming in his eyes as he smiles.

"That's great. It should take a few hours for his birthing slit to close and return to normal. The more he feeds, the faster it should happen," he explains distractedly, making more notes.

"The babies have voracious appetites. I bet Nik will be back to normal quicker than ever."

"Yes, multiple births aren't common on Aquilia, so you may be right. Twice the sucking action." He types a few more notes.

"What about names?" Saxon asks, and I shake my head.

"I'm sorry, my friend. I don't know. We didn't get a chance to discuss it."

He looks disappointed. "Never mind, I can't wait to meet them. How long do you think they'll nap for?" He looks longingly at the water, and I stifle the smile that wants to cross my lips. Who would have thought General Saxon would be so excited to meet babies?

"I'm not sure. Nikos was exhausted. It certainly wasn't as easy as laying kraken eggs. Why don't we all go have something to eat and check on the children? I'm sure they are nagging Ghosie to come visit, and then we can all return. If we write a list of names that we like, maybe that will help them with a decision."

Xavier has been quiet all this time. I could tell he was still trying to figure out how he could get to the bottom of the pool. I'm sure if we were much longer, he would have conjured a bubble of air around his head and teleported into the pool, but my suggestion has him swinging his attention back to everyone.

"Caspian is right. We are excellent at naming babies and should definitely write a list of suggestions."

One of the grandpas snorts indelicately, and Xavier scowls in their direction but can't figure out which one it was. I'm almost certain it was Eric, but I decide not to drop him in the shit. I do wonder if Xavier will be so open to "suggestions" when it comes to naming his offspring.

William plays a card, and the rest of the men at the table groan loudly. He smirks and pulls the pot closer to him then starts to shove his winnings into his pockets. "Sounds like a great idea to me. I'm ready to eat something," he announces.

"Of course you are," John grumbles. "You just took us for all our money."

I climb out of the pool, staying in my half kraken form, and Link tosses a towel at me so I can dry off. I'm eager to go back to our suite and snuggle with my own children and tell them about their new brother and sister. "Maybe the kids might have some name suggestions as well," I say, tongue-in-cheek, knowing that if they had their way, our new babies would definitely be named after one of their favorite cartoon characters.

"It won't hurt to have a list. With as many mates as Lila has, I'm sure there will be many more children," Eric says gleefully, rubbing his hands together. "Lots and lots of grandbabies to spoil, not to mention many Adams to help with the circus. Maybe one day we will have enough that we won't ever have to hire any acts.

Right, brothers?" He slaps John on the shoulder, who nods his head.

"Wouldn't that be lovely?"

Everyone makes their way up the stairs and back to the suite. There are a lot of names being tossed around, and I feel a small amount of pity for Nikos, but not too small, because I had to deal with the same thing, although it all worked out in the end.

Two hours later, Tirrian and I return to the Aquilian pool with three excited little kraken babies who are just about jumping out of their skin. The rest are going to follow in an hour or so, but they decided we should have a swim first so as not to overwhelm the new ones. I'm not sure if it's the right decision, but Jack, Cordy, and Cally wouldn't take no for an answer. Tirrian also has a list of names on the tablet tucked under his arm.

We leave it on the card table in the bottom cavern before the babies shift into their kraken forms. They don't have a half form yet, but I caution them to be gentle with their new siblings and tell them that they are their protectors. I'm not sure if it will work, but thankfully the new little ones seemed quite sturdy when they were playing with my tentacles, so I'm hoping it won't be too much for them. The four of us enter the water and wait for Tirrian to shift. He strips off his clothes, and before I can blink, he shifts into his water dragon form. I haven't seen it before, and I know he is usually much bigger, but he has taken a smaller size so he can swim around the pool. Unlike his air dragon, this one is turquoise green, but his eye color is the same as his other dragon. His body is long, like a serpent, and his four legs don't look like they could hold him up on land. This form doesn't look to have wings, but he has webbing between each of his toes, and long, mustache-like tendrils draping down on either side of his elongated snout. He slithers elegantly into the water, barely splashing, and swims toward us, using his legs to propel himself through the water. The children swim around him, and their cries of delight are loud in my head.

*Look at Daddy Dragon. He is so pretty*, Cordelia says, brushing her body against him. *So shiny.*

He blows out a breath, and bubbles encase the children, who squeal with delight. I wince at the piercing sounds rattling my brain. They frolic a little, but then I remember that the others are sleeping, so I caution them to be quiet.

*We need to be quiet now. We don't want to give the new babies a fright. How about you jump on Daddy Dragon's back, and we will go meet your new brother and sister?*

All three of them suction onto Tirrian's back, and the five of us swim downward. It's not far to the bottom, and when they see the anemone, I can feel their curiosity, even though they stay silent.

We're almost to the formation when Lila swims out with a huge smile on her face, and she opens her arms wide. *My babies, I missed you. Come give Mama a cuddle*, she calls to them. She looks radiant as the three krakens swarm her, giving her tentacles kisses. I can hear them chattering inside her head, asking question after question. She just laughs and does her best to answer them before swimming toward Tirrian and giving him a kiss on the nose.

*Hello, beastie. I missed you too. I haven't gotten to see you in this form since the mating dome*, she teases him, and I remember the story of the large, horny water dragon and chuckle.

He blushes adorably, obviously able to hear her in his head too, and sticks out his tongue, slowly dragging it over her body. I see her shudder and wonder if it's in disgust or a lustier feeling.

The children are impatient, and Jack tries to swim into the anemone but stops as soon as he brushes against one of its tentacles and it stings him. He starts to cry, and Lila quickly gathers him into her arms, soothing him.

*You can't swim in there, it will sting you. You have to wait. Daddy Nik will bring the babies out to you, but remember they are smaller than you, so you have to be gentle*, she tells our children, and Jack stops sobbing and promises to be gentle.

*How is he doing?* I ask our wife, and she beams at me.

*He's wonderful. The babies have nursed every half*

*hour or so, and his body has mostly recovered. He slept through most of it, but I have been watching over them. They have big appetites.*

*Have you named them yet?* Tirrian asks, his eyes not shifting from the anemone. I can see the longing in his gaze. I think his dragons are as desperate as my kraken was for Lila to lay their eggs. He may get a chance sooner than the others too, because he will share the job of sitting on their nest. Lila won't be solely responsible like she was for most of our pregnancy.

*No, not yet. Nikos would like everyone's input.* Lila screws up her nose slightly. *Not that I think that's such a great idea, but he insists.*

I chuckle and feel a rush of love for our merman. He has certainly lost that selfish streak, and I'm proud of him.

*That's lucky, since everyone definitely has their opinions. There is a list on a tablet back in the cavern if you would like to read over it,* I tell her, and she rolls her eyes, laughing.

*Of course there is.*

Before either Tirrian or I can respond, Nikos pokes his head out, and a smile lights up his face when he sees Tirrian and the children. He turns back the way he came and calls, *Come on, little ones, come and meet another daddy and your brother and sisters.*

He swims farther out, and I scan his body. Lila is right, his tail has mostly closed up. There's still a slight line, but even that's not as long as it was during labor.

He still looks a little tired, but that's to be expected. My attention soon swings to the two beings following him, and a smile creeps across my lips. They are perfect, miniature versions of their parents, and it seems like they may have inherited their boldness too, because instead of waiting for the dragon and our other children to come to them, they dart around their dad faster than any of us expected and swim directly in front of the smaller yet still intimidating dragon. Our little krakens leave their mother's side and swim over more cautiously than the merlings, and I can feel their curiosity and nerves. Instead of being their usual bull-dozer selves, they wait and watch.

Nikos quickly gets over his surprise and swims over to them. *This is Daddy Dragon*, he tells the two little ones, rubbing a hand over Tirrian's snout. I watch with amusement as the water dragon leans into the affection. *And this is Jack, your brother*. He points to my son before gesturing to each girl in turn. *And Cordelia and Calypso are your sisters.*

The merlings study their new family members seriously, and I hold my breath in anticipation. Tirrian huffs a breath of air that creates a multitude of bubbles that swirl around the little ones. They giggle and swat at the bubbles with their hands, which is enough to jolt the krakens into action. They join the fun, and the five of them zip in and out of the bubbles and around the dragon like they are playing a game of tag. Once the merlings are capable of speech, they will all be able to communicate inside their heads like we do, but that won't happen until after their first shift. Link said it takes about two weeks for them to shift for the first time, similar to my babies. He thinks they will probably be human-sized toddlers as well, with advanced speech, unlike human babies.

*Well, that looks like it's going well. Shall we go to the surface and look over the list so we can finally give our babies names?* Lila asks, putting her hand around Nik's waist and leaning her head against his shoulder as we watch our babies play together, the delighted dragon blowing bubbles for their enjoyment.

*I would love nothing more*, he replies, no sign of the ditsy airhead he portrayed so effectively.

# CHAPTER SIXTEEN

## Lila

"We would like to introduce you to our babies," I announce to our gathered family. Everyone is here, Bubby having set the autopilot so he could be here like I requested. Even Ghosie, who is still subdued after his interaction with Zeydan, is here, looking at the merlings with so much longing, it hurts my heart.

"This is Typhoon," Nikos holds up our son so everyone can see him, and the cranky little boy waves both his arms around and cries at being lifted out of the water, much like the furious storm he's been named for.

There are cheers and cries of welcome from our family. Link looks surprised then proud, because he was the one who suggested the name. Nik and I couldn't think of a more appropriate name.

Then it's my turn to lift my mini me out of the water so they can see her, including her delicate tail flukes. "And this is Hali," I tell them, keeping with our nautical theme. "It means from the sea, and I couldn't go past it. It's so pretty and perfect for our little angel." My gaze moves to Saxon, who was the one who presented that name. They were all allowed to propose one boy name and one girl name, otherwise the list would have been crazy, but Nik and I had the final decision.

Saxon puffs out his chest and looks smug as the rest of them coo and call to our mer princess, trying to get her attention.

"What wonderful names," William congratulates us as we place the children back into the water. The kraken babies encourage them to swim over to the little ledge, and once there, they shift back into their other forms. The merlings look startled for a moment, but the babies babble to them in childish voices, introducing them to their daddies one by one. Each man gets dragged into the water so they can give the new little ones a proper welcome. Even Zeydan, Ghosie, and Silac get introduced to our new little ones. They look slightly overwhelmed, and I decide that's probably enough introductions for the day.

"Okay, it must be pretty late. How about we call it a night, and you can swim with Hali and Ty in the morning?" I tell them. There are a few tears, and Jack crosses his arms and sits his butt down in the water, refusing to move, but Xavier just scoops him up and carries him up the stairs, his wails echoing back down to us. The girls are better behaved, and with a sloppy kiss for each of their siblings, they let Saxon and Tirrian lead them away.

Neither of my cats got into the water, and I can see the merlings looking at them with curiosity in their eyes.

"Daddy Echo and Daddy Maxsim aren't very good with water," I explain, but I'm not sure if they understand. "You can have cuddles with them once you shift for the first time."

Ty's face falls, and he starts to swim backward, but Hali screws up her face in concentration, and I gasp as she shimmers and her mer body disappears, replaced with two legs. She still has scales on her body and face, but so does Nik in his two-legged form. She claps her hands with delight, hurries through the water, and climbs out before she stumbles over to the two lightning cats. She's unsteady, but Maxsim leaps forward and gathers her into his arms. His expression of shock must match mine.

"Is that supposed to happen?" Echo asks, pointing at the little girl before looking at Nik. Nik shakes his head.

"No, not for a few weeks." He sounds flabbergasted.

"Kitty!" Hali shouts in a musical voice that has us all sighing, and I feel my body relax.

"Whoa, her song is powerful." Nik looks at Link, who is busy scanning Hali's body, checking her over.

He nods and looks back at us. "Just as I expected, she shows the same kind of DNA markers as the krakens. She is perfectly healthy, I promise."

Only the cats and Link remain, the rest of them having retreated upstairs, so it's not so loud and chaotic down here now.

"Should we try to get her to change back?" I ask Nik, not sure what to do.

Ty is watching on with a frown on his face, but he has made no move to attempt the same. Hali is busy running her hands over Maxsim's fur, babbling happy sounds at him. I snicker at his shocked expression, but Echo quickly joins the cuddles and starts purring as he rubs his head against her little back, scent marking her as he likes to do to all of us. She squeals with delight and wriggles around in Maxsim's arms and pulls on Echo's whiskers. He winces and softly untangles her little fingers, whispering about being gentle.

"I don't know. I've never heard of a merling who shifted before the first two weeks. I still need to feed her." He sounds lost, and I wish I could call Nixie and ask her, but that's out of the question.

Link must be on the same wavelength as me. "Shall we contact your family to announce the births and ask if they know of any instances of merlings shifting within the first twenty-four hours?"

Ty must be getting tired, because he swims into Nik's arms and nuzzles against his chest. He shows no inclination whatsoever to follow his sister, and I don't think that's a bad thing. Now I have three headstrong girls, which must make all their daddies' assholes pucker. I smother the smirk that wants to break free, since now is not really the time to gloat about that.

"No," is Nik's very abrupt response before he clears his throat and answers a little calmer. "No, I don't want to contact my family. I haven't heard a word from either my mother or Nixie since we left. I think that shows how much they care about me and my babies. If you could, please do a little more research. I'm sure you have access to medical journals or maybe contact the Celestians." He looks hopefully at Link, whose eyes soften as he nods his head.

"Of course. I'll go to the med bay and explore all my databases and contact the queens to see if they have any suggestions. Will you be okay here?" He looks between us, his concern making my heart ache with love.

"We will be fine," I assure him, flicking my tail and swimming toward the ledge. I allow my fins to fade away so I can climb out and collect our little girl, who is now busy chasing both Max's and Echo's tails, but they keep them moving quickly so she can't grab them, a look of indulgence on both their faces.

"Come on, my little guppy, let's get you back in the water and feed you." I scoop her up, and she squeals so loudly both the cats clamp their paws over their ears.

"Wow," Echo murmurs. "She has a set of lungs on her."

She kicks and screams and wiggles like crazy, but I manage to wrestle her back into the water. Just like that, her legs disappear, reforming into her tail. I guess she isn't able to control it consciously yet, thank goodness.

She's still wailing and bashing against my shoulder as I will my own change and sink beneath the water, cutting off her external noise. It now switches to screams inside my head, and I grimace as she makes her disappointment known. Her vocabulary is mostly still baby babble, but I make out the word "kitty" and "mine." She's going to have a fight on her hands if she thinks she has exclusive rights to my lightning cat mates. Her big sisters and brother will not stand for that. I'll make sure I have another important thing to deal with and let the guys sort that out.

I see Nikos and Ty swimming next to us. Ty is latched onto Nik's nipple and feeding as Nik brushes a hand over his head, looking calm and serene. Well, at least we have one calm baby. We settle back into the anemone, and I pass Hali over to her father once she calms down and decides her hunger is more important than her righteous anger. While he feeds them, I close my eyes and nap. I know I'm going to need to take as many cat naps as possible to keep my energy up. I'm also going to have to up my intake of blood and sex for the next trials we have to face. We're only a few days out from Fluxx, and it's time to deal with Silac's problems. Hopefully that job will be quick and easy, and we can focus on returning to Earth and rescuing Brannock's Chloe from Agent Smith's clutches.

✴

When our ship finally docks at the space station high above Fluxx, both Hali and Typhoon have shifted and made the move from the large pool to our suite. They still spend plenty of time in the water, but the pool in our suite lets them have longer stretches before returning to the large pool.

Watching the relationships develop between our five children has been amusing as well as frustrating. Ty and Jack have bonded despite the couple of months age gap and are as thick as thieves, but we are constantly breaking up fights between the girls. There's been hair pulling and biting that has required me to shift and heal Cordy when she wouldn't let Hali have her turn riding Maxsim's back. I didn't think merlings had the same sharp teeth as adult Aquilians, but Hali put that idea to rest after she took a large chunk of flesh out of Cordy's leg. I was horrified and cried to my mates for over an hour.

They just laughed it off and told me that it was normal, and that they were trying to form a hierarchy and I should let them. As much as I don't disagree, I draw the line at permanently maiming each other. Hali was punished and was not allowed any contact with

Maxsim or Echo or allowed to play with the other children for two days. She was sent to the big pool, where Cas, Tirrian, and I took turns supervising her punishment. Do you know what the little shit did? Well, she didn't care one little bit and spent the whole time picking the gems off the wall of the gem cavern and hoarding them in a little coral rock cave she found in the reef. Tirrian was super proud of her hoarding, but I had to explain to them that the gems didn't belong to either of them, and that Nik would be upset if he found his beautiful cave destroyed. Again, a tantrum ensued, both Hali's and the dragon's, but he calmed her by telling her he would help her start a hoard when we got to Fluxx and visited his family.

I was speechless, but he growled at me when I tried to intervene. Heaven save me from overprotective daddies. I can't even imagine what he's going to be like if we have a clutch of eggs for him. It's a disaster in the making, but he assured me all of his babies would have their own hoards, so I felt a little mollified after that.

"Lila, honey, you look exhausted," Mira, Caspian's mother, says to me as I enter the space port from our ship.

She and Murphy insisted on greeting us. My grandpas are going to stay with the ship for now to look after my grandma, and Zeydan and Ghosie both decided to stay behind and assist, but they are on call if we need them. They think their presence may cause more chaos than we need, and I guess they aren't wrong. A living, breathing god and a man who can turn you into a sex puppet with the brush of his fur probably aren't the stealthiest teammates. Echo, for obvious reasons, is also staying behind. Nobody wanted to risk him in his delicate state, and he was happy to comply. I think he has plans to pump Zeydan and Ghosie for more personal information.

I debated whether or not to bring the children with us, but Mira and Murphy insisted they would look after them while we were attending to Silac's family drama. Caspian and Nikos will stay as well, and I'm sure they will enjoy swimming in Cas's home waters.

Before I can answer, her focus switches to the group behind me, and she gasps, putting her hand to her mouth as tears well in her eyes. I follow her gaze and smile at the sight. Caspian, Nikos, Xavier, Saxon, and Link all have a baby in their arms. There was a small argument over who would carry whom, but it was finally sorted. Tirrian is still frowning that he lost out, but he got plenty of time in the water, or that was Xavier's argument. Brannock and Maxsim just look amused at the whole situation, while Silac is tense and ready to get this show on the road. He's been surly, but deep down, I know he understands the need for the delay.

There's a flurry of movement as Mira and Murphy crowd the guys while Caspian introduces the children to one set of grandparents. Mira cries openly as she swings Cordelia around in her arms, remarking on the beauty of all our babies.

"Good job, Lila. That should keep Mom and Dad off the rest of our backs for the next year or two at least. Just make sure there are plenty of visits." I chuckle as Malik hip bumps me and swings his arm over my shoulders. He is planning on leaving with us once we take care of the basilisk problem. We had to mess up his previous plans, but he wasn't upset. He knew what we were doing was important.

"You wait. I have a friend I'd like you to meet. You never know, your kraken might pull an act like Caspian's, and you'll be the one getting all the praise." I smirk at him as he shudders, but I still have every intention of introducing him to Magenta. Last time I spoke to her, she was sad about Nixie, and things weren't going all that well with Hale and Velorina. She informed me they decided to form a clan with Saxon's brother, Xenos. I found that weird, because there was an air of hostility between the two groups, but I guess things can change quickly. It doesn't look like they will be returning to the circus. When I talked about it with Saxon, he told me not to worry and said his aunt would find us another troupe, which was a huge relief to me.

"Not anytime soon, I can assure you," he swears, but I see longing in his eyes as he strolls over and snatches Jack out of his father's arms and lifts him in the air, telling him that he's going to be his favorite uncle.

God, I can't wait for every day to be like this one, when all of the drama is behind us.

# CHAPTER SEVENTEEN

### Lila

We get everyone settled at Mira and Murphy's and try to make contact with Xavier's parents. We get no response from them, which is worrying. Xavier said he hadn't heard from them since they first advised us that Silac's father had been turned to stone and was being held for ransom, but he said he hadn't been concerned because that's not unusual for his parents, but for them not to respond now that we are actually on the planet has his magic sparking wildly.

"The only reason they wouldn't respond to me is if they had also been turned to stone." He stalks back and forth across the warehouse office. We are using Caspian's family's warehouse to make our plans. It's located near the naga shipyards. It's why Cas and Silac have been friends for so many years. They grew up in the same circles.

"We need to get eyes on the place and get an idea of what kind of forces we are up against before we step inside to make negotiations." Saxon is in general mode, and he's looking over blueprints. "The last thing we need is for all of us to be turned to stone as well. I'm assuming that's what the basilisks want to do, so they can fully take over your family business. Have you been able to reach out to your mother or siblings?"

All eyes are on Silac when Saxon poses this question. He is in half form, and his tail twitches behind him, and his hood flares and retracts every couple of beats. He's barely keeping himself under control. "No, I haven't been able to reach any of them since Cronus advised us that my father had been turned to stone."

"This is not good. We don't know how many are on their side, and they have hostages. I'm assuming that if they destroy the stone statues, then they will kill the person inside, yes?" Brannock looks at Silac for confirmation. He gives a little hiss and flick of his tongue and nods.

"Yes, it is a permanent death."

"We need a plan so we can avoid any casualties on our side, and possibly a greater force. It was different when we could rely on the warlock king and queen, but now it seems like they have been taken out of the equation." The Aaz'axian looks at our small group. There are only seven of us in the rescue party, and despite our combined skills, Brannock is right, we need more intel.

Xavier sparks with fury at the thought that his parents have been turned to stone, but I guess it would be an effective way of taking them out.

"We will head to my family compound. My father will gladly help. He has been complaining about the basilisk family for many years, but they have not gone so far as declaring war, and that is exactly what they have done if they turned the warlock king and queen to stone. He will readily lend assistance." Smoke drifts from Tirrian's nostrils, and his eyes flare with anger.

"That's probably a good idea. We need more help, and I'm assuming your father has probably been keeping tabs on their operations?" Link's keeping a cool head, as usual. I wanted him to stay behind, but he assures me he is capable of fighting but prefers healing. He also said it is easier to hack into surveillance systems when he's closer to the source. He and Silac have been trying to gain access to the cameras so we can get a better idea of what we are walking into.

"Yes, he should at least have a list of the current family members. The family relationships are turbulent, and leadership changes hands regularly. They turn their own family members to stone for a while to assert their dominance. I have no idea who is in charge at the moment. It may not even be Sissolic, but one of his brothers."

"Sissolic is the father of your fiancée, right?" I ask Silac.

"Yes. He was the one who issued the ultimatum that I was to return and marry her immediately in exchange for my father being reanimated."

"Well, why don't we just give him what he wants? Then we can crash the wedding and rescue whoever needs to be rescued and take out as many of the basilisks as we can," I suggest, but Saxon shakes his head.

"We still need to know the key players so we don't end up hurting any innocents who may attend the wedding. I'm assuming it will be a fancy affair?"

"Yes. Sissolic or whoever is in charge will want to make a show of them grabbing our families business from us. It's a power play more than anything else. Sadly, my father's desperation didn't let him see the catches."

"I'll teleport us to the dragon compound, and hopefully King Tysar will be able to assist." Xavier waves us all closer, and we gather around him, each putting a hand on one another so we'll travel together.

With a flash, we move. The dragon compound is located in the mountain ranges of Fluxx, and Xavier has obviously been here before, but when we rematerialize, we find ourselves surrounded by sword brandishing warriors with dragon scales flickering across their skin and wings tucked into their spines.

"Stand down," a voice shouts behind us, and I wait for the guards to follow the instructions before I move —I don't want anyone to get trigger happy. They are quick to respond though, and they all melt back against the walls of the throne room. "That was quite an entrance, warlock. Luckily I was expecting you, or you might have been BBQ and a late supper for our dragons," a rumbly voice calls sardonically.

Tirrian pushes his way to the front, grasping my hand firmly in his, and walks to the smiling man who bears a striking resemblance to him. "Papa, meet my mate, Lila Adams. Lila, this is my father, King Tysar of the dragon clan," he announces as we reach the formidable man.

Before he can respond, though, there is a commotion behind him. "That's the bitch who got my son shunned from the circus and dragon kind. How could you betray your family by taking her for a mate?"

As one, Tirrian and his father turn to face the newcomer. Unlike the two men standing with me, who are both built tall and broad and have the same stunning pink and black wings, this man is slimmer and shorter and also bears a resemblance to his afore-mentioned son, Dylan.

"Destir, I suggest you mind your tone when you speak about my son's mate. We all know the circum-stances of your son's disgrace. Keep that in mind if you don't want to join him in exile," Tysar cautions with a low rumble.

Destir sneers in my direction. "Your son has been fooled by the Skarrian slut before you. Maybe he is no longer in his right mind to be your heir."

A low growl rumbles from Tirrian's chest, and smoke drifts out of his nostrils as his whole body tightens in preparation for an attack. I reach forward and stroke a hand gently between his wings that have spread out to block me from his uncle's view. His scales shimmer in the gap between his wings, and his body shudders. I smirk, thinking of what I'm doing to him in front of an audience before pulling my hand away now that I have his attention.

"Ignore the jealous, bitter man. His words really don't hurt me. I am Skarrian and, by my very nature, slutty, but you also know I am picky, and only the best males will do for me. It's probably why Dylan attacked me. He knew he never stood a chance with me or turning Caspian's attention back his way." My words are said quietly, but I know dragon hearing is super sensitive, so there is no way Destir doesn't hear the implication that his son was never good enough for me. That should be a big enough of a hit to his ego that not even a slutty Skarrian would think his son was worthy. Besides, we have way more important things to worry about.

"I saw Dylan recently making deals with a Madovian. He wasn't looking so great, so I wouldn't cast stones in glass houses, if I were you. How can I fault my wife for her nature when your son goes against everything dragon kind stands for? Mates, women, and children are to be cherished, and your son tried to claw Lila's eggs out of her body," Tirrian says loudly for everyone to hear, and it gets the reaction he was looking for.

There's a large gasp, and when I look around, the

throne room is actually more crowded than I thought. Not only are the walls lined with guards, but there are also courtiers sitting around tables piled high with food. None of them look impressed by this announcement. In fact, they look downright lethal with fangs bared, smoke drifting from their noses, and wings arched up amongst the gathered.

The long table behind the king not only has Destir seated at it—or he was seated, because he's now standing and leaning aggressively toward us—but there are two slightly older females. I'm going to take a guess that these are Tirrian's mother and Destir's wife. They have opposite expressions. Tirrian's mother is looking at me with glistening tears—I'm not sure if they are from joy or sadness, but I guess I will find out eventually—while the other woman glares at me with as much venom as her husband. I move my gaze to the younger people at the table. I know Tirrian said he has siblings, but there seem to be a lot. Maybe some of them are Dylan's siblings too. I try to figure out which ones, but none of them seem to show any venom like their parents, just mild curiosity. Perhaps I'm not the only person who hates Dylan. Although he sure had Tirrian fooled when he first arrived, maybe Tirrian's had time to convince the rest of his siblings and cousins that I'm not a mate stealing whore.

"Outrageous accusation! What proof do you have?" Destir scoffs, and I feel Xavier's power crackle behind me as he takes a step closer.

"I witnessed it. Are you calling me a liar?" he

snarls, and this has Destir's black skin turning a pale shade of gray. He sits down quickly, shaking his head.

"No, I must have been mistaken," he mutters, and I hear Xavier scoff behind me.

"That's what I thought."

"Well, now that the little bit of drama is over, let me be the first to welcome you to the family, Lila." Tirrian's father holds out his hands, taking both of mine and giving me a kiss on each cheek. "I can't tell you how thrilled Tisa and I are that Tirrian finally took a mate, and what a beautiful mate you are. He tells me you can shift into dragon form. We would love to see it."

There's a rumble of voices, and I hear a few skeptical mutterings from the courtiers.

"I would be happy to shift for you if we could beg a moment of your time when you finish your meal. I'm afraid this is not exactly a social call." I can tell by the knowing look on Tysar's face that he knows exactly why we're here. I'm sure Tirrian has briefed him on the reason we are on Fluxx.

"Shift and share a meal, then I and my dragons will assist with anything you request. You will be queen of them one day, and I'm sure they will jump at the chance to curry favor with their future queen." He winks when there are more mutterings from the surrounding court, and I smother a chuckle. I get the feeling this man likes to stir shit, much like Xavier's father. I wonder what dinner will be like with both men at the table, and goodness knows I probably shouldn't let either of them babysit, let alone together.

With a snap of his fingers, chairs are placed along the opposite side of the table from the already seated guests. I find myself sitting next to Tirrian and across from his parents.

"Lila, we are so happy to meet you, but where are your babies I've heard so much about?" Tisa, Tirrian's mother, asks, smiling widely. I look at my dragon mate. He's blushing adorably. It's fun, his cheeks turn the same pink as his wings so it's not hard to miss.

"We left them with their fathers at Caspian's parents' place. We didn't think it would be safe bringing them with us until we had dealt with the basilisk problem," Xavier, who is seated on my other side, explains.

Her smile droops, and I feel terrible. "Don't you worry. Tirrian has promised to retrieve them and bring them back to see his hoard as soon as we have," I add, hoping that will make them feel better.

"That is excellent. We have arranged for six more caverns to be dug out for their own treasures. They are ready to be filled immediately," Tysar tells me, taking a sip from the goblet in front of him and leaning back casually.

"Six? But I only have five children at the moment. And they really are too little to be collecting a hoard." I look between the royal couple, and Tisa smirks.

"Yes, but you're part dragon now, dear. You're going to want your own hoard."

"And it's never too young to start. It is a tradition that everyone in the dragonling's family donates something out of their own hoard to help start the new one, so all of us will be presenting them with something to start their collection," Tysar explains, waving his hand up and down the table.

"Usually it's not six items at once," one of the men on the right of Tisa grumbles, but I can hear that it's good-natured instead of resentful.

"She already has one, it's just full of men." The girl sitting next to Tisa winks at me cheerfully. "Hi, I'm Tallon, Tirrian's sister. It will be nice to have more girls in the family. I only have brothers." She points at the two males on her other side. "That's Titas and Thorn." Both brothers give me a cheerful wave. Titas is the one who grumbled about giving up his treasures.

"We can't wait to meet our nieces and nephews. Tirrian is the first of us to have children, and on behalf of the rest of us, we thank you." Titas grins broadly as plates of food are placed in front of us newcomers and liquid is poured into the ornate goblets at each of our settings.

Thorn stands up. "A toast to Tirrian and Lila, may their lives be full of happiness and their nest full of eggs." The crowd shouts their toasts, and there are cheers and laughter as Tirrian blushes once again.

"You know he's always dreamed of having many children. His dragons were so fussy, but obviously they were holding out for the right one," Tallon says in a fake whisper, and Tirrian growls at her, but she just laughs.

I hear a grunt of disapproval on the other side of Destir. "The throne can't be handed to a non-dragon. She is going to have to prove she can give birth to a purebred before you get too excited."

I turn my attention to the sour-faced woman, but before I can even form a response, someone else does. "Now, Mother, don't be like that. Uncle Tysar and Aunt Tisa have other children who will get the crown before any of us. You need to stop with your scheming, or you're going to be accused of treason," the female dragon sitting next to her hisses before turning an apologetic smile on me. "I'm sorry for my mother. Dylan's treachery surprised us all. We hadn't realized how unbalanced his dragon had become. Can you please forgive us?"

"No one blames you, Dacia," Tirrian says to the female. "It was not your responsibility as his sister to make sure he was sane, nor yours, Darcan. Maybe your parents should have been paying more attention than spending so much time plotting." Tirrian glares at Dylan's parents, who glare back just as fiercely.

The male next to Dacia inclines his head. "Nevertheless, we don't want you thinking everyone in this family supports our brother. As far as I'm concerned, he's as good as dead."

His mother, whose name I still don't know, gasps and stands up.

"I can't listen to any of this. Are you happy now?"

she spits at Tysar. "You've turned our children against their brother and us. You should be ashamed of yourself."

Tysar stands up, his fists clenched. "Brother, I suggest you get your wife out of my face before she says something she cannot recover from, and the two of you find yourselves joining your son in exile."

Dylan's parents quickly remove themselves, throwing looks of utter loathing at me.

# CHAPTER EIGHTEEN

## Lila

Dinner continues with comfortable conversation. Tirrian's family is welcoming and friendly and nothing like I assumed they would be considering the asshole he was when he first arrived at the circus. Saxon, Link, and Xavier take great joy in telling his family all about it, while Tirrian grumbles beneath his breath, my hand clasped firmly in his. He hasn't let go of it once, so I guess he's feeling a little territorial. I allow him the boon and manage eating with one hand.

Brannock joins the conversation. He has stayed in his human glamour, which is basically as solid as one of my forms, not wanting to alarm the dragons, though the royal family is aware of his alien status. I hear him talking with both Titus and Thorn about what Earth is like. They are curious, and it wouldn't surprise me if we get one if not two tagalongs once we leave Fluxx.

My gaze slides to Silac, and I can see how tense he is, barely touching his meal. He's on two legs, but he keeps hissing and flaring his hood, and Dylan's poor brother and sister keep jumping. He apologized, but I don't think we should make him suffer any longer.

"I'm going to shift to prove to those gathered that I can, and then we need that meeting," I say to the king, who is quick to agree.

"That should stop most of the negativity as well. There was some speculation on whether or not Papa would rename his heir when the general public heard that Tirrian did not mate a pure dragon," Tallon tells us quietly.

Tirrian scoffs next to me. "They should know better. The mating bite usually fixes that, and even if it didn't, she's a mimic."

"Not always. If you mated another shifter, you know there's a fifty-fifty chance they'll take after one parent or the other, and as far as the gossip goes, Lila is a low powered mimic and doesn't have many forms," Tisa whispers quietly so the whole room isn't privy to the conversation.

"Well, shall I prove to them that Tirrian and I can give them pure dragonlings?" I roll my eyes and stand up, pushing my chair back.

Tirrian stands with me and puts his hand on my shoulder. "You know I don't care about that," he says firmly, looking me in the eye, and I snort with amusement.

"Yes, you do. You want a brood of eggs, and I understand that. I can't guarantee a brood, but I can tell you this, buddy—you will be the one sitting on them. I have way too much on my hands to spend weeks nesting, but I'm sure you're up to the task." I pat him on the shoulder and walk off the raised dais to the large space Xavier teleported us to. When I look back, Tirrian is watching me with stars in his eyes, and I can feel my beast's hunger for him and desire for more babies pulse inside me.

*You are all going to have to wait a little longer. We still have a few more tasks on the list to complete before I will consider getting knocked up again by anyone, so slow your roll.*

They all settle down, except for my dragon, who is chuffing to come out, so I let her take over. The change is just as painful as the first time, but I clamp my teeth together, refusing to show weakness in front of the predatory, judgmental crowd.

My body reshapes and reforms, and we stretch our wings, brushing one of the guards against the wall, who yelps and steps back when Tirrian growls at him. Our whole body shakes, and then she stretches like she's doing the downward dog. I'm almost certain she's just showing off now, and Tirrian's growls get even louder. Her happiness at his jealousy has me rolling my eyes. I don't sink back and allow her to take complete control. We may end up causing a galactic incident if we do that, so I monitor the driver's seat in case I need to take hold of the reins.

I tune into what the crowd is saying.

"I've never seen a dragon that color before."

"Isn't she stunning?"

"She looks like a rare dragon's eye stone. I haven't seen one of those in years. I would love one for my hoard." Ah, so that's what my cave gems are called. Isn't that ironic? I gave one to Tirrian. I hadn't heard anyone call them that.

"I would love her for my hoard."

"The crown prince is really lucky."

"She's a bit small, isn't she? Hardly fit to be queen, and she's kind of ugly."

There are loud gasps of shock, and a small tittering of laughter. We drop out of the stretch and search the crowd for the person who said that last part. Of course it's a pretty female, and she's looking down her nose at us. Most people have stepped away from her, not wanting to get caught in any crossfire.

I feel my mate join me, stroking his hand over my side, and I quiver with joy. I have no desire to play into this one's games, so I just ignore her and nuzzle my mate, but he obviously feels like he has to defend me.

"Still bitter I turned down your proposition I see, Ioldres? Be glad that I did, because neither of my dragons would accept you, and you would have been killed before you could even blink. Get over it and move on, otherwise you are going to find all the eligible bachelors are no longer available," Tirrian says calmly, and I admire how neutral he sounds. Hopefully she lets it go, because I can feel how furious he is.

Her gaze moves, and when I follow it, I find she's staring at both of Tirrian's brothers, who look like deer caught in the crosshairs of a hunter's rifle. Tallon is laughing, quietly amused at their terror. I huff out my own breath of laughter, smoke swirling around us, and a small hiccup of flame falls to the floor. Ioldres yelps and steps back a little. Yup, I totally meant to do that. My dragon rolls her eyes at my antics.

"Maybe lower your ambitions slightly. Neither of my brothers are looking for mates, and if you push it, their dragons will also kill you. You know this. Our dragons will not stand for human manipulations and calculations. They are primal and don't understand those kinds of machinations."

She huffs, and I can tell by the stubborn set to her shoulders that she hasn't listened one bit. I change back, and Tirrian quickly strips off his shirt to throw over my naked body. His shirt has room for my dragon wings, which I keep on display as a reminder to the petty bitch. We turn our back on her, not willing to give her any more attention, and walk back to the table.

"I'm not sure that one is going to give up," I whisper. "She had a look of determination that I recognize."

He leans his head in and whispers, "No, but I won't be sad to see her gone either if one of my brothers' dragons eats her." I chuckle as Tysar stands up and gives his wife a kiss on the cheek before leading us away from the throne room to what Tirrian tells me is the security and surveillance room.

The rest of my mates have joined us as well at Tallon, Thorn, and Titus. "When you apprised us of the situation, we sent in some of our ground drones." Tallon is the one who starts up the conversation, bringing a big screen on the wall to life.

"Ground drones?" I ask, and Link is the one who answers.

"Small automated spy robots designed to look like insects, or small creatures from specific planets. It's a side project my father created years ago. While my mother concentrates on the leisure industry, my father put nanobots to more practical uses, like the automated drones that care for our crops or households. These ones are aimed at home security."

"Or spying," Thorn says unapologetically. "Most savvy businesses or people with shit to hide screen their place of business or abodes twice a day for these kinds of measures—we certainly do. They are easy to track with the right system."

"There are also effective countermeasures. This room contains them. The walls send small bursts of EMT pulses every few seconds. It's a small enough burst to keep all the machines inside the room safe, but anything attached to the walls, floor, or ceiling automatically short out," Titus explains.

"It's not something that can be utilized in a large scale because of the potential to ruin everything, but to protect important meetings, it is definitely effective." Tysar takes a seat at a long table and gestures for all of us to sit. "Tallon has video feeds to show you. The basilisks are obviously unconcerned about being discovered or have more important things to worry about, because they don't have countermeasures."

"These feeds are from when you first apprised us of the situation. I can confirm your father has been turned to stone, I'm sorry to say, but for now, he is in one piece," she informs Silac, pausing on a screenshot that shows us exactly that. It's an office, and Silac's father is in his half form. He looks like a statue from some Greek inspired garden. "Obviously we didn't catch what happened, because we didn't have surveillance on them at the time, but we were able to catch what happened next."

She fast forwards the film, and I can tell by the time stamp that it is a period of a few days. Finally, she slows down when Xavier's parents appear in the video of the same office. Silac's dad's statute is nowhere to be seen. They are having a meeting with six big basilisk snakes. They are in their half form, and unlike the nagas who have a hood, they have large spike-like crests on their heads, slightly like a dragon's and creepy as fuck, with white eyes with black pupils.

What starts off as a friendly negotiation goes downhill rather fast, and before any of us can blink, both Cronus and Xylene are turned to stone.

"How?" I mutter, still shocked. "Cronus and Xylene are mega powerful."

"They are, but they are also arrogant because of it, and I guess they didn't even consider it might happen to them." Xavier combs a hand through his hair in agitation, staring at the paused image of his petrified parents. I can feel his anguish. It's bitter and unpleasant, and it's all I can do to stop myself from wrinkling my nose.

"That's how quick it can be and why they must be stopped. We did some more digging and found this." Tallon switches out the video, and I blanch at what I see. It's a huge warehouse, and it is filled with hundreds of stone statues.

"Holy fuck, is that what I think it is?" We all lean forward, but it's Saxon who asked the question.

"We think this is probably everyone who has opposed the Bravalanas over the years. Your parents are all stored here now." She brings up an image of them at the front of the warehouse.

"We need to get Lila in there and everyone freed before tomorrow night's wedding ceremony. That's the only way we can be sure they are safe." Brannock is in planning mode.

"I am required to present myself to the family this evening. I will create a distraction so you can do that." Silac has a stubborn set to his jaw, and I know there is no talking him out of this. He still wants to make sure his fiancée, Kinga, gets out alright. He insists she doesn't want this any more than he does. I'm not sure it's the right choice, but none of us can dissuade him.

"Excellent, and once we free everyone tonight, we

will crash the wedding tomorrow, rounding up all the basilisks we can." Tysar sounds excited at the chance, as is everyone else in the room. The room practically sparks with anticipation. "It's been a while since we could let out some aggression on a foe."

"I've developed some glass with mirrored reflections for everyone. The basilisks can't change you if they can't see your eyes. I'll make sure we have enough pairs for all the troops tomorrow." Link points to a suitcase that he carried from the ship. I wondered what was in it.

"Lila, you need to fuel up for a few hours. We don't know how long it's going to take you to change all of those people back to flesh."

"How exactly is Lila going to do that?" Thorn asks, sounding skeptical. I'm pretty sure he's asking me how I'm going to change the people, not fuel up, because there is no way I want to share that I have to fuck to power up with Tirrian's brother.

"Did you get what I asked for?" Tirrian's gaze is on Tallon, and she nods.

"Yeah, secure in the dungeon. Shall we go there now?"

"You have a basilisk?" Link sounds excited. "Good, I can test my glasses then too." He grabs a pair and slips them onto his face, and we follow Tallon through the mountainside complex to a lower level.

"How did you catch one if you can't risk looking them in the eye?" Max has been mostly quiet, observing and taking everything in, so I almost jump when he asks this question.

"Tranq dart," Tallon says wryly. "They aren't particularly observant about their surroundings. We caught this one coming out of a fast-food place in the capital. We kept him sedated until we got here, but it should have worn off by now. Are you sure you're going to be able to mimic him without being turned to stone?" she asks, unable to hide her concern. "The last thing we want is for that to happen, and for Tirrian and the rest of your mates to lose their shit." She gives Brannock the side-eye. We haven't hidden his race from the royal family, and so far, they've been happy to accept him, but I understand them being wary about him going berserker, even if we aren't fully mated.

"I don't need to look them in the eye. I can just as easily look at them through a viewing window. Do you have a two-way mirror?"

"Yes, we can activate one. We can see them, and they can't see us. Our cells allow us to do that."

"They are the same as the ones on Earth. The barriers are tech based," Xavier explains to me.

"I'll wait until Lila has mimicked him before I test my glasses. That way, she can always unfreeze me if I get turned to stone," Link decides, and I heave a sigh of relief.

"Can a basilisk reverse the process? Do we know this for sure?" I ask as we enter the containment area.

"Yes, they can. Most of the time, they choose not to. It's horrible, because although they are frozen, their minds are very much active inside the stone. I can't imagine how much counseling all those people are going to need in the warehouse." Silac sounds furious.

"We will seize all their assets and liquidate them to compensate any of the victims. By the time we're finished, the Bravalana family will be done," Thorn assures us.

"Make sure you are positive of guilt. Silac says that not all of them are happy to be involved in any illegal doings," Saxon cautions.

"Kinga should be able to help us with that. The Bravalana basilisks aren't a huge family, but they are still significantly bigger than us nagas. There are other basilisk families that live perfectly legal and normal lives." Silac is staring at the male who is in half form on the other side of the two-way mirror. I don't even think he knows we're here.

I step closer, and I stare at him, giving my mimic abilities a nudge. They surge forward. I haven't asked them to mimic any new forms for a long time, and they are almost champing at the bit to mimic this one. I feel my body shift, my bones realigning, and can't stop the groan that leaves my mouth. I see someone reach out for me, but Saxon jumps in and stops them.

"Leave her, she can do this. The first change is always the worst."

My legs fuse together and elongate, my hair shrinks away, and I feel bony protrusions growing from my head. My mouth fills with razor-sharp teeth, and my vision changes, the sounds of everyone's heartbeats becoming more pronounced. My nature becomes more primal, and it's all I can do to control myself from lunging at one of the warm-blooded creatures in the room.

The dragons and Saxon feel different—not as warm-blooded as the others—and when my focus slips to Silac, his cold-blooded nature calls to mine. I hiss, my tongue flicking in and out, but I keep my gaze firmly on the two-way mirror in front of me and the creature on the other side. I'm not sure how to control turning someone to stone, so I'm going to have to do some experimenting. There's no time like the present. I'll practice with the creature I just mimicked.

"Step out of the room and let me through," I say, my voice changing. It's lower, and the S's are very sibilant.

"Are you okay, Lila?" Tirrian asks, knowing it's a struggle to control my more basic instincts in another form.

"Yes, just go and let me practice on him." I still don't risk looking at any of them—not only because I'm afraid of turning them to stone but, if I'm honest with myself, I also don't want to see them looking at me with horror in their eyes.

"We don't need to step out," Tallon says, her fingers flying across the control board. "I've adjusted it so you can pass back and forth, and you can leave when you have what you want," she explains, and I nod that I heard her, still not wanting to risk looking at them.

I slither into the cell, and the captured basilisk goes on alert, rising and hissing at me.

"Who are you? What do you want? Where the fuck am I?" he demands.

"How do you activate the petrifying power?" I ignore his questions, and he hisses at me, lunging forward with his mouth open. Jesus, he has way more fangs than an Earth snake. I hadn't even noticed my own mouth. I react quickly and slap him on the nose, and he yelps and slithers backward again. I use my tongue to feel around my mouth, but my teeth are normal. I guess we can will them to change on command.

I see his eyes swirl, and I feel a wave of power, but it seems to slide right off me. Basilisks can't turn each other into stone. I knew that instinctively, so I didn't even flinch, but with him trying to demonstrate it, it triggered the innate knowledge inside me, just like my mimic powers are supposed to work. I now know how to petrify a person, but most importantly, I know how to reverse it—a drop of basilisk blood placed on the forehead of the victim. It looks like I'm going to bleed a lot tonight.

"Who are you? I know all the basilisks on Fluxx, and I don't recognize you," the snake man demands, but I ignore him. I have what I came for, so I turn and slither back the way we came. Link stands in front of everyone, wearing his mirrored glasses.

"Look at me, Lila," he demands when I keep my eyes on the ground. I've mostly wrestled the more primal nature of this creature into submission, but there's a scent in the air that makes me hungry. I flick my tongue out to taste it and groan as the flavor reaches my taste buds, my eyes zeroing in on who it is —Silac. My basilisk wants to lick him all over, but I grit my teeth and avert my eyes, even though I know how to trigger the powers now. I have to be patient. Our time is coming, and it won't be as a basilisk.

I look up at Link and activate my powers, staring directly into his mirror-covered eyes. I feel the power creep out, but it quickly rebounds when it hits the mirror, and Link remains flesh and blood and nanobots. I heave out a sigh of relief that it didn't work, and a wide grin spreads across his lips.

"Excellent. Just as I thought. You can change back, Lila," he tells me, and with a sigh of relief, I let the form go.

"Right, if we're all done here, then I have something I need to show Lila. We'll meet you at the launch pad when it's time to leave for the warehouse." Tirrian grabs my hand and drags me out of the room before I can even speak. I hear everyone else laugh as we leave the containment area and move deeper into the mountain.

# CHAPTER NINETEEN

## Tirrian

My dragon has been riding me hard since Lila changed in front of everyone else. I hated that she had to prove she could, but I couldn't help feeling immensely proud when everyone admired her. I knew she was going to ignore Ioldres, the bitch not even worth the air my mate breathes, but I wasn't going to stand for any of her petty behavior. I also don't like the way she looked at my brothers. She's cunning and conniving, and I have no doubt she's going to end up roasted or as a meal for one of their dragons. Mine pushed for that, but we don't have time for a diplomatic incident. We have more important matters to worry about.

I feel for Silac. I would feel the same if it were my

parents suffering, but my dragon is not patient, and he wants to show our hoard to our mate.

With her hand clasped in mine, I drag her deeper into the mountainside. All dragons in our clan keep their hoards here. It's the safest place for them, and they are easily accessible when dragons feel the need to be one with their treasure. It's almost like a bank with rows and rows of vault doors coded to each individual dragon in the clan. Some are more impressive than others, but together, they hold an eye watering amount of wealth and are guarded well.

I nod my head to the guards who stand at the entrance to the facility. They are all smart enough to keep their eyes cast downward and away from my scantily clad mate, but I can't stop the rumble in my chest. My dragon is making sure they keep their gaze there.

We move farther into the repository, since the royal family vaults are the farthest away from the entrance. We get to the separate section that contains my and my family's. There are five sealed doors, and I see six more new vaults, their doors wide open and ready for the children and Lila to start their own hoards. I can't wait for the babies to visit so they can pick out what they want from mine to start their own collection.

First, though, I need to fuck my wife on top of my own hoard, allowing her scent to fill the room. Lila shivers behind me, and I realize how cold it is down here.

"God, I'm sorry, I forgot that you would be cold.

Come here." I pull her into my arms and allow my heat to warm my own body, giving her the warmth she needs. She shivers again and snuggles into my arms, which has my dragon roaring with delight.

I push my finger onto the sensor spike, and it absorbs my blood before I hear the door click open. I shift Lila to one arm and use the other to pull the door wide enough for us to slip through before sealing us in. I turn us around to face my treasures, and this time, I can't stop the purr that escapes my mouth. My dragons are pleased at seeing all their treasure and that our mate now knows how well we can provide for her and our children.

"Holy fuck!" Lila's mouth drops open, and she steps out of my embrace as she takes in the vault with wide-eyed astonishment. "I feel like I've stepped into Scrooge McDuck's vault," she mumbles, and my dragons growl.

"Who is this Scrooge McDuck, and why were you in his vault?" I demand, and she giggles, waving a hand at me.

"I wasn't, and he's not real." She waves me off as she takes a step closer to the massive pile of coins, gold, and jewels that make up the majority of my treasure. "Where did you get all this?" she asks me, and I puff up my chest.

"I have worked hard for the dragon crown for many years, and these are my rewards," I tell her, and she turns to look at me, arching an eyebrow.

"Really?" she asks skeptically, and I grin. That's

what I love about my mate—she's high intelligence wrapped in a sexy package.

"Well, I mean, the Carevasta bears aren't the only ones who excel at pillaging and plundering. Anyone who dares to get on a dragon's bad side knows they stand to lose anything of value as well as incur their ire. Spoils of war are fairly won, my love." I slide my hands up and down her naked body and nuzzle into her neck as I wrap my arms around her from behind.

"Now what I'd really like is to fuck my mate on this pile and watch the gold shimmer on her wings," I cajole her, nipping her skin and stroking a finger between her wings, which she left in place after she changed to basilisk and back.

She shivers at my touch but screws up her nose. "Doesn't look very comfortable to me," she argues halfheartedly, and I pull away and scramble up to the top of my pile and wave a hand to my nest. It's large enough for my dragon to settle in and plenty big enough for the two of us to roll around in. It's full of furs and soft furnishings, much like Echo's nest.

"Why don't you come and find out?" I taunt her, opening the zipper of my pants before dragging them down my legs, taking my underwear with them. I stand before her naked, my cock throbbing and leaking precum. I know my wife, and I know her desires, and there's no way she will refuse me. I smirk at her, and she huffs but starts to climb up the mound of treasure. She stops every now and then to admire something, and my dragon huffs with pride, making note of what she looks at so we can gift them to her.

Finally, she makes it to the nest and looks around with wide-eyed amazement. "This is nice," she tells me, bending down and fingering the soft furs, her inner dragon and lightning cat enjoying the sensations. I watch as she flutters her wings, and my cock throbs harder, and I can't wait any longer—I lunge at her

She squeals and giggles as I drag her down into the bundle of furs, tearing the shirt I gave her off her body before nuzzling her breasts. Her hands run through my hair as I take one of her nipples into my mouth, rolling the tight nub with my tongue before sucking on it. She groans and wraps her legs around my body, her core hot against my throbbing dick. I can't wait to fuck her hard and deep, but first, my dragons insist on a few things, and if I don't do it for them, they'll be sulky dicks. I pull away and give her a quick kiss before getting up and scrambling down my pile of treasures.

"Hey!" I hear her call behind me, but I find the piece of treasure they are looking for and scramble back to my mate. She's leaning back on her hands, looking at me in confusion.

"What are you doing?" she asks playfully, tilting her head to the side.

I place the delicate tiara on her head and smirk at her. "What is a queen without a crown? You are definitely my queen," I tell her and lean in to kiss her again, but I jolt in frustration and growl, my dragons now encouraging me to get another thing for her.

"Be right back." I kiss her on the lips, and she frowns again before I move in a different direction, finding the bit of treasure they are insisting on, and when I get back to her, I drape a necklace made of rare black diamond-like gems called dnomaids from a planet almost at the end of the galaxy. It's inhabited by an asshole race that is hated by most of the galaxy, but their gems are stunning and worth a lot, because like Husadavia, nobody wants to go there and mine them.

"Wow, this is gorgeous." She runs a finger over the gems that sparkle like they are filled with glitter. "But I don't need any of these things," she tells me, holding out her arms to coax me back into the nest. Grimacing, I shake my head.

"I know, but my dragons are insisting," I snarl apologetically, but she just giggles and shrugs.

"Okay, and honestly, my dragon is very happy too," she tells me as I spend the next ten minutes covering her from head to toe in gems. Basically, the only spot that doesn't have anything on it is her pussy. She's lying flat now and spread out, looking slightly uncomfortable. I wonder if I can convince her to pierce her nipples and clit hood so she can wear our gems all the time. My dragons purr internally at the idea.

"You look gorgeous covered in our treasure," my dragons growl, but I shove them back as I kneel down and push her legs apart, swiping my tongue through her folds.

"Finally," she says and reaches for my hair. I love her tugging at it while I feast on her cunt. It makes my cock throb and precum leak out. Her hands drift to my shoulders and out to my wings, and she runs a fingertip along the edges. I growl into her pussy.

"Yes," she exclaims as I lengthen my tongue and jam it deep into her dripping channel, curving it up like a finger to brush against her G-spot. Her pussy clenches, and she arches her back, screaming as her release gushes out of her and into my mouth. I lap at all the sticky delicious fluid, not wanting to miss a drop, before climbing up her body and kissing her mouth, letting her taste herself. She groans and clamps her legs around my waist as I thrust into her tight core. It's a struggle, and it takes a couple of thrusts until I'm fully seated deep in her hot, throbbing cunt. My balls throb, and my spine tingles as the aftermath of her first orgasm ripples around my dick.

I swirl my hips as I tongue her mouth like I did with her pussy. Her hands stroke my wings, and my teeth ache at the sensation. I reach out to run a finger along the edge of one of hers as the jewels she wears scrapes against my skin with each thrust, creating a sharp contrast to the pleasure my cock feels. It's a heady combination, and I pick up my speed, her own hips thrusting up to meet mine. The sounds of jewelry jingling and our damp bodies slapping together create a soundtrack of us fucking.

"Love you," she cries out as another stroke of my finger against her wings sends her careening into another orgasm. She screams and grips my own wings as her channel convulses around my cock, setting off my orgasm. I fill her with my hot seed, and she groans and sighs in pleasure as my barb scrapes along her G-spot. I keep filling her with my seed, looking forward to the time when it will be in dragon form so I can breed her.

She relaxes underneath me as my seed floods her womb, her hands stroking gently up and down my back. "That was good," she murmurs, nuzzling into my neck. I tip my head to the side, giving her better access, and her tongue probes the thick vein there.

"Yes, it was, but we're just getting started," I purr. "Bite me, Lila, and drink deeply, because you're going to need your strength," I tell her as I adjust the tiara on her head, which is a little lopsided after her thrashing about.

She doesn't argue, just bites me hard. Her venom is a straight shot to my dick, and it quickly fills with blood, the telltale sign of an orgasm tickling my skin.

I pull out of her and take it in my hand, stroking it a couple of times before I'm erupting with a roar. This time, I paint my cum all over her body, rubbing it into her skin with my other hand. I want her to smell like me for days.

She finishes drinking and seals the wounds before looking down at her body. The gems and her skin are a sticky mess, and she giggles again. "I guess they are definitely mine now. Nobody is going to want them covered in cum."

# CHAPTER TWENTY

**Lila**

Fucking Tirrian on his mounds of treasure was like something out of an *Arabian Nights* fantasy, but the whole time, my dragon rumbled her delight and had her eyes on any number of his gorgeous trinkets. It was almost distracting, but he really does have a way of keeping my attention completely on him, especially when he kept covering me with jewels so he could admire his treasures while getting his dick wet. If I didn't have my own dragon soul, I may have been offended, but instead, I admired them right along with him and plotted how I could stick them in my prison pocket to smuggle them out of his vault.

In the end, smuggling wasn't needed, and he readily gave them to me and showed me how to activate my own vault, locking them safely away. My small pile of jewels looks pitiful on the floor of my vault, and my dragon has started plotting how we can get more. I'm not sure anywhere is safe until I have a significant amount of treasure to call my own. Luckily for me, I have ready access to a jewel cave. I will need to return to Rilu so I can bring some of the gems back with me.

We have to go to the basilisks' compound first. I wonder if they will have any other treasures apart from the warehouse of petrified people. They are the main priority. I am going to reanimate them, and Xavier is going to teleport them to the dragon compound. From there, Link and Tysar are going to facilitate returning them to wherever they belong.

Tirrian, Saxon, Brannock, Silac, Xavier, and Maxsim will be on the away team with me as well as Tirrian's brothers, Thorn and Titus, and his sister, Tallon. Once done, Xavier will create an illusion to make it look like the statues are all still there.

We teleport to the warehouse. Everyone is on high alert, and all are wearing special combat armor the dragons supplied. It's made of dragon scales and is virtually bullet and magic proof, and it will shift with a person if they need to, so that means even I'm wearing it. I haven't changed forms yet, because I'm going to be in it for a while with that many people to unfreeze, and I don't want to run out of juice. Beings that primal are also a little hard to control without losing some of myself.

"Holy shit." My voice echoes in the warehouse despite the vast amount of stone statues. "That video did not do the amount justice. I'm not sure if I can get them all done in one go."

The warehouse is way bigger than I anticipated, and the amount of people must be in the thousands, not the hundreds. It's going to take way more time to change them all back.

"Start with my father and Xavier's parents." Silac points at the familiar statues, and I feel a pang of sadness at seeing the two vibrant, full of life warlocks trapped like that.

"Do you think that's such a good idea?" Brannock asks before I get a chance to change forms.

Silac glares at him, but Xavier looks thoughtful as he scratches his chin. "Of course it is. Why wouldn't it be?"

"No, Brannock is right. What if they come to get them as leverage to make sure you go through with the ceremony? I certainly would," Maxsim agrees, and what he says makes sense.

"Kind of like Han Solo trapped in carbonite and on display for Jabba," I remark, and everyone looks at me with bewilderment. "Never mind." I wave a hand, putting Star Wars on the family movie night list.

Xavier continues. "Maybe if she unfreezes them, we can ask them what they know before repetrifying them. It's going to seem too suspicious if they disappear, then the Bravalanas will be on high alert."

"But then I'll have to go through with the marriage to Kinga to stop them from killing them." Silac looks at me hopelessly, and we can all hear the desperation in his voice.

"What about an illusion of them as well?" Maxsim suggests.

Xavier shakes his head. "They won't be able to pick up an illusion and move them. If they were already in place, it wouldn't be a problem."

"What about a spell that temporarily freezes them with the illusion of them being stone attached to their bodies? Then, when shit starts to go down, they will unfreeze and join the fight," Saxon suggests.

"Hmm, that's not a bad idea. Both of those things are simple spells, so easily doable," Xavier agrees.

"Let's do that then. Can you please turn my father back?" Silac pleads with me. Tirrian's brothers and sister have been keeping an eye on the perimeter to make sure we aren't interrupted. They shifted as soon as we arrived and are doing aerial surveillance, and they will let us know if anyone gets close, but I would like to get started.

"I'm not sure if I'm going to be able to reanimate everyone tonight. I'm definitely going to need blood and sex," I tell them, not meeting any of their eyes.

"Hey, don't you dare act like that. You have nothing to be ashamed of." Saxon puts his finger under my chin and lifts it so I'm looking him in the eye. "That's why you have all of us. Trust me when I say it is no hardship to power our wife up." He grins, and the rest of the guys chuckle except for Silac and Brannock. Silac just looks uncomfortable, and Brannock looks hopeful. Ah, yes, I guess now will be as good a time as any to knock one or two mutual orgasms out of the park.

"As long as you're willing."

"I'd rather wait," Silac says, and the others glare at him, and my stomach sinks.

"Of course," I agree, even though we are less than twenty-four hours away from him being rid of his fiancée problem. What does a girl have to do to get some snake action? I'm beginning to think that he's not all that interested but still needs our help to untangle himself. Maybe he lost interest when he saw me change into the basilisk. They are pretty fucking ugly compared to the nagas, who are straight up gorgeous for a slithery, fanged creature.

I brush off the hurt and let my mimic powers wash over me. I need to work out how many statues I can change before I need to power up, and I need to be able to change back before I do. I don't think any of my guys would appreciate needing to fuck me in basilisk form—except for maybe Xavier, since he's such a kinky fuck. Silac also probably wouldn't mind if he was on the ride a Lila train, but he's not, so he's out.

I slither up to the first statue, prick a finger with one of my fangs, and smear a bit of blood on Cronus's forehead. I feel the power spark that goes with it, and his body shimmers. He gasps for air before roaring loudly. Holy fuck, he could rival Maxsim with that noise. I step back quickly as his power throbs against my body.

"Where the fuck is he? I'll kill him," he shouts and locks eyes with me before lunging with his hands out to grab my neck.

"No, Dad, that's Lila!" Xavier shouts, and Cronus halts inches from snapping my neck. He cocks his head and looks at me. I hold perfectly still, not wanting to set the furious warlock off, but I do give him a little smile.

"Hi, Dad," I say to him, and his whole body relaxes as his hands drop from my neck. He wraps his arms around my body as he hugs me.

"My dear girl, thank you. It was horrifying being trapped and unable to get out. I couldn't even get my magic to work. Quick, do Xylene, will you?" He steps back and gestures to his wife. The puncture wound on my finger has sealed, so I repeat the process with my fang and drop it on Xavier's mom's forehead. She reacts in much the same way as her husband but is quicker with her magic, and it's only Xavier's quick thinking of putting a shield between me and her that stops her from obliterating me.

"Love, that's Lila. Stop." Cronus jumps at his wife and wraps her in his arms, holding her tight. They cling to one another, and we give them a moment to recover without our attention on them. Xavier joins their huddle, and I hear him telling them what happened before they turn to face us.

"Lila, thank you." Xylene grabs my hand and gives it a squeeze. I don't blame her for not hugging me, I'm a fucking mess. Basilisk half form is not attractive at all.

"Okay, Silac's father next. Do you want to get close so you can stop him from killing me?" I raise an eyebrow at the naga, and he moves into position. He's changed forms, and I guess he's going to need it since his dad is in half form. My mimic powers throb, and I grit my teeth and clamp down to hold the form I'm in. Holy crap, it wants me to mimic Silac desperately. I won't do that. He's been very insistent on waiting, and if it comes down to it, I don't need a naga form. He might only be interested because it's his only chance. I don't want to be wanted because it will get his father off his back. I have enough mates who want me for me, not because I can change into the same race as them. Hell, Caspian, Xavier, Saxon, and Link all wanted me when they thought I was a boring old no powered Skarrian.

I feel his tail slide against mine, and it gives me goosebumps. It's an incredibly erotic feeling, and I almost groan out loud. I don't think he did it on purpose, but I move anyway. I don't need any more temptation, and the primal basilisk part of me wants to fuck and bite and wrap him up in our tail so he can't get away.

Xavier quickly steps between me and Silac with a pained look on his face. Both Cronus and Xylene look uncomfortable, and this time I do groan out loud in embarrassment.

"Can you all feel that?" I hiss at my warlock mate, who gives me a subtle head nod.

"Fuck my life," I mutter, and Cronus chuckles

before Xylene smacks his arm and hisses at him to shut up. I really like my warlock in-laws.

I go through the process again and slither back so Silac's father doesn't catch sight of me straight away. It takes him a little longer to recover than the two warlocks, but soon, he and Silac are embracing, and he's apologizing profusely for getting him into this mess.

"It's okay, Dad, we have a plan. King Tysar and my friends, as well as the king and queen of warlocks, are going to make sure the Bravalanas can't cause any more trouble permanently."

Silac's dad pulls back and frowns at him. "But what about your marriage to Kinga? We can't derail that."

"Dad, you know neither of us want that marriage," Silac argues, and his dad gets a stubborn look on his face.

"No, son, you have to go through with the marriage. It's our only chance at continuing the naga line, you know this. Without it, there will be no more chances of nagas," he blusters and waves his arms around, his hood flaring up and down with his emotions.

"Actually, that's not true, is it?" Tirrian steps into the conversation, and I brace for Tirrian to tell him about me, but what comes out of Tirrian's mouth kind of floors me, and I feel my mouth drop open. "A shifter can bite a non-shifter mate, changing them into a shifter. Silac or any of your children don't need to mate within the same species to be able to continue the naga line. Even if they do mate a shifter, there is a fifty-fifty chance their children will be nagas as well."

Oh snap. How did any of us forget about this? I have my dragon from Tirrian's bite, not because I mimicked his form, and it's the same with my kraken. I was a kraken before I knew I was a mimic.

Silac narrows his eyes and takes a step back from his father. "You told me that it doesn't work like that for nagas."

Silac's father glares at Tirrian. "It doesn't," he insists vehemently.

Tirrian shakes his head. "He lies."

Silac moves back slightly from his father, his face wary now.

"Caspian tried to tell me the same thing, but I argued with him. How could you lie to all of us like that?" Silac looks at his dad with devastation. "Why would you make your children think they didn't have any chance at finding a compatible mate? You insisted nagas weren't capable of changing their mates."

"Don't be an idiot, Silac. The dragon doesn't know what he's talking about. If you bite your potential mate, there's a chance our venom could kill them. It doesn't work the same way for venomous shifters." His dad is insistent.

Tirrian scoffs. "There's an antivenom for naga venom. You just dose the partner up before you bite. He'd have to do the same thing for his fiancée since she's a basilisk. What are you hiding? Come on,

Suzuth, tell us the real reason you tried to marry your son into that family."

Tirrian's right, it is all becoming very suspicious. Suzuth squirms with our attention on him, but he keeps his mouth closed. I guess Cronus gets tired of waiting and goes digging in his mind, because soon enough, he's scoffing.

"Kinga comes with a huge dowry. It seems like maybe your father has a bit of a gambling problem, and the shipping business isn't doing so well."

Silac gapes at his father. "How can it not be doing well? It's one of the biggest shipping companies in the galaxy. Its net worth is astronomical."

"Apparently your father has made a few bad investments and has been shipping products for certain families for nothing. You've been in bed with the Bravalanas for a long time, and it finally caught up to you, didn't it?" Cronus has nothing but disdain for the naga father.

"You sold me? How could you do that to our family? Does Mother know?" Silac asks, and I hurt for him despite our own rocky relationship.

"You won't tell her a thing. Once your marriage to Kinga is finalized and the basilisks have been dealt with, it should be no problem to regain our former glory," Suzuth hisses at his son.

Silac shakes his head. "No. I will not be marrying Kinga, and you will be stepping down as the head of Snakebite Logistics."

"And what then? Do you really think you are

capable of running it? You ran off to the circus instead of taking up your responsibilities. You will do no better than I did," the naga sneers aggressively at his son, who just looks hurt but shakes his head.

"No, Dad, I will not be running the company. My life path is different. Siskar, however, has the brains and know how, and with Simu and Slorun to back him, hopefully they can recover our family company. I think it would be a very good idea if you took an early retirement."

His father splutters and hisses aggressively, and I have the feeling he doesn't like that idea at all.

"If you don't, I will tell Mother all about your gambling habit."

"He likes whores too," Xylene says dryly, and my eyes widen. Holy fuck, they are not holding back.

"You cheated on Mom?" Silac's hood flares, and he rises up above his father, who cowers in the face of his son's aggression.

"They meant nothing to me. I had to portray a certain position to get the basilisks on board. None of them are faithful to their partners."

Silac shakes his head. "And to think I was impatient to get back and save you. I should have Lila turn you into stone again."

I push my way through and glare at the man who recovers his fight and sneers at me. "And who is this basilisk bitch that you're throwing everything away for? What's the difference between this one and the one I arranged for you? I'm sure you had fun sticking your cocks into her to get her to cooperate."

"Oh shit." Xavier snickers. "Please, Silac, let Lila show your father what she can do. Please. I promise when it's your turn to have babies, I'll look after them once a week so you can have one-on-one time with Lila."

I glare at my husband before turning my attention to Silac. I can see all his hurt and anger, not to mention feel it viscerally with my warlock powers, which must be reacting to the other three warlocks who are here.

He sighs. "Go ahead, Lila. Show my father exactly what I have thrown away my chance with Kinga for... what I am so very happy to throw it away for if you will ever forgive me for being such an ass and pushing you away until this had been dealt with. I was trying to be honorable, but now I know how ridiculous that was, considering my father wouldn't know honor if it bit him on the nose."

I've never changed from one form to a new form before, but I don't even have to think about it. I loosen the reins on my mimic powers, and I feel the power rush over me. My tail changes slightly, growing thicker and longer, and the horned ridge on my head shrinks and I feel a hood form. Something happens in my pelvis region, but I don't get a chance to check before the mist fades. I look down to make sure my breasts aren't exposed to Silac's dad in this form, but sure enough, like the basilisk, I have scales covering my chesticles. I'm the color of all my other creatures, the same as the dragon eye stone.

"You're gorgeous," Silac whispers reverently while his dad stares at me in horror. "Dad, I'd like you to meet Lila, whom I'm hoping will do me the honor of being my mate if I haven't fucked everything up too badly. Even if I couldn't bite her to change her, she can mimic my form, and we can continue the naga line without any question."

# CHAPTER TWENTY-ONE

## Lila

I don't stay in my naga form and change back to my basilisk quickly. Silac's dad alternates between yelling at him and pleading for forgiveness. The man doesn't know if he's Arthur or Martha at this stage. I think the dragons would like to arrest him and throw away the key, and the warlocks are of the same mind. Silac said it was up to his mother to make that decision, but he wanted nothing more to do with him.

After about ten minutes, I couldn't stand it any longer, so I used the basilisk power to petrify him again.

The sighs of relief as silence descended on the warehouse were almost comical.

"Lila, can we talk?" Silac corners me after they move his father to one side, and I get started on unfreezing the rest of the captives. The first five are reanimated, and the rest of my gathered men and family are trying to calm them down and ascertain where they need to be returned to. This is going to be a long ass night, and I only just started.

"Not now, Silac. I don't have the time if we want to get this finished and still make it to your wedding. In fact, weren't you supposed to be heading there now?" I ask, just wanting him to go away, and he grimaces.

"Yes, Xavier is about to take me over there, but I was hoping we could talk before I go."

"I'm sorry for all you have learned today, and I respect that you made the decisions you did, but the whole hot and cold is wearing on me. Come see me once you officially break everything off with Kinga, and then we can talk."

He looks devastated, but now he knows how it feels. Only minutes ago, he was refusing to help refuel me, which I completely understand, but it doesn't make me feel good. Does that make me cruel? Maybe, but I don't have time for head games, and that's all I feel like our relationship has been. After showing me all that affection one night, barely letting me move off his lap, he went back to giving me the cold shoulder. I don't have the emotional fortitude for that shit. I've dealt with people who were indifferent to me all my life in foster care, and I'm not allowing those behaviors to be a part of my life anymore—not when I have people who want to be a part of my family.

He must realize how serious I am, because he leaves me be when Xavier tugs him away from me. The two of them teleport to wherever Silac needs to go, but Xavier will be back to help with this clusterfuck.

Tirrian called in more dragon guards to assist with the process. I unfreeze ten people at a time, and they guide them off to the side where the rest of my mates and Tirrian's and Xavier's family work to gather their information. It's then the warlocks' job to transfer them to the dragon compound so arrangements can be made to transport them home or, in some cases, to jail. Xylene and Cronus are scanning all their minds to make sure they are innocent victims and not more trash that need to be taken out. Some of them are rival criminals the Bravalana have taken care of. We check records and outstanding warrants, and if they have none, we let them go with a warning. If they have them, then we contact the relevant authorities and transport them to the dungeons of the dragon keep to await collection.

This process takes way too long. I've reanimated approximately two hundred people nearly three hours later, and I've been pushing the last few lots. I feel my basilisk form fade away and I groan, needing blood, food, and sex.

"Lila, are you okay?" Saxon asks as the rest of my men surround me.

I shake my head. "No, this is going to take a lot longer than I thought it would. I can't hold my basilisk form anymore. I'm going to have to feed," I say quietly under my breath, but of course my father-in-law won't stand for that.

"What's wrong with Lila?" Cronus demands. "Can we do anything?"

Xavier chuckles while I blush.

"Thanks for the offer, Dad, but Lila's problems can't be solved by you."

"Actually..." Maxsim turns to the warlock king. "Would you be able to teleport me back to the dragon keep? I want to organize some food for Lila. She needs to keep up her strength. Maybe you and Xylene could show me exactly what someone with lots of power needs to eat to increase their strength." He guides him away, and I say a small prayer of thanks to the gods for my alpha mate. He distracted the nosy warlock for now as he ruminates on the best food for power levels.

Tirrian smirks at me. "How about I gather our troops and have them do a perimeter check to ensure no one is sneaking up on us, and you and Brannock can make use of that office over there? It's not much, but it will provide a bit of privacy." He gives me a kiss before rounding up the dragons and hustling them out the door.

"But Brannock can't power me up," I argue.

"No, but it will get a few more of those pesky orgasms out of the way and closer to bonding him permanently." Aww look at him being a team player. "Xavier or I will tag in after and provide you with a power boost, or do you need more than one of us?" Saxon asks, and I shake my head.

"There is no way I'm going to get through everyone tonight. I'm not even sure if I can change to Aaz'axian form. Do you think it would work if I filled a container with my blood and everyone went around and put a drop on the statues' foreheads?"

Xavier looks thoughtful. "Your blood has power, but I'm not sure if that's the only thing that does it, or if there is some innate magic that activates when you do it, but it won't hurt to test the theory. It would certainly help get through this quicker if that's the case."

"Okay, here's the plan then. I'll refuel, then I'll fill a small beaker with my blood when I'm back in basilisk form, and we can give it a try. If it doesn't work, I'm only going to continue until I run out again. The rest can wait. They've been here this long, so a day or two won't hurt. Tomorrow, we can round up the bad guys and Silac can free his fiancée."

The three men agree, and I notice Xavier and Saxon grimace at my comment. I cross my arms in annoyance. "What, do you think I was too harsh on him?" They are quick to shake their heads.

"No, I think what you said was perfect. Hopefully he will pull his head out of his ass, but he's also the kind of guy who just may go through with it so she's not left in an awkward position, and despite what he said to his father, he seeks his approval. It's why he agreed to the arranged marriage in the first place. He wanted to make his daddy happy," Saxon warns me.

I groan and throw up my hands. "I just can't right

now. That's what I told him and what I'm telling you both. Tomorrow will be what it will be."

Saxon places a kiss on my cheek. "Remember we all love you. Brannock, make sure you show her how much."

Brannock is in is human glamour, and he blushes slightly but doesn't argue as he tugs my hand and tows me toward the office. When he closes the door behind us, he pushes me up against the wall and kisses me. It's slow and sensual, and I shiver in his arms. Holy crap, this man is a good kisser. It's also kind of strange kissing him in this glamour. I'd grown used to the real him.

"Do you think you can just change your lower half to your Aaz'axian form? Would that take less mimic power than the whole lot?" he murmurs when he pulls back from my lips. When I can see the love and concern in his eyes, I pretty much melt. I wonder if we can knock out four mutual orgasms right now? What is an Aaz'axian's recovery period like?

My eyes widen in surprise. "Oh, that would be a good idea. I can try." I concentrate on my Aaz'axian form, but only around my pelvis, and what do you fucking know? It works... or I think it does. I guess I'll find out if he rips me to shreds.

I start to strip off his clothes, impatient to feel his naked skin under my palms. "As much as I want to take my time, we are running short on it. I promise I will make it all up to you in the future many times. Right now, I need fast and furious. I don't want to be here all night," I mutter against his lips as he strips my outfit off. Despite being made of dragon scales, they are flexible and easy to remove, and we're soon both completely naked.

"I will hold you to that," he grumbles, taking one of my nipples into his mouth as he wraps his large hands around my thighs and lifts me. I wrap my legs around his waist and grind down against his cock, the barbs still lying flat, but my cunt drips the lubrication it needs to take his cock deep inside me, exactly like it's designed to do.

"Want to taste you," he growls and starts to drop me, but I shake my head.

"No time. Next time," I promise him and slam my mouth against his again as I coat his cock in the wetness dripping out of me. He slides a finger into my channel, stretching me slightly. He pulls away and pops it into his mouth, tasting me like he wanted. I smirk as his eyes roll back.

"Fuck, you're delicious. I can't wait to take my time and drink you down," he rumbles before taking my nipple into his mouth again, sucking harder.

"I can't wait either. Maybe I can suck your cock at the same time, and that will be another mutual orgasm to get us that much closer to being mated in the Skarrian way," I tell him shyly. "If that's what you want." Sure his cock is likely to rip my mouth to shreds but I have stellar healing abilities and it's not like blood freaks me out. I'll give anything a try once.

He pulls his mouth away from my nipple and

looks me dead in the eye. "I would like nothing more. If we had more time, I wouldn't let you walk out that door until I was yours and you were mine, but I have waited this long, so I can wait a little longer."

He tips his head to the side. "Drink, Lila, while I slide my cock into your pussy. I want to feel your fangs in my neck."

"My venom will make you come," I warn him, and he nods.

"I can't wait to fill you with my seed. My own toxins will set off your orgasm, but let's get you close first." He holds me away from him slightly, and I notch his cock at my entrance. He slowly lowers me down, and we both groan simultaneously at the feel of him entering me. He's thick, hot, and hard, and it feels fucking amazing. My pussy pulses as he retreats before pushing in again, this time going a little deeper. He's not quite there, but I am already rippling. The backward slide has his closed barbs brushing against my inner walls in a way that creates a delicious kind of friction unlike anything my other men can do. It's equal parts discomfort and pleasure.

He works up a bit of speed once he's fully seated, and I drip with need, panting with the anticipation of what's about to happen. Although it's unlike any other orgasm, it's still a little intimidating knowing exactly what is going to happen.

His hands grip my thighs hard, and he rolls his hips with a delicious motion, sliding in and out of me in a rhythm that is exactly what I need. I feel his finger brush against my asshole, and I imagine one of my other guys fucking me at the same time as Brannock, and my cunt clenches. Sweat beads on our flesh, the scent of desire thick in the room.

Brannock groans and presses his forehead to mine. "Look at me, Lila," he demands, and I force my eyes open. "Are you ready?" he asks me, and I shake my head.

"Dude, just do it. I don't want a warning." My body stiffens because I know what's about to happen.

"That's my good girl, so fucking perfect, taking my cock that's made just for you," he praises, and I feel my body start to relax again.

"Such a pretty perfect pussy. Watch my cock slide in and out of it, Lila. You were made for me." He forces my head down so I can watch us. His cock glistens with slick, rippling with every thrust, distracting me from what's about to happen.

He tips his neck and pleads, "Bite me, Lila." This time I do, sinking my fangs into the pulsing vein just beneath his flesh that calls to me like no other. His blood floods my mouth, salty and sweet and spicy. That flavor surprises me every time—sriracha peanut butter cookies.

"God," he groans, his hands tightening on my thighs as his thrusts get harder and faster. "Going to fill you with my seed."

I can't help but freeze as his barbs activate, that fiery feeling ripping through my body. I tear my mouth away from his neck and scream, forgetting to close the holes, so his blood keeps flowing, trickling over our bodies. My instinct is to fight him, even though I know the pleasure is coming, but he wraps his arms around me to hold me in place as his barbs rip through the walls of my pussy like they are designed to do. The pain quickly morphs to liquid ecstasy, and I sag against him as I ride the waves of pleasure as they pulse through my body.

"Fuck yes!" I scream, leaning my head back against the wall and closing my eyes, rolling my hips so I can wring every exquisite moment out of this. His movement falters, and I feel his cum flood my walls, seeping into them and prolonging the intense pleasure. My body pulses with energy, and I feel amazing as I lap at the stream of blood on his chest. One of his hands strokes my hair as he whispers dirty words of praise and thanks to me. I love a filthy mouth, and Brannock gets an A for effort.

# CHAPTER TWENTY-TWO

### Lila

Saxon pops his head in to tell me that Maxsim and the warlock king and queen have returned with food for us, but I drag him into the office and ride him like a pony while I drink from his vein. When the three of us emerge, Xylene looks at us with a bemused smile.

"You've got a little something..." She points at my lips, and I freak out, swiping at where she pointed, thinking maybe I missed a drop of Brannock's cum when I sucked him off while I rode Saxon—yes, it's possible as long as he strokes himself to completion on my chest—but nope, when I look at my finger, it's just a drop of blood. I heave out a sigh of relief.

I know everyone around us has sensitive noses and can probably smell what we've been doing, but they are all too polite to mention it as I dig into the sandwiches they arranged for all of us.

I'm embarrassed to admit I eat three of them before I finally change forms and get ready to unfreeze more people.

Tirrian stalks up to me and holds out a small beaker. "Put some blood in here, and we'll see if we can help get this done a little faster."

I change forms and hold out an arm to Maxsim. He draws a claw across my wrist, and we watch black blood drip into the small glass tube. It kind of freaked me out when we first started because basilisk blood looks very similar to Madovian blood. At least it's not acidic like theirs is.

My wrist doesn't take long to close up, and Tirrian moves over to the next statue in the row, using a pipette to drop a small amount of blood on the statue's head. I'm sure everyone holds their breath as we wait to see if it works, and there's a large exhale of relief when the statue shimmers and reanimates.

"Thank fuck, and praise baby Jesus," I whisper to myself. "Can someone get me more jars? I don't want to have to return here tomorrow. I have too much other shit on my list."

Xylene gives me a hug. "Just one step at a time, Lila, and don't forget to breathe. Also, you have people you can lean on. Stop putting everything on your own shoulders."

I hug her back, sinking into her warmth. I love my

mates, but there is nothing better than a hug from a maternal figure, and I am very lucky both Xylene and Mira love me as much as I love them.

"Thanks, Mom."

She gives me another squeeze, but by then, Xavier has made a whole heap of beakers appear on a table off to the side.

"Okay, I'm going to go drain a vein, then I might need to suck on another neck or two. Tirrian, maybe if you change to dragon form, I can really fill up. I'm not sure how, but you seem to have much more blood in that form."

"I will do that for you, my beautiful mate. I much prefer that over you snacking on anyone other than your mates, and half of the ones here are already tapped out." He snickers, looking at both Saxon and Brannock, and I notice they both look well-ridden and a little pale.

"Maxsim and Xavier are still good to go," I grumble, but he just presses a kiss to my head and shifts for me, waiting patiently while I alternate between bleeding myself and bleeding him.

His brothers snicker like prepubescent boys, but his sister just smacks them both on the backs of their heads.

"Shut up, assholes. I bet if you had a Vilaxian lover, you'd be happy giving up your vein too. Just be glad the venom doesn't affect him in shifted form."

They wrinkle their noses, and I giggle at the thought of his dragon having a raging boner before splattering dragon cum over his two brothers. That would be fucking hysterical.

Once the blood has been handed out, it only takes another three hours to reanimate everyone. The process is smoother, and once everyone is transported to the keep, we return, and I collapse into bed in Tirrian's room. It's not quite as big as his nest in the vault, but it's not far off. It smells of his dragon, and I quickly fall asleep surrounded by my equally exhausted mates.

⋈

The following morning, after what feels like not nearly enough sleep, we make plans to infiltrate Silac's wedding. We left his father at the front of the warehouse in a petrified state, assuming that Silac would demand proof of life before going through with the wedding, with the rest of the warehouse covered in an illusion to make it look like all the other statues are still there.

Tallon informed us we were right, and that they collected Suzath, Cronus, and Xylene this morning. The two warlocks used a spell to take on the appearance of being petrified and frozen but have the ability to shake it off when the time is right. Everything is falling into place. We even replaced some of the staff at the function with dragons.

Once all the basilisks are in the room, we will

spring our trap. We're hoping to get out of this without any casualties, but the dragon guards have been told to shoot to kill if they have no other option. I was originally worried about having the actual authority for any of this, but apparently the punishment for turning the king and queen of warlocks to stone is the death penalty, so if any of them survive, they can call it a win.

We haven't had any communication with Silac, but the plan is to wait until whoever is in charge of officiating the wedding starts, and then all hell will break loose. The warlocks plan on freezing everyone, but I'm on standby to change into my basilisk form to reanimate anyone who needs it.

The raiding party is hidden by an illusion placed by Xavier, and it covers scents as well as sight, so that we are not sniffed out before go time. We watch on as Silac's dad is placed to the side of the raised dais where Silac and a couple of unknown basilisks wait by a pretty flower arch. There is no sign of Xavier's parents. They must not have thought they were necessary to keep Silac in line. I'm sure they'll make themselves known when the time is right.

"One wrong move, naga, and your dad is toast. You will marry my daughter with a smile, and if you even hesitate to say yes, then my guy has the order to smash your father." All of the basilisks are in half form, which is kind of creepy considering the rest of the guests and Silac aren't. I wonder if the fiancée will walk or slither down the aisle.

"The Bravalana must not know that the Snakebite Logistics is in the red otherwise they wouldn't be going to so much trouble to overthrow Silac's family," I murmur to Brannock who is closest to me.

"I don't think they care as long as they can ship their own contraband throughout the galaxy," he whispers as I feel Saxon's hand on my back as more guests take their seats. Xavier is here, as is Tirrian, but Maxsim returned to the ship. Being away from his pregnant mate was wearing on him, and he was getting snappy. After his last close call, I didn't want him to make a mistake because he was distracted, so I agreed it was the right thing to do. He did argue halfheartedly, but in the end, I think he was relieved.

Tallon asked me if it bothered me, and if I felt like I was less important than Echo, but I was quick to tell her that wasn't the case at all. I have enough men that I don't play favorites, and if I was the one who was pregnant, I'm pretty sure he would be the same way. Heck, even though he didn't like me at the time, he was pretty damn protective when I was pregnant with Cas's babies.

"It must be nice to be loved like that," she murmured over our morning coffee as we waited on everyone, her eyes sliding to a group of guards who were waiting for their orders from her this morning. I learned that she was the equivalent of a general for the dragon clan much like Saxon is for the Vilaxians.

"I have no complaints," I replied as I studied the group, noticing that two of them kept looking at her out of the corners of their eyes. They were all trying to be subtle, but it was glaringly obvious if anyone looked closely.

"Dragons are mostly monogamous, aren't they?" I asked her, and she turned her attention back to me.

"Yes, it's one of the things that sent a ripple through our society when they heard that Tirrian mated you and was not your only mate. Occasionally, there have been triads, but most matings only involve two people. There were a few who called for Tirrian to be replaced by one of us as Father's heir because they claimed his focus wouldn't be on the good of the dragon clan. Dad immediately shut that talk down, not to mention both of my brothers would run screaming if they thought they had to be responsible."

I felt a pang of guilt but also a rush of gratitude that King Tysar was so supportive of everything. "It might not be a bad idea, but Tirrian has to be the one to make that decision, not anyone else, and I support him no matter what he chooses. And why does it have to be one of your brothers? Why can't it be you?" I asked her, and her eyes widened in surprise.

"Nothing says it can't, but I am the youngest, so traditionally, it would be one of them first."

"Yet you're a general and your brothers are comedians." I nodded at them. They were pretending not to listen, but I knew they were. The looks on their faces at my last comment proved it, and I chuckled. They flipped me off in unison.

"I really love your family. It's awesome," I told them all, and I meant it.

It's comfortable, and I don't feel like I have to be someone I'm not. I thought maybe royalty would make them aloof, but that's not the case at all. Much like Xavier's family, though maybe amongst their subjects, it's different.

The mission got the green light, and we needed to move into place before we could continue that conversation. I hope she's happy no matter what she decides to do, and I hope those two dragons grow a set of balls and take a chance on her. I'd like to see my new friend happy. I get the feeling most dragons avoid her because of her status, and she implied as much when she said that female dragons can be increasingly catty when they get to mating age.

It looks like nearly all of the guests have gathered as the venue seats are mostly filled, but a cry from the foyer has everyone turning to look. It doesn't sound happy, and the man up front who threatened Silac waves a hand at one of the women seated in the crowd to go see what's happening. Silac tries to follow, but the large basilisk clamps a hand down on his shoulder and growls at him not to move.

I decide to follow her and have a look myself. There is no chance of me being discovered if I stick to the walls and stay out of the way.

What I find in the foyer makes me livid. There's a pretty dark-haired girl in a wedding dress, and she's sobbing her eyes out. "Please don't make me do this, please," she begs the woman who had been dispatched to see what was wrong. She backhands the girl in the bridal dress, and her head snaps back. She gasps, clutching her cheek as she looks at the woman with shock, but it does stop her crying.

"Get yourself together. It's a great honor for Father to choose you to do this. I wish he'd chosen me. Silac is filthy rich, not to mention handsome, so you could do much worse, and nagas have two cocks as well. Don't be ungrateful."

The man standing behind the bride clenches his fists and glares at the woman. I'm assuming he's a bodyguard, since he has that kind of look to him.

"Well then why don't you take my place? I'll gladly swap. I'll leave, and you will never have to see me again," the girl pleads, the red handprint on her face doing nothing for her bridal look. Hell, if my sister slapped me like that, I would have punched her in her nose.

"I wish I could. I begged him to let me take your place, but he is insisting. He says it's to teach you your place." The sister looks from the bride to the bodyguard behind her, and he stiffens ever so slightly. The bride does the same thing. Oh, okay, I see how it is. Star-crossed lovers. Well hell, now not only do I want to help Silac, but I also want to help this woman too. "And you've always wanted children, so who cares if they are nagas or basilisks?"

"I don't care at all, but I want them to have two parents who love each other. That is not me and Silac."

"Shut up, Kinga. It's a done deal. You just have to get your ass down the aisle before Dad comes out here and drags you down it by your hair. It will be so much worse if you disobey him," the sister hisses, obviously tiring of the conversation. She whirls around and stalks back into the other room.

I feel someone behind me, and when I turn, Xavier has joined me. *It's all very dramatic,* he says dryly, obviously having heard most of the conversation. He must have followed directly after me.

*Isn't it? How about we do something about it?* I reply. I share with him the plan that hatched while I was watching the drama unfold, and his lips tick up with amusement.

*Well, look at you being all devious. Silac's going to be livid when we don't stop the ceremony, and I thought you were over his hot and cold ways.*

I sigh. *I am, but the heart wants what the heart wants. I'm hoping if I take Kinga's place and marry the guy, then he's going to have to give in to whatever is between us. He wanted to set Kinga free anyway, and if he decides he doesn't want it after it is all said and done, I can grant him a divorce. It's not like we're mating straight away.*

*Alright, you know I like a bit of mystery and intrigue, so let's do this.* Xavier waves a hand and freezes everyone inside the church, then he peels back the

glamour on both of us, and the bride and her body
guard startle at our sudden appearance.

"Who the fuck are you?" the burly bodyguard
demands, pulling out a gun and pointing it at us.

"Whoa, calm down. I have a proposition for you."
I hold up my hands in a nonthreatening way and cross
my toes that they will listen to my suggestion.

# CHAPTER TWENTY-THREE

## Silac

My heart races as I glare at the man standing next to my father, poised to tip him over. The warlocks aren't here. They didn't drag their statues along, but they aren't frozen like my father is, so hopefully they will appear at any moment.

I was devastated to hear that my father has driven our company into the ground and been cheating on my mother. She is going to be heartbroken. I don't want to be the one to tell her. She's not here, and neither are my siblings, thank goodness. I also can't believe Dad convinced all of us that a naga can't bite an intended non-shifter mate to change them, saying that we were the last of our kind and marrying a basilisk was the only chance for naga children.

He really had the wool pulled over my eyes.

Caspian tried to tell me in the past that biting was an option, but Dad's argument about the venom sounded valid. How could I have been so stupid? I thought he had our family's best interests at heart. Instead, he just wanted the money that comes with Kinga.

Poor Kinga, I know she doesn't want this any more than I do. She's in love with her bodyguard, a griffin shifter. I told them to run away, but her father threatened to kill Andre if she did, so she stayed, and here we are, only moments from being married to each other.

There was a commotion out in the entry, and Sissolic sent his other daughter, Klotho, to investigate. I fidget, my mind drifting to Lila's heartbreaking reaction last night. I really fucked up. She was right, I was all over the place. I desperately wanted to be with her, but I wanted to do the right thing by Kinga before starting anything, and I came off very hot and cold. I just hope I haven't fucked things up completely. The minute this marriage is done with, I plan on begging Lila to add me to her mates. Caspian muttered something about me needing to woo her now that I've been such an asshole. He gave me a list of her favorite foods and flowers, and a few suggestions on what I can get her to make things right.

Tirrian also whispered something to me about her new vault and how it needed to be filled, and as a shipping magnate, surely I had some kind of treasure that might be useful for this. Normally we would have, but if Cronus is right, and our family is broke, then I may not be able to procure anything of value for her vault.

My mother is the bookkeeper, and I just can't see how we could be broke without her knowing about it. I would really like to have a conversation with her. I was expecting her and my brothers to be at the wedding. It kind of hurts that they aren't, but I understand if she's trying to keep the others safe.

Klotho returned five minutes ago, and the crowd is starting to get restless. "Go see what is taking so long. Put a hole in the bodyguard to get the bitch moving," Sissolic mutters to one of his men, but before he can slither away, music starts up, and all the guests turn to face the entry to the church. Kinga appears in the doorway in a beautiful white dress and veil. As the music plays, she walks slowly down the aisle in time to it and mounts the steps to stand next to me. She hands her flowers to one of her father's goons. There are no attendants for the wedding, just her father and his men making sure it takes place.

I'm tense, waiting for the others to spring their plan. I know that there are dragons in the crowd, waiting to round up all the Bravalanas, but that's not what happens. The official starts the ceremony, which is very quick since there are no vows from either of us, and before I know it, he's asking me if I take this woman, blah, blah, blah. My mind tunes out, and I feel nauseous. Why hasn't the plan been sprung? I'm going to have to marry Kinga if I want my father to live. As much of an asshole as he has been, he doesn't deserve to die in such a horrible way.

The officiant is waiting for my answer. My throat

closes up, and I can't respond. Shit, they'll kill my father if I don't hurry.

Kinga reaches out and takes my hand, giving it a squeeze. "Say yes, Silac," she encourages. "Everything will work out, I know it."

"Please forgive me," I mutter under my breath, and her hand tightens in mine, even though it's not her I'm begging for forgiveness. "I do," I say, voicing the words that will seal my fate, and I hear her exhale with relief. What else was her father hanging over her that she actually wants to go through with this?

The official turns to her and gives the same spiel, and she is much quicker to respond. "I do."

"I now pronounce you man and wife," the officiant announces. "You may kiss the bride."

I hesitate, and I hear her father hiss a warning, so I lift her veil and stare into the familiar eyes of my childhood friend. They glimmer with tears, and she smiles gently at me. "It's okay, I promise," she assures me like we both didn't give up our chance at happiness. Andre may be alright being Kinga's sidepiece, but there is no way Lila will ever want to be my mistress, nor would I ask that of her.

I lean in and press a kiss to the lips of the woman who is more like a sister to me. I intend for it to be short, but she wraps her arms around my head and holds me in place, licking at my lips for entrance. I gasp in surprise, not expecting Kinga to assault me like that, and she pushes her tongue in. I groan as her flavor hits my taste buds and she presses herself into my body.

Her breasts rub against my chest, and her tongue strokes mine so unexpectedly, it makes my cocks rapidly harden, and I feel wicked guilt.

"Oh fuck." I pull away and look down at Kinga in shock. Never in our relationship has she ever insinuated that she felt anything but friendship for me. She gives me a cheeky wink and wipes at her lipstick with a finger, looking very pleased with that kiss.

The crowd cheers and shouts their congratulations as we are ushered back out into the foyer and then into another area where there are tables and chairs set up for the reception. Food and drinks are brought out, and music starts up, with guests taking to the dance floor to celebrate our marriage.

Kinga and I are at the head table with her father and his men. Andre, Kinga's bodyguard, is nowhere to be seen. I guess the commotion was her finally letting him go, just like I'm going to have to let go of Lila. I'm married now, and that might not mean anything to a lot of people, but I won't break those vows. I will be the very best husband my friend deserves, especially if it means protecting my father. Speaking of my father, he is still in stone and being wheeled to a prime position in the room.

"Unfreeze my father," I demand of Sissolic when I finally catch my breath. "You got what you wanted, and now it's time to follow through on your promise."

Sissolic shakes his head. "Not until the marriage is consummated and you bite my daughter. Getting out of a mating is way harder than a divorce. Once that happens, I will gladly unfreeze your father. He already signed Snakebite Logistics over to us."

"Then why the fuck did you need us to marry?" I demand while Kinga stays quiet next to me.

"Leverage. You can never have too much of it. Your mother and brothers have mysteriously disappeared, and with them, the books. I need those ledgers back. They have all the account information."

I can't admit to him there is no money. There's nothing stopping him from tipping Dad over and smashing him to smithereens.

"Well, there's no time like the present. Shall we retire to our suite?" Kinga announces, standing up and holding out a hand to me. Her father smirks at her and nods his head approvingly, rubbing his hands together gleefully.

"So glad you came around to my way of thinking. Now you're acting like a real Bravalana. I'm proud of you, my girl."

I stare at her in horror. Despite the somewhat surprising kiss, which I will chalk up to an overabundance of emotions, I have no desire whatsoever to fuck and bite my friend. I'm not even sure I can rise to the occasion so to speak, but she ignores my look and drags me through the reception, not stopping until we get to the elevator to take us upstairs to the reserved bridal suite.

How did we get here? Everything has gone wrong. What happened to Lila and the guys and all the dragon backup?

The doors close, and Kinga approaches me with a smirk on her face. I back up, not quite sure how to react. Had she been faking her reaction to the marriage? Was she secretly going along with the plan the whole time? What happened to Andre? I thought they were together. I guess I've been fooled by everyone.

She slides her hands across the lapels of my jacket I'd been stuffed into. "Hello, husband," she says, her voice husky with desire. I grimace and push her away.

"Kinga, no. How did we even get here? You know I love another. I told her this was not going to happen. I've broken my promise to her. How could you do this? I thought you loved Andre!" All of my inside thoughts become outside ones now that we are alone, and I can't help the venom in my tone.

"Oh, are you sure? Wouldn't it be easier just to give in? I'm certain we could be good together. Once we're mated, Dad will let you continue to run your family business, and we could have snaklets, and maybe they would be nagas. I could give you anything." She stalks toward me, and I stumble as my knees hit the back of the bed, falling on top of it.

"Who are you? Did I even know the real you? I told you I'd fallen for someone else." I stare at my friend in shock. Did I even really know her?

"Please, you'd be one of many with her," she sneers, waving her hand around. "With me, you'd never have to fight to get your cocks seen to," Kinga says crudely. I don't even recognize the person in front of me. She was always so sweet and gentle and never used language like that.

I shake my head. "I could be one of a hundred and still want to be in her life. She calls to my snake. I didn't think I had to explain that to you. I thought that's what Andre was for you—your soul mate."

"Is it because of that kraken? The one you had a dalliance with years ago? Is it because he's mated to that whore as well?" She puts her hands on her hips before running a finger across the top of her cleavage, which is pushed up in her dress.

"I can give you snakelets, and he can't. It's the same reason he chose that whore. His kraken implanted his eggs in her. He couldn't have done that with you, but he'll never love you like I can."

"I couldn't care less if I have children or not. I never cared about continuing the naga bloodline. That was all my father. I knew there was only a fifty-fifty chance when Dad arranged this marriage," I argue. "Lila is my world, or I think she could be. I've tried to keep my distance out of respect for you."

"It's too late. I have you, and I am not giving you up." She lunges at me, throwing her body across mine and pinning me to the bed. I feel my fangs descend, and I hiss at her, getting agitated. I can't stop the change when my body shimmers into half form, shredding the suit I'd been wearing. She groans and rubs against my cocks, and I close my eyes, willing them to stay soft.

"Performance issues?" she asks as she drags a hand

across the slit in my scales that thankfully refuses to open for her.

"Because I have no desire to fuck you," I snap at her, throwing her off my body. "Keep your fucking hands to yourself, or I'll kill you, best friend or not."

She throws her head back and laughs loudly. "Ah, Silac, I guess you passed the test with flying colors. Xavier had no doubt. I'm going to owe him now, which he's never going to let me forget. Never wage anything with a warlock, especially our warlock. He's a smug fucker when he's right." Kinga's voice is different as her form shimmers, and Lila is suddenly in the wedding dress. "Turns out I can mimic just about anyone." She smiles at me, shrugging her shoulders as I stare, speechless.

"What? How? But..." I stammer, not sure what I'm saying. Did I marry Lila?

"Hi, hubby." She gives me a cheeky wink and a finger wave. "Hope you're not too pissed."

# CHAPTER TWENTY-FOUR

**Lila**

"Hi, hubby." I wink and wave at the clearly irate and stunned naga. I let the charade go on a little long, making him suffer unnecessarily, but I consider it payback for all of his hot and cold ways. Now, we can start this marriage with a clean slate. I'm only hoping he's not pissed I tricked him into marrying me.

"Lila," he murmurs before throwing his arms around me, pulling me against him, and circling his snake body around me so I have no chance of escape. "Thank fuck it's you. I thought I ruined everything." He pulls away and frowns. "I did marry you, right? You didn't sneak in sometime after we said our vows and signed the papers?"

I shake my head. "No, that was all me. Xavier

transported Kinga and Andre to the circus ship, and I took her place. The poor thing was beside herself, and her bitchy sister slapped her. She was in no condition to marry you. I promised them a safe haven, and they'll be traveling with us for a while. I'll find something for them to do."

He strokes a hand down my hair and nuzzles into my neck, his tongue flicking out to taste my skin. "So you're my wife?" he asks, his coils tightening ever so slightly, and those oh so delicious bumps in his pelvis region I've been curious about start to harden.

"Yup. I hope that's what you wanted, because you're kind of stuck with me now," I tell him, running my hand over his naked chest and tweaking one of his nipple rings, which has him shuddering in response.

"Well, we're supposed to consummate this marriage, and I need to give you a mating bite to free my father," he reminds me.

I wave a hand in the air. "I wouldn't worry too much about that. As soon as we left the room, the guests were rounded up, and Xavier was going to scan their minds for guilty and not guilty. Right about now, Sissolic is going to be more concerned about his own safety than worrying about his supposed daughter and her new husband."

"Oh, okay." He recoils slightly, and his grip on me loosens like he's disappointed.

"But I'm okay with us, you know, fucking to save your father and everything. We would be remiss not to at least have proof just in case Xavier, Saxon, and

Tirrian didn't round up all the basilisks," I blurt, feeling my cheeks turn pink. "I mean, we are married, and it is our wedding night."

"It is our wedding night, and I agree, we would be careless not to cover all our bases." Silac's hold tightens on me again as he chuckles. His tongue flicks out to taste my skin, and I squirm while I consider what that tongue would feel like on my clit.

"You're already in half form, so should I change too?" I ask, kind of wondering how we're going to do this. I've fucked both Caspian and Tirrian in half form. Tirrian's half form isn't too extreme, but Cas's tentacles sure are, and I'm kind of curious about snake sex.

"I won't need to bite you to change you into a naga because you have your own form, but I will still need to bite you to seal the mating bond... That's if you still want to mate," Silac replies, but he won't look me in the eye.

I put my finger on his chin and make him look at me. "Of course I do. Would I have gone through all the trouble of marrying you if I didn't? Please bite me and make me yours."

"You will have to bite me back too," he says, and I can get on board with that. I can't wait to see my bite marks scar his skin. I love seeing my marks on Nikos and my cats. Maybe I need to bite the others just to put my mark on them.

"Okay, let me go, and I'll change." I pat his body wrapped around me, but he doesn't release me completely, just loosens his hold. He drags down the zipper on Kinga's wedding dress. It's not easy, but I manage to shimmy out of it, and he tosses it to the floor. Now, I'm just wearing panties and nothing else. His heated gaze skims my form, and he groans.

"God, you're beautiful." His hands slowly caress my skin, his touch cooler than my body temperature, making me shiver. His scales warm beneath me as my heat sinks into them, and I feel those two lumps I've been fascinated with under his skin hardening. I'm finally going to experience naga sex.

I can't say I didn't google some galactic porn, desperate to know about half form snake sex. All shifter snakes have a hemipenis, which apparently means they have two cocks. He's a whole amusement ride on his own. I shimmy down a bit and run a finger over his slit, which is exactly in the same spot it would be if he were in human form. Much like Nikos and his tail, Silac has a sexual slit that should open and allow his dual cocks to poke out.

The porn I watched had an alien female riding a basilisk's pronged cocks, with one in each of her holes. Double penetration for the win, but I'm not sure if it was real or fake. I was also interrupted before I could watch any porn with both participants in half form, so I have no idea how it works. I also didn't have time to explore my basilisk body when I changed to reanimate all those people, so I'm not quite sure how we are going to fit together.

Silac moans and loosens his hold on me even more.

"Change, Lila. I can't wait to stick my cocks into your holes."

Holes? Do I have two? Or does he mean asshole and pussy? Oh, why didn't I do more research? Do snakes have assholes? I'm sure Earth snakes only have one hole they do everything through. I try not to screw my nose up, but I obviously don't succeed, because Silac chuckles.

"Change, and I will give you a hands-on naga anatomy lesson." He releases me completely, but not before he strokes my naked body with his tail, flicking the end over my nipple, as he slides off the bed and shoves it to the side.

"We're not going to need that," he tells me when I raise my eyebrows. My mouth falls open in surprise, but I quickly get my shit together and slide my panties down my legs—no point in destroying them if I can avoid it. I release my hold on my mimic powers, and once again, it's like a playful puppy as it swiftly washes over me, taking my naga form with happiness. It's painful, but not anything that I haven't experienced before, and I blink with amazement as the mist dissipates. I'm that same beautiful color pattern of the dragon eye gems, but this time, scales don't cover my breasts. There is, however, a thick line of them that runs between them, down my belly, around my belly button, and then blend into where my tail starts.

"You're gorgeous." Silac slithers toward me, circling my form, his long body dragging against mine. His tongue flicks out to taste the air, and my own tongue does the same thing, taking in Silac's taste. The slight hiss of scales on scales sounds through the bedroom as my eyes roll back at the sensations this elicits. Wow, that is something. My nipples tighten, and something inside throbs with desire.

There's also something inside me that is screaming at me not to give in so quickly. She wants him to prove he is worthy of us. She wants to be pinned down and strangled by his coils. I hiss at him, my hood flaring with aggression, and he chuckles and pulls away. I lunge at him, baring my fangs, and he quickly shuffles backward, holding up his hands as he tries to calm me.

"Easy. Naga females like to be dominated. It proves to them that their mate can protect them and their future offspring. It usually involves wrestling and then being pinned and fucked." He points a finger at what was my pelvic region. "May I?"

I still feel agitated and restless, but I need to know the mechanics of this, so I nod. He slithers closer and runs a finger down my scales, brushing over the ones between my breasts. It sends a shiver of pleasure to my core, but I hold still.

"Naga females are made for naga males. A lot of serpent shifters form poly family groups, and females can store their partners' sperm for months at a time, choosing when they wish to get pregnant. In half and full form, you have two sexual slits to accommodate a male's hemipenis and a vent for waste. Sexual coupling can only be achieved with our bodies wrapped together because of it. Unlike a lot of shifter species, pregnant female serpents cannot shift. Pregnancies often result in multiples, and they are born live. There is not enough room in a female's body to accommodate if they shift back into their two-legged form. Pregnant female serpents usually hibernate during this period, typically two to three months depending on the species, and the males will tend to their every need."

"I get to nap for two to three months?" I ask, focusing on the positive. "That sounds like my sort of pregnancy, though not something we have time for right now," I warn him, and he smiles and nods.

"No, I understand. I just hope that you will be open to bearing one or two children for me one day." I think I'm going to have to sit down and work out how long I'm going to be pregnant for so each mate can at least have one offspring. I'm hoping if I can give them all at least one, then they won't want any for another fifty years or so.

"So no kinky positions for snakes, just the horizontal mambo?" I ask as he runs his finger up and down my closed slits, which is very much like him running his fingers over my clit, only twice the pleasure.

"Not in half form, but the male naga is adaptable in case their female is not a shifter. The base of the penises will rotate and sit vertically, meaning that dual penetration can occur in bipedal form." I think about what he said, and my eyes widen. It's just like the porn I watched. Nice to know my research paid off.

"Well, that sounds like a lot of fun and definitely something we should explore. Anything else I need to know about?"

He winces. "Yes, they will swell and vibrate, and because our bodies will be entwined, making thrusting difficult, they will thrust for me, locking us together for quite some time to ensure proper fertilization, which you don't have to worry about because of your contraception for now. You'll want to bite and squeeze me, and you should let yourself do that. I need to prove to you that I can handle your venom and your strength."

I shrug as I run my tongue over my fangs. These ones are like long, thin needles, but I can't taste any venom dripping from them. "I'm a little bit of a biter in any form."

He reaches up and cups my cheeks, drawing my head closer to him, while his long body slides against mine. I shiver as our mouths join and his tongue flicks out to tangle with mine. It's a strange feeling, because they are both long and forked, and they literally tangle together much like our bodies. Silac twines his length around mine until we're twisted and it's hard to move. That's when the other side of me pushes forward. I pull away, wincing as our tongues pull apart, then I hiss at him viciously, and something starts to rattle. I look down and discover that the tip of my tail is vibrating violently and making that sound.

"Lila, you are so sexy," Silac mutters as I roll us so I can be on top, and then I lunge, biting into his shoulder. "Yes, make me your mate." He moans as I feel my venom sink into his system, and his soul melds into mine. "Your venom causes my slit to open." I feel exactly what he means as our lower bodies align, and his cocks try to push out of his slit, but he's not aligned properly with me yet, so there is nowhere for them to go. "Now it's my turn." His eyes narrow, and his mouth widens before he bites into my shoulder, his arms and body tightening as our mate bond clicks firmly into place. I hiss, and the tip of my tail rattles harder as we begin to roll around on the ground. I try to get away from him, the primal part of me not happy even though I can feel his cocks brushing against my slits, which feels fucking amazing. I groan and rub that part of my tail harder against him while still trying to escape. It's all so confusing.

His tongue flicks over his bite mark, and my body relaxes. I feel slick drip out of my slits, which are opening for him. "God, Lila, you feel amazing. I love you so much. I'm so glad I waited," he tells me as his tongue wraps around one of my nipples. It feels rougher than most of my mates' tongues, but not as rough as the cats'. I shiver and squirm, not sure if I want more or want to get away from him. My primal mind is really messing with me.

I moan and struggle a little more. I want to get away, but I also want to get closer. I really can't make up my mind, but then Silac takes the decision away from me. His cocks get more forceful, and suddenly, they breach my slits as he seems to grow bigger and rolls so he's on top of me, his hands forcefully pinning my shoulders to the ground as his tail tightens, forcing his cocks deep into my slits.

"Oh my god." I throw my head back and give up on the fight. It might make me a sad naga female, but this feels amazing, and I am so here for it. His cocks slide in and out, and they are rough like his tongue, sliding along every single sensitive nerve inside my slits. It's like the whole thing is a G-spot, not just a small section on the front wall. I want to move, but he has me completely pinned, his tail wrapped around mine so we are immobile.

His mouth finds mine, and the kiss is a furious battle for domination that my body can't give, but his cocks start to thrust fast and swell bigger, and my orgasm rips through me, and I scream.

"Are you ready, Lila? I'm going to fill you with my seed and breed you. I want to see you swell with my babies." His voice has become very sibilant much more than normal, and I know his animal is pushing his needs on him. They all have a breeding kink, but as my own pleasure pulses, I know they aren't the only one. As long as it's only role-play for now, I love it.

"Fuck yes! God, Silac, so good. Breed me, I want it," I ramble as he grunts and groans, and I feel him flood both slits with his cum, his cock pulsing and thrusting in what feels like a never-ending orgasm.

It swells even more, and I know I'm not going anywhere. The thrusting slows, but his cocks start intermittently pulsing like a goddamn vibrator, and every time it does, it triggers another orgasm.

"Yes, God, yes!" I scream as another one crashes over me. I push him at the same time I try to wiggle my pelvis to get more of it. My body can't make up its mind, but after it happens a few more times, I'm too exhausted to struggle. I relax in his arms, and he whispers words of praise and strokes me all over. I sink into a sort of sexual coma and drift away.

# CHAPTER TWENTY-FIVE

**Lila**

When we emerge from our room a few hours later, we find the reception hall empty except for Xavier, Saxon, Brannock, and Tirrian with his brothers and sister—oh, and Silac's dad, who is still petrified. Silac stayed in half form, since his suit was shredded when he shifted, but I slipped the wedding dress back on. It seems that I glamoured myself as Kinga and didn't assume her form, so when I changed back, I didn't destroy the wedding dress. It's a bit floofy for my tastes with heaps of layers of tulle, but the only other option was a robe or staying in half form. I'm pretty sure Silac wouldn't keep his hands off me in half form, so the dress it is.

"Congratulations." Xavier stands up and starts clapping, and the others follow suit, hollering and hooting. I didn't hide the bite mark on my neck, happy to show it off next to the others. I pretty much look like a chew toy now, but I really don't care.

"Come join us and let us fill you in." Tirrian gestures to a couple of spare seats.

"There's plenty to eat, and we are barely putting a dent in it." Saxon points out the buffet, which is still full of food. Obviously, nobody had a chance to dine before shit hit the fan. Everyone at the table has a plate in front of them. They must have had something to eat while they waited for us.

"Can we send it back to the dragon keep? I'm sure there are plenty of hungry dragons who won't let it go to waste," I ask Xavier who nods.

"The guards who helped with the raid would think you were a goddess." Thorn chuckles. "The sure way to get a male dragon on your side is through their stomach."

"They better admire her from afar," Tirrian grumbles, smoke drifting from his nostrils at his brother's teasing.

"Then that's what we'll do." I sit down on a chair, and Silac moves the one next to me out of the way so he can coil up next to me.

"So how did it all go?" I ask as Tallon passes me a glass of champagne. We clink glasses as Brannock answers.

"All the guests were scanned. Those who were innocent of any foul play were released—mostly women and children and non-related guests. Some were business associates whom the Bravalanas were trying to woo, but they weren't complicit in any of their illegal trades. Maybe they were trying to go legit, we will never know, but I highly doubt it. None of your family members apart from your father were in the building," he tells Silac, who nods.

"I didn't think I saw any of them. I'm actually worried about them," Silac admits, and I grab his hand and give it a squeeze.

"And those who were complicit are currently residing in the dragon's containment block, awaiting transport to Westalin." Saxon takes over as he grabs a plate and fills it before putting it in front of me.

"Mom and Dad want to make an example of them. They have a reputation to uphold, and the basilisks are going to pay the price for their mistakes. Nobody fucks with the king and queen of the warlocks and lives to brag about it," Xavier explains.

"Where are they?" I ask. "I thought maybe they'd be here as well."

"They got word from one of their loyal followers that while they were petrified, Atrax tried to take the crown. That's Elyan and Aryan's father, who has been one of my father's advisors for years despite knowing he is plotting against him—the whole keep your enemies closer bullshit." His power crackles with agitation.

"But even if they were out of commission, you are still crown prince," I point out.

"Apparently I am being charged with crimes

against a harem member and am not fit to hold a royal title."

"What the hell? You had every right to kill her." That bitch didn't suffer enough as far as I'm concerned.

"I thought attacks against one's intimate was a grievous crime," Tirrian rumbles, smoke drifting out of his nose. He really does have a short temper.

"It is, and so is trying to overthrow the king and queen. He must have gotten word that they were petrified and assumed there was no chance they would be reanimated. He's going to wish he wasn't born by the time Mom and Dad are done with him. They will also clear me of all charges and have told me that neither of us have to appear before the tribunal. They will handle it all."

I sag in my seat, the relief I feel immense. "That's one less task we need to take care of. It's just the Vilaxians now and that bullshit clan stuff. I hate those bitches. I'm feeling all kinds of negativity towards the Vilaxians at the moment. They fucked up one of my acts."

"I'm sorry," Saxon apologizes, and I hear his guilt.

I shake my head, waving a fork at him. "Not your fault. Thankfully Vilax is on the way back to Earth, otherwise I'd tell them to kiss my ass, and they could wait until we've rescued Chloe." I look at Brannock who practically vibrates with excitement. "Now that we're done here, we can do that."

Xavier winces and looks apologetically at Brannock. "We need to make a short stop at Skarr for supplies and to recall the rest of the circus. The call went out already."

"What? Why wasn't I told?" I ask, frowning at my warlock.

"The grandpas made the decision during Nik's birth. They decided if we were returning to Earth anyway, then we may as well resume our tour."

"Yeah, sure, that's if they don't declare war on us once we raid Area 51," I mutter sarcastically, glaring at the others, even though it wasn't their decision. "What were they thinking?"

"Don't forget this is a business as well, and it's already taken a few hits this year. If we don't resume soon, the acts are going to find other employment." I hate when Xavier is the voice of reason. It makes me unreasonably furious, but he's not wrong.

"Okay. Let's wrap things up here and head to Skarr. I guess with the recall going out, I'll know for sure how many acts we're going to replace. Fuck, we're going to have to do that before we head to Earth too."

I stand up and start pacing, which is not easy in this froufrou dress. Smoke even starts to drift out of my nose. Well, I can't really throw stones in glass houses with Tirrian, now can I?

Tirrian stands up and steps in front of me, stopping my pacing.

"Easy, your dragon is still new, and if you're not careful, it will take over. I don't think this reception center will accept you destroying it if you shift inside. They are already pissed that we raided it earlier."

His hands on my arms ground me, and I breathe in and out. "Okay, sorry. I'm good now." I reassure him, and he releases me. Everyone else stands up as Xavier waves a hand, sending the buffet back to the dragon keep.

"How about we fly back? It will give you time to calm down, and there's nothing like flying with a wing."

"Wing?" I ask him, slightly confused.

"Yeah, that's what a group of dragons is called," Thorn says, taking off his shirt and tossing it at Xavier. "Be a pal and bring our clothes, will you?" He finishes stripping and saunters out one of the patio doors, shifting before taking off. If I looked at his pert ass on his way out, I'm only a red-blooded female, and it was there.

Xavier grumbles but gestures to us all to pass him our clothes. The other dragons strip and head outside while I give my guys a quick kiss. I get to Silac and throw my arms around him, hugging him. "Bye, hubby. See you back on the ship. Make sure you move into one of our rooms." I have a moment of panic and look at Saxon and Xavier. "Are there any spare rooms?" I haven't been keeping track.

"No, but we've booked for the ship to be refitted during the time we are on Skarr. It should only take a day or two, which is how long we plan to be there."

"Okay, well, we'll move your stuff in later. You can

sleep in mine for now." He beams and hugs me back, dragging the zipper of my dress down and letting it pool at my feet. I'm not wearing any underwear, and I feel the room grow heavy with lust from my guys.

"Wait," Brannock calls as I start to walk out the door. "What about him?" He points at Silac's father, who is still standing in the corner, petrified. Whoops.

Silac heaves out a sigh. "I'm going to have to stay behind and figure out what happened to my mother and siblings. I'll catch up with you on Skarr. If you could reanimate him, I'll take it from there."

I feel a pang of agitation, knowing I'm going to be separated from him, but it will only be a couple of days. The flight between Fluxx and Skarr is just a few hours. "We'll leave the grandpas' shuttle in the space port. That way, you don't have to wait for a scheduled one," I tell him, giving him a kiss. I let the basilisk form wash over me and prick my finger on my fang before dropping the blood on Silac's father's forehead. I don't wait for him to unfreeze before shifting back to OG Lila.

"Toodles." I wave and skip out of the room naked, changing quickly to dragon form when I get outside. Tirrian follows me, growling aggressively. Aren't shifters okay with nudity? I bet a whole heap of female dragons have seen him naked. Smoke starts to drift out of my nose at that thought, and my dragon growls at him, nipping his tail as we take off. Our flight home involves a lot of nipping and chasing, and it's the most fun I've had in ages. I'm breathless and worn out by the time we get to the keep.

As it turns out, we didn't have to wait for Silac. He found his family at their family home. His mother refused to be involved in any of his father's dealings and had apparently already known about the cheating and stealing. When Silac and his father arrived, she told him she was taking over the business, which wasn't as in the red as he thought. She had been hiding the funds so he couldn't lose them all. They are mated, and that mating bond is painful to break, so she kicked him out, and they will live separate lives for now. Silac's brothers are now fully involved in running the business, and Silac also told them their father had been lying about the mating bite not changing a non-shifter female, so they have hope for future naga offspring as well. When he returned to the ship, we had a video call with his mother and siblings and made plans to have dinner next time we are close to Fluxx. I liked them all, and they seemed to like me too, so I call that a win.

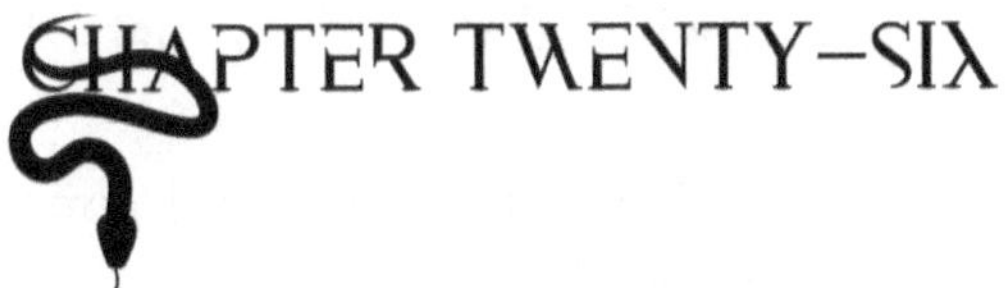

# CHAPTER TWENTY-SIX

### Ghosie

After the successful rescue mission, we move from Fluxx to Skarr late that night. We arrive in the middle of the night, the journey a lot quicker with the circus ship. The Adams brothers decide to take their wife to their home on the planet, claiming she might wake up if she's in more familiar surroundings. They invite all of us to stay with them.

It's still winter on Skarr, but the minute they wake up the following morning, Caspian and Nikos herd their children out the door and into the freezing cold water. It's completely different from Fluxx, which was warm and balmy. I can hear the children squealing from inside the house as they take to the water.

Echo and Maxsim also change forms and disappear to run up and down the icy, snow-covered shore. Both

Xavier and Tirrian stayed behind on Fluxx to help facilitate the transport of the prisoners for the king and queen of warlocks. They, as well as Caspian's brother Malik, will be joining us in a day or two.

That leaves Brannock, Saxon, Silac, Link, Zeydan, and me to help Lila with all the things that need to happen.

"I think our best bet is to divide and conquer," Link says as we all enjoy a hot beverage once the children have departed. "I scanned Liliana this morning, and I'm happy to announce there is more brain activity. I really think she will wake soon, but we need to keep busy instead of hanging around, waiting for it."

"Okay, well, we need supplies. William gave me the master list, and all his suppliers are here on Skarr. I'm going to take care of those orders today. If I go in person, then there's a higher chance of me getting them now instead of having to wait a week or two," Silac tells me, tapping the tablet on the table in front of him. He's in charge because shipping and logistics are kind of his thing. "Saxon, maybe you can come with me to provide intimidation?"

Lila rolls her eyes. "I'm pretty sure your half form causes enough intimidation, especially if you flare that hood, hiss, and shake your tail feather, but sure, why not."

"I was planning on greeting all the returning performers. They'll need physicals, and I want to make sure they all have the proper documentation to travel, and that none of them have records or warrants." Link looks at Lila's newest potential mate, the earth god. "Could you help me with that? Even with your reduced powers, you can scan minds like Xavier, right?"

The god nods. "Yes, I can make sure people are who they say they are. I would be glad to help out. I've been feeling useless, unable to contribute to this family."

"Wouldn't want to let another Madovian on board," Lila mutters. "Thank you, because that would ease some of my worries. I don't want any possible Syndicate members or hellacious she-beasts getting near my babies. Also, Zeydan, you are not useless. Every member of our family is important and valued. We just have to find something that you want to do or don't. I really don't care, I just want you to be happy."

He has this frown on his face, like he can't decide if Lila is being genuine or not, but that's the thing I love so much about her. She wants your happiness as much as she wants her own. Take Silac's ex fiancée Kinga and her partner Andre, for example. Lila offered them positions with the circus, but it turns out Kinga is amazing with children, and she will be the children's nanny, freeing up the parents to work on the show during the day now that we are resuming our schedule on Earth. Xavier decided that their children probably needed a bodyguard, so that's Andre's job now. It worked out brilliantly. They can spend all their time together while making sure the babies are safe and occupied.

"Okay," he agrees slowly. "I would like to spend more time with you this evening if you are not busy."

"Like a date?" Lila's eyes light up.

"Yes?" Zeydan is clearly not sure, but Brannock slaps him on the shoulder.

"That's a great idea. I'm sure Eric can give you some ideas on great places to eat here on Skarr. Why don't you talk to him before you return to the ship?"

The poor god looks completely out of his element, but I can see how happy his suggestion has made Lila. The poor girl didn't get much in the way of courting with most of her mates. I know she loves being mated to them, but a bit of romance never goes astray. I hope my big gesture is received well.

"We need to go shopping for the children and Chloe. She's going to need things." Lila turns her attention to the Aaz'axian, who is in his human glamour. He seems more comfortable like this. I guess maybe he got used to it when he was on Earth. It also doesn't cause people to run in fear on planets that know what an Aaz'axian looks like.

"Good idea. I'll ask John to borrow the vehicle and find out where the closest mall is. If you have a list, I'll grab everything we need," Brannock assures her, and she frowns.

"I thought that maybe Ghosie and I would come with you." She looks at me, and that's my cue.

"Well, actually, I've made other arrangements. I hope you don't mind, but I took the initiative and have arranged for auditions. I was provided with a list of resumes and contacted the ones we thought might fit the show best. They are all waiting to perform for you this morning at a local theater," I say, not quite looking her in the eye while bracing myself for her reaction.

"You had all the acts come to Skarr to audition?" she repeats slowly, and I wince before nodding.

"Yes?" I answer cautiously.

She jumps up out of her chair and shouts, "I fucking love you!" She throws her arms around me without caution, and I melt into her embrace. God, it feels nice to be hugged, but then she starts to squirm and rub her breasts against me, and I curse the fur I've been born with. I try to pull away, but she hangs on.

"Lila, stop. It's not you," I tell her, looking for help from the others, but they are just watching with amusement.

Silac chuckles and shakes his head. "Nope, not a valid excuse. I can feel how much she's attracted to you, and she knew what your fur would do. I say go for it. I know how much you want her too. Don't make the same mistakes I did and take the choices out of her hands."

I look to the others for help, but none of them do anything to interfere.

"Silac is right. Take her to her room and have your way with her. I think you've both been tiptoeing around it for too long," Link agrees.

"I can feel how starved you are for affection," Zeydan chimes in. I growl at the nosy god, but he ignores me.

"But it's taking away her consent," I argue, and she pulls back from me. Her body shimmers, and when the mist clears, she's in her Carevasta bear form. My cock was already throbbing inside its sheath with her rubbing against me, but seeing her like this makes it start to worm its way out.

"Does this even the playing field?" she asks, throwing herself back at me, and when her fur touches mine, I just about come all over her. She's activated the aphrodisiac qualities in her own fur, driving my senses insane.

I pick her up and stride down the corridor toward her bedroom in this wing, leaving the others cheering behind us.

"Don't forget, you only have an hour and a half until the auditions start," Saxon calls after me.

"They knew about this?" Lila asks between kisses. I pant, my mind foggy with lust.

"Yes, they suggested it would be a way to help you." I can't stop my hands from running all over her body, feeling how soft her fur is. I've felt male bears before, but none of them were ever as soft as she is.

"You have no idea what that means to me," she murmurs against my mouth before shoving her tongue inside and kissing me.

All conversation halts as the aphrodisiac floods our systems, turning us into mindless rutting animals. Her hands rub over my belly, and I try to suck it in, but she shimmies down and rubs her face against it.

"God, I love your belly. You're so fucking cuddly,"

she purrs, and I feel my chest puff up with pride. For Carevasta bears, a big belly is a sign of being a good provider, but that's not how most societies work, so knowing it turns her on makes me very happy.

My eyes roll back in my head as she turns her attention to my cock, which has pushed its way out of its pocket. It's one of the only places on my body that doesn't have fur, and when she runs her tongue over the length, my knees give way, and I sag onto the bed. She pushes me back and straddles my legs.

My cock dribbles continuous precum, and not just from the tip. All the ridges and bumps on the shaft are self-lubricating. Lila laps and sucks at it like it's her favorite meal. "Tastes so good, like strawberry candy. All those bumps and ridges are going to feel so good," she mutters as I reach down and run a finger through her slit, which is hidden by all her fur. I find it easily since her fur is dripping with slick and slide a finger into her channel. My cock might be covered in bumps and ridges, but so is the inside of her pussy in this form. They act like the clit does in human form, and every time I brush over them with my own bumps and ridges, it will stimulate them. I can't wait to feel it gripping my cock.

She takes my dick deep into the back of her throat, and I growl, grabbing hold of the top of her head to guide her up and down, thrusting slightly with my hips. She doesn't gag, but tears do stream down her face as she swallows around my thick length.

I feel my balls tighten. They are internal, so she

can't touch or feel them, but I know it means I'm going to come soon, so I pull her off my length. I want to be deep inside her when I come.

I sit up and push her off me, moving behind her and pushing her down so she's on all fours. She looks back at me, her pupils blown wide.

"Please fuck me. I need it. It hurts," she begs, and for the first time, I don't feel guilty that Lila wants me because of what my fur does.

A growl leaves my mouth as I lean over her and thrust my cock into her channel. We both shout out at the sensations, and an animalistic urge over comes me. I ride her hard, my body pinning hers to the bed as she screams and shouts her need. The sensations are like nothing I've ever experienced. Her ridged inner walls must do something to mine, because the pleasure is so exquisite, it borders on painful. She gets tighter and tighter, and I can't hold out. I roar and almost stop in shock as my teeth grow bigger, and I bite her shoulder. My pleasure nub pushes out and sinks slightly into her asshole. She shouts her surprise before growing pliant in my arms as I spill my seed deep inside her. I keep thrusting through my shock, even when I feel Lila's soul fill my chest as a mating bond clicks into place. I had no idea we could form mate bonds, but I am super excited about it. My cock pulses more cum, and I feel it leak out and drip down the backs of her thighs.

Lila snarls and groans as her cunt continues to ripple with every stroke. Her orgasm will continue until I pull out. She reaches back with an arm and pulls me closer. I lean over her, and she turns her head and bites my neck, her large teeth marking me as they sink in. My cock pulses, and I fill her with another load of cum.

I groan and roll my hips, both of us snarling and panting like animals. Eventually, I pull out and watch as cum drips out of her cunt. I push it back in with one of my fat fingers. Lila's voice is husky as she groans again before I roll her onto her side and spoon her, slipping my still hard cock back inside so I can keep my cum in her. I stroke her fur.

For a brief time after copulation, the aphrodisiac qualities recede—I guess it's so we don't fuck to death—and I'm able to hold my mate in my arms. I can't believe we mated.

"Are you okay?" I ask her, and she turns her head so she can look me in the eye.

"We mated. Were you expecting that?" she asks, not sounding upset, just curious.

I shake my head. "No, it's been so long since we had females, I think the fact that it was possible faded from our everyday knowledge. I also never bit any of the men I fucked in the past, nor do I remember any males mating."

She turns her head back and snuggles into me. My cock pulses, and she shivers, but we don't move or talk. We just enjoy our new bond, the reciprocal feelings on a constant loop between us.

# CHAPTER TWENTY-SEVEN

### Lila

I've locked down one more mate when we emerge two hours later. It was a surprise, but not a bad one. I'm really happy. I can feel him inside my chest, and he is a genuinely good, happy soul.

I am a very happy Lila, and so is my mimic. She practically preens with smug pride and keeps trying to get me to change forms. It doesn't matter which one, she just wants me to make use of the power. We're running late for the auditions, though, so it will have to wait, but it's not like they can start without us, and it was for a good cause.

Ghosie and I settle in seating a few rows back, giving us an excellent view of the stage. He has a tablet sitting in front of him.

"Okay, the first act is an animal act. We still haven't

received confirmation on whether or not the Aquilians or Vilaxians are returning, correct?" he confirms.

I shake my head. "No, Nik is going to call his mother this evening to ask. They keep refusing to answer any of my calls. Saxon and I will speak to his aunt when we stop in Vilax on the way to Earth. Saxon is still willing to perform, but without any others, it will be a fairly short act."

"I will happily join him for that act if the Vilaxians don't come through for you. It's not like it's much different from mine," a voice in the wings calls, and I stand up and squeal.

"Mags!" I hold my arms out for my friend, and she rushes to hug me, a huge smile on her face.

"Ugh, I missed you." She tips my neck to the side as she pulls away and whistles. "I need to hear about all the things." She turns her gaze to Ghosie then leans in and whispers, "And I want to hear all about that delightful hunk of man meat and where he came from. Does he have a friend?"

I frown, thinking about the last time I'd spoken to her. Was that before he kidnapped me? Fuck, I am a bad friend.

"Well, I want to hear about everything you've been up to while I've been preoccupied. I heard a rumor that none of the Vilaxians are returning to the show." I cock a questioning eyebrow, and she glares at me.

"We will not be talking about bloodsucking or scaled assholes."

I give her another squeeze and change the subject

for now. "Okay, so how did you know we were here?" I ask as we take a seat. I ensure she is on the other side of me so she doesn't accidentally brush against Ghosie. I don't want to cut my friend when she starts rubbing up on my bear. I make introductions, and they wave to one another.

"We've already met," she tells me. "When I got the recall notice, I called the ship to see if there was anything I could do to help. It's not like I have anything else going on," she mutters bitterly. "And X put me in contact with G here. He suggested I help you with auditions and said that you could probably use some company of the female variety."

"God, yes." I quickly kiss the bear next to me. If I only brush my lips across his, I get a warm, tingly feeling, but no desire to jump him like a horny dog. "Thank you. I've had Tirrian's sister, Tallon, the last few days, but I'm always happy to see you."

"What about me, bitch? Or am I that easy to replace?" another voice calls behind us.

Frowning, I stand up and peer into the darkness. That can't be who I think it is. As they emerge from the shadows, my stomach flips with joy.

"I'm pretty sure you're irreplaceable," I reply and scramble over the seats, not waiting for Susie to get to me. I hug my friend, her corkscrew curls tickling my face as tears stream down my cheeks. "I missed you."

She holds me tightly. "I missed you too, but we have a long trip back to Earth, so we have plenty of time to catch up, and I can play with all the babies. I can't believe you're a mother two more times." She pulls back and looks over the length of me. "How do you keep that figure?" She winks, and we dissolve into giggles as I lead her back to sit with us.

"It helps when one of my husbands did the heavy lifting this time," I reply, and she and Magenta wave to one another. I'm so glad my girls get along. I know they haven't had a lot of interaction, and we still haven't had our girls' night out. I'm going to try to rectify that as soon as possible. I'm just sad that Nixie isn't here, but she turned out to be different than the person I thought she was anyway.

"Ghosie, this is my sister from another mister, Susie. She and her fiancé have recently made the transition to alien as well." I gloss over their story, sure we can get into it later.

"Hey, G," Susie calls, and the two of them exchange an air fist bump like they are the best of friends already.

"Have you two already met?" I look between them, and Ghosie shrugs sheepishly. "The guys put me in charge of communicating with them and telling them we were returning to Earth to bring down Agent Smith, and I asked if they wanted to be involved."

I look at my friend. "Is everyone here? What about Mark?" I ask, knowing his parents probably weren't happy letting him out of their sight after only having found him a few months ago.

"Yes. Aura wants Pleasure Inn back. I'm not sure what that means for all of us." There is sadness in her eyes. "Mark and I kind of wanted to join the circus. I don't think we're cut out to run a brothel. We both want to use our medical skills, and I have some cool new abilities that may come in handy."

"You got powers?" I gasp, and she nods her head, looking shyly at Magenta.

"Yeah, turns out I can fly, amongst other things."

"Whoa, yeah, girl!" Mags holds up her hand for a high five. "I can totally work with you on that. Maybe we can turn my act from a solo to a double. It would be fun to change things up a little and have another person to help with Saxon's act if the Vilaxians choose to be uncooperative."

My heart is almost overflowing with love right now. My two best girls are here and not going anywhere for the near future. Both of their lives seem to be chaotic, but I'm here for them. My grandma is getting close to waking up and making my grandpas the happiest men in the galaxy, and I've locked down all but two of my men, with only one of them being a work in progress, which only leaves the mysterious god. We have our upcoming date, which I'm excited for but also super nervous about, and hopefully on our flight from Skarr to Earth, we can get to know each other a little better.

"Okay, shall we get started?" Ghosie says, tapping the tablet. "I'm not going to give you any insight to the act. We're going to watch it, and I would say it's the best way to judge whether it wows us or not, right?"

"That sounds great," I tell him, desperate to pat his

hand. One thing I'm going to do when my grandma wakes up if she turns out to be the goddess of life as well, is beg her to help the Carevasta bears and the Aaz'axians—not that there are many left. Both races have suffered long enough, and it's been close to seven hundred years since the war.

"Audition one can start," Ghosie calls to the stage manager, who is assisting with the auditions.

I watch with barely contained excitement as the house lights drop, and the ones on stage light up.

A female walks out onto the stage. She is humanoid, but on her head, she has a mohawk of fur. On either side of it, her head is bald, but it has patterns like a leopard. She has a thin, whip-like tail, and I can see webbing between her fingers. She's wearing a body-suit, which hugs her body, and she has two sets of breasts and wide hips.

"Oh, an Elgrug." Magenta leans forward, and I can feel her excitement. "This should be good. She can take the place of my act if I end up helping Saxon."

She places her hands together and starts rubbing them back and forth. I can see something is happening but can't make out what. She starts singing a hauntingly beautiful melody.

"Elgrug are an amphibious species who make their homes around lakes and rivers. The females are the hunter-gatherers and are fierce. Their men are pampered little princesses who have their every need catered to." Magenta rolls her eyes, not taking them off the female in front of us.

Her hands stop rubbing, and she begins to pull them apart, forming a large, adult-sized bubble. She flicks her wrists, and the bubble detaches and floats on the spot.

"They use the bubbles to catch prey and entice mates."

"Entice mates?" Susie asks, sounding bewildered.

"Yes. If they can catch a male and keep him inside their bubble for fun times, then they are likely to be a good provider. Their bubbles are good and strong, and if they stand up to vigorous fucking, then they can trap any kind of large prey animals. Females will create life- sized bubbles and trap potential males for weeks at a time, hoping they will accept their suit."

I frown, watching as she taps the bubble, and it bounces in time to the music. "But I'm not sure that is going to make a good act. We're not providing adult entertainment." Although I must admit, I am intrigued. I'd like to coerce one of my mates into the bubble for some floating fun times.

She waves her hand, and the stage manager steps back onto the stage, looking a little nervous. She keeps singing but gestures for him to stand still. She then pushes the bubble at him, and it speeds toward him, surrounding him with a large pop. The stage manager waves to us through the translucent bubble. She does a quick little dance around him, shimmying and shaking until she gets behind the bubble, then she lifts it into the air and gives it a push. It gently floats out over the audience. We follow its trajectory for a moment before we notice her forming another bubble. She steps into this one herself and is able to make it move by gently applying pressure in the direction she wants to go.

We watch as her bubble also drifts out over the audience. She is able to control the other bubble from inside hers somehow, and they dance together in a breathtaking motion of sound and movement. They eventually come to a stop above us, pressed against one another, and she steps from hers and into the bubble of the stage manager, letting hers pop above us. I gasp and applaud as the bubble now containing them returns to the stage.

It pops, leaving the two of them standing on the stage unharmed. The volunteer looks slightly green, but that's nothing that can't be trained for. She will need an assistant or maybe a volunteer from the audience.

"I can make and add as many bubbles to the act as is required to make it longer," she calls out, her voice as melodious as her singing was. "I can also put any number of objects in them to wow the audience. I would really love to travel the galaxy with you." That last declaration sounds kind of desperate. "I'm not ready to settle down and join our mating season. There is so much I'd like to do first, and I also don't want a mate that I have to fawn all over. Is it wrong to want an equal relationship where he cares for me just as much as I take care of him?"

God, I feel for her and completely understand. It must have been so hard for her to come here today to audition and go against her society to want something more.

"As long as you can clear our background checks, I would love to offer you a position," I call out, not even conferring with the others.

"Could you give her the relevant forms to fill out?" Ghosie asks the stage manager, who quickly agrees and escorts her off stage.

"That was thrilling," Susie says, her eyes wide with amazement. "It's so exciting seeing it with the truth."

I hated that we had to erase her memories the first time around, so it's wonderful for me that she can be here and know the truth.

The next act is adorable. There are these small German shepherd like creatures that have sheep faces, but they have green leaves on their bodies instead of wool. The tip of each leaf and both cheeks have pink spots. Their trainer has them doing typical kind of agility things, but then the act changes and they start to merge with one another, and they create a horse-sized leaf sheep creature. That's when the trainer climbs on its back and performs jumps and dressage movements to music. It's not quite as elegant as dressage, but it's still fun. He then jumps off, and the stage manager wheels a large hoop onto the stage. He steps out of the way, and it lights up with flames. The large creature leaps through it, and it sets his leaves on fire. I scream and stand up, about to use my warlock powers to conjure water to put him out, but the trainer waves me away. The creature seems to absorb the fire, and his leaves turn from green to red, and instead of pink tips, they have little flames at the end of each leaf. The creature then separates again into seven miniature flaming versions. One by one, they cough up a ball of flame that dissipates before he sets anything on fire, and they return to their green color again.

They all bow in unison, and we applaud.

"Whoa, okay, not what I was expecting but still super cool," I say to Ghosie, who smirks.

"I've never seen anything like that before," Magenta says. "Where did you find them?"

"They sent in an audition tape. They are from a small planet at the far edge of the galaxy. The animals are bred and traded to control forest fires, but it's still a very new process. They are hoping the circus will drum them up some business."

"That's smart," Susie murmurs, and I have to agree with her. Earth could certainly use whole herds of them.

I end up offering him a spot in the circus on the spot as well. The last act scheduled today also gets an offer. It starts with the lights off, and when slow droning starts, they turn on, showing the stage covered in rocks.

"Well, that's a little underwhelming," I mutter, and Ghosie snorts.

"Wait," he whispers.

The low droning continues, and one of the rocks start moving. Susie and Magenta gasp.

"Oh, I know what this is," Magenta says, leaning forward.

One by one, all of the rocks start to vibrate, and then they begin to roll around the stage. They seem to be making patterns or following a routine, but from this angle, I can't see it. In the circus tent, it won't be a problem though. They freeze, and then suddenly, they roll toward the largest rock in the middle of the stage, and as they touch it, they seem to meld together. My mouth drops open as it forms a being with two arms, two legs, a body, and a head. The head rock forms facial features, and the being grins and waves.

The stage manager wheels out more rocks, and the being proceeds to give us a demonstration on his strength.

"Okay, a rock strongman, I like it," I remark at the end of the show and also offer him a position. "I like what we've got so far. What do you all think?" I ask my co-judges, and the two girls agree with me while Ghosie points at the tablet.

"There are three more scheduled for tomorrow, but we've made a good start. Shall we head home and see if everyone else's day was as successful?"

I invite Magenta and Susie to join us, but they both beg off. Susie and Mark are staying at a hotel until they need to be on the ship, trying to get some distance from Aura and company to see how they really feel. Magenta admits to being in a funk and not good for company, but promises that once the circus gets underway, she will be over it.

I let them go, although I'm worried about both of them, and add fix their problems to my list.

Ghosie leans in and gives me a brief kiss. "Lila, you don't have to fix everyone's problems," he says gently. Damn intrusive mate bond.

I grimace sheepishly. "I know. I'm a fixer, okay? I'll try to do better," I promise, and we leave the theater behind and head back to our family.

# CHAPTER TWENTY-EIGHT

### Lila

The auditions exhaust me, and when I get home, I ask Zeydan for a rain check on our date, mostly because I want to be able to focus on him, and right now, my attention is scattered. Instead, I suggest we have family dinner and game night. It feels like it's been forever since we were all in the same room together. Xavier and Tirrian arrived from Fluxx, so we're all here, but Nik is insisting on making the call to Aquilia first. He wants to see if they are still going to provide some Aquilians for their act.

He's quite agitated as we sit down in front of the large screen that doubles as a TV and a video conferencing device. "You know, even if they don't, we have the makings of a cute little act right here," I tell him, rocking Hali in my arms. Thankfully she's asleep for now, because she does not stop. Ty is a lot calmer, which is so funny considering his name. We certainly got that wrong. We should have called him Tranquil or Millpond or something more appropriate.

"Wouldn't it be fun to have you and the children in the act? Maybe we can incorporate the krakens into is as well."

He looks thoughtful, but before he can reply, the screen lights up, and his mother is staring at us, wearing an expression that makes her look like she smelled something bad.

"What is it, Nikos? I'm pretty sure I made it clear that if you chose the path you did that you would no longer be welcome on Aquilia."

My mouth drops open in surprise, and I gape at my husband. "You never told me that. When did she make you choose?"

He sighs, brushing a hand over sleeping Ty's small head. "A few days before I gave birth, she answered one of my calls and gave me an ultimatum. If I gave you full custody of the children and returned to Aquilia, she would make me crown prince again, and I would be forced to marry an Aquilian woman of her choice. She was planning on claiming my babies were stillborn, as they are the rightful heirs to the throne with the way Aquilian succession goes. It's supposed to be the firstborn."

"You hag, what a horrible thing to do to your son," I sneer at his mother, disgusted by her ultimatum. "You are no better than that slug of a husband. You probably would have kept me in the dungeon and pimped me out too if Tirrian hadn't saved me," I say, knowing that's what her husband planned to do with me.

She shrugs. "You would have been a good money earner," she remarks nonchalantly.

"Mother, I thought if you saw the babies, you would change your mind." Nikos holds up Typhoon so she can see him. "This is my son, Typhoon, and Lila is holding our daughter, Hali." I don't bother disturbing our child by holding her up. I don't want this woman to have anything to do with my babies.

Her eyes light up a little at the sight of Typhoon, but it's with greed and not joy, and I feel ill. Yup, not letting her anywhere near them. Her attention turns to me and my beautiful girl, and she wrinkles her nose again.

"What is wrong with her coloring? That's not the coloring of an Aquilian." The only part of Hali she can see is her hair, which is the same as mine.

"She takes after Lila, which is dictated by the dragon eye gem. She is the keeper of their mine," Nikos brags, and I wince. Damn it, she didn't need to know that. I can see the greed in her eyes multiply at possibly having access to the gems.

"Fine, you can bring the female child with you too, and I expect a delivery of the dragon gems once a quarter as payment for letting them return."

I stare at the woman, completely gobsmacked by her audacity. She wants me to pay her to take my mate and children back. Does she expect me to just be okay with this? She didn't mention anything about me going with them.

"Mother, where is Nixie? I'd like to introduce my sister to her niece and nephew." Nikos doesn't give her an answer to her demand, and I reach out with my warlock powers to see how he feels. He looks very calm, and I will kill him if he is even considering it. I shouldn't have worried, though, because inside him is a ball of fury, and I can feel his worry for his sister.

His mother huffs in disgust. "She turned out to be as useless as you. She is unavailable to see your spawn, as I have her locked in the dungeon for some correctional behavior. I've given her womb to General Mallon to use. He expressed interest in breeding her when I initiated bidding rights."

"Are you fucking serious?" Nikos explodes, waking up Typhoon who wails with fright. He glares at his mother before standing up and shushing Typhoon, bouncing him up and down to sooth him. "I cannot believe you. After how Father treated you, you're now acting as badly as him."

"Being nice doesn't pay, Nikos." His mother smiles contemptuously. "Now that I'm in charge, we're doing things my way."

"But who are you going to have as your heir?" I ask the mer bitch, still rocked by her attitude. She smiles, and it makes me feel ill. It's slimy and reminiscent of her dearly departed husband. I shudder.

"Nikos, your friend Hurricane is a captain in our

armed forces, isn't he?" Queen Nerissa asks, and I brace for wherever she is going with this.

"Hurry? Yes, he's stationed at the barracks near the trench. His unit is in charge of making sure none of the creatures escape." My mate sounds confused.

"He has twins in his family, right?"

Nikos nods as Typhoon falls asleep, although there is a small hitching of breath as he still sobs in his sleep. My poor baby. "Yes, he has younger twin sisters. They must be in their mid-teens now."

"Excellent. He will be a suitable breeding partner. I will have him relocated to the palace immediately. I'm still young, and who knows, the next lot of spawn we give birth to may actually be competent." She pushes her hair back behind her ear and flutters her eyelashes girlishly.

Nikos's eyes widen with horror, and he looks at me. I can feel his desire to warn his friend of his mother's plans. I decide I've had enough of this whole interaction. Time to cut it short.

"Well, good luck with that." I brush off her announcement like it means nothing to us. Narcissists like her only want attention, and I am not feeding into that. I'm thankful she's not going to be in my children's lives, because after that little performance, there's no way she is spending any time with them. "Nikos and our babies will be remaining with the circus. I take it you no longer want to be associated with the Galaxy Circus, Queen Nerissa, so I shouldn't rely on Aquilian performers returning now that the show is resuming its tour, correct?"

I'm done playing games. I don't want this woman anywhere near any of us.

"No Aquilian will demean themselves by performing in that freakshow anymore." She curls her lip in disgust.

"Fine, I'll have the council made aware of your stance so that when we refuse to bring the show to Aquilia, they will know why. I'll also share your decision with my in-laws. That would be the ruling families of Vilax, Westalin, and Iceen as well as Snakebite Logistics and the suppliers of suva, to name a few. I'm sure they will agree that a boycott on anything Aquilian will be appropriate since you consider us all freaks."

Her entitled look drops, and she starts to sputter.

"Oh, and I'll make sure my mate, Zeydan, the god of earth, lets his brother know that the ruling royal on Aquilia approves of selling females for breeding purposes. I'm sure Tito, the god of water and your patron god, will be interested to hear that. He may even decide that Aquilia needs a reset or, at the very least, a new ruling family," I bluff as I pass Hali to her father and stand up, putting my hands on my hips as I glare at the now pale woman on the screen. "Watch your back, bitch. Nobody messes with my family and gets away with it."

I wave my hand to turn the screen off, feeling spitefully pleased at the shocked look on Nerissa's face.

"I need to call Hurry and warn him about my mother's plans, and I need to go rescue my sister," Nikos tells me, juggling both children flawlessly.

"Wow, so that did not go well," Xavier says, leaning against the kitchen counter and drinking a beer. Saxon and Tirrian are sitting at the dining room table with their own beer, and they were thankfully quiet through the whole conversation. We didn't need to add fuel to the flames, but I can feel Nikos's embarrassment.

"Not sure your mother is any better on the throne than your father," Caspian points out unnecessarily, and I glare at his tactless ass. He just shrugs.

"How long do you give it until the Aquilian people rebel? They must have thought their luck changed when Marlin was dealt with. They are not going to like what she's doing," Saxon muses, and Nikos nods.

"Yes, I don't doubt Mother will have to quell possible civil war. She should have kept Nixie as her heir. She is the beloved princess of Aquilla. Our people will not be happy to hear she will be replaced."

Xavier puts his beer down and walks over to us, making grabby hands for the children.

"Give me my guppies. I'll watch them while you call your friend." He's so grabby for all the children, and he spoils them rotten. I think he's been secretly working on a spell to help him breathe underwater. I heard him muttering when he thought nobody was listening, and he was considering getting Caspian or

Nikos to give him a mating bite so he could shift and swim with them. Talk about extreme measures.

Nikos hands Hali to Xavier, and I take Ty from him.

"But you can't leave to rescue Nixie. Is there no one else you trust on Aquilia who could help you? What about this Hurry person?"

"He would, but if my mother caught him, he'd be just as trapped as Nixie. There isn't really anyone else. I didn't make myself too popular with that idiotic act. It kept away true friends as well as those who only wanted to be with me because of my status. Hurri was the only one who saw through it."

"And it's not like we can send any random mercenary team to break her out, because I'm assuming she will be kept in the castle at the bottom of the ocean." Saxon pushes back from the table and takes Ty from me, putting him over his shoulder and swaying on the spot. My merman starts pacing back and forth across the floor, pulling at his hair.

"What am I going to do?"

"Do you think they are treating her badly? Like, would your mother torture her or anything?" I ask, stepping in front of him and blocking his path. I wrap my arms around him and rub his back, hoping to calm him slightly.

He shakes his head. "No, I don't think so. It will just be an out of sight, out of mind kind of thing. She often told us she couldn't stand to look at us when she was having a particularly bad day. It's why she didn't argue when we decided to leave for the circus."

"Okay, well good, so she should be fine where she is for now. It's important that you warn your friend so he can hide or maybe go off world for the moment until your mother sets her sights on someone else. She won't be able to wait too long to produce an heir, or maybe one of your father's other bastards will make a play. This should keep her busy until we can do our thing on Earth, and then we can rescue Nixie," I suggest, and I feel him take a large breath before he pulls away and sighs.

"Okay. Yeah, you're right. I'm not leaving our family for the moment, and Nixie will be okay."

"Lila," William calls as he emerges from their wing of the house. The kitchen and dining area is centrally located and shared by both wings. He's frowning down at a tablet in his hands.

"Hi, Grandpa Will. How's Grandma?" I ask him. The three men mostly stay close by in case she wakes. Link disappeared into their wing not too long ago to run some more checks on her. "Are you ready for dinner and family game night tonight?"

I finally have everyone where I want them, and tonight, we're attempting to play some of the games I brought from Earth. There's Twister, Game of Life, Clue, Monopoly, Jenga, Go Fish, and Operation. I'm going to set up stations, and we can take turns playing the games. I've also arranged drinks and snacks. I can't wait.

He smiles, but it almost looks like a grimace, and I wave a finger at him. "Nope, you're not getting out of it," I tell him before he can even wrangle an excuse.

"Fine, but I just got a funny alert at the dino sanctuary. I was wondering if you could drive out there and check it out. Most of the staff go home in the evenings, and they rotate who stays overnight. I tried to get in contact with Connor, who is supposed to be on shift tonight, but he's not responding. I'd go, but I don't want to leave Liliana when she may be close to waking."

"Yeah, okay, I have time to run out there before dinner is ready. Maybe Zeydan can come with me since we didn't get our date tonight."

He and Brannock were in the library before I sat down with Nikos, so I head in that direction. I've never been out to the dino sanctuary before, but I've been granted access to all Galaxy Circus holdings. Hopefully I can find Connor, and he can show us around. I'm sure he's probably just seeing to an animal and can't come to the phone, but I don't mind a little one-on-one time with Zeydan. I really like him and want to know him better, and this will help with that.

The library has an open fire that crackles, making the room toasty warm. Zeydan and Brannock are both curled up in plush chairs with books as they read quietly. I love that neither of them feel the need to communicate with one another to be comfortable. I think Zeydan has spent so much time alone that he struggles in big crowds now, and let's face it, our family is loud and demonstrative and loving, so he's going to need quiet time regularly to decompress. Brannock must be the same, used to isolation because he and Chloe lived separate from society the last year. It's nice to see them bonding.

"Hi." Both of them look up when they hear me. Brannock gives me that smile that makes his eyes crinkle at the edges, and my heart go pitter-patter. God, I love this man.

"Hey, baby, are you coming to join us?" He points at the plush chair that has my romance novel on it. I left it there earlier, so I knew where to find it next time.

I shake my head. "I'd love to, but I have to run an errand for William, and I was wondering if you wanted to come with me," I ask Zeydan, who quickly puts a bookmark in the place he was reading and stands up.

"Sure, I'd love to."

"Do you need anyone else?" Brannock asks, but I shake my head.

"No. Enjoy your peace and quiet, because I guarantee game night is going to be anything but." I laugh as he winces. I know it's not really his thing, but sometimes we need to sacrifice for the good of the masses.

# CHAPTER TWENTY-NINE

**Saxon**

I'm peering into the fridge, looking for a blood bag to drink, when my wife and Zeydan walk into the kitchen. I close the door and smile at them. I don't know much about this man yet, but he seems to be enamored with my blood rose, so that's good enough in my book. I felt sorry that they didn't get their chance for a date tonight. I'm also intrigued because he smells delicious, like liquid ambrosia. I wonder if Lila has drunk from him yet. I'd love to know if he tastes as good as he smells. Is that weird? I probably shouldn't be eyeing this man as a meal replacement, but just like Xavier, his scent calls to me. While the other men in Lila's harem have helped me out when she hasn't been able to, and their blood is nutritious, none of them are as tasty as hers or the warlock's. I think this god's blood may come close though.

I watch as Lila grabs a key fob for one of the vehicles the Adams brothers keep in the garage. "Where are you off to?"

"William got an alert of some kind of disturbance at the dino sanctuary. The staff member isn't answering any calls," Lila answers, and Zeydan frowns.

"A dino sanctuary?" he asks, looking between the two of us.

"Earth people call the animals that inhabit Reccedea dinosaurs. Dinos for short. We have some that are bred and raised for use in the circus," I explain, and his face brightens.

"They were some of my favorite creatures to create. I always wondered if they could be domesticated. I look forward to seeing this sanctuary."

"Do you mind if I tag along?" I ask, feeling shitty that I will interrupt their one-on-one time, but I don't like the sounds of a possible break-in or worse, a breakout. I know that the two dinos from the show are back in the sanctuary until the circus leaves again. In fact, Viggy probably needs to be transferred from the sanctuary to the ship tomorrow or the next day. The circus is planning on leaving Skarr in three days. Htaed has proven to be too erratic and will be left behind. I'm not sure what that means for Lila's cousins, Phillip and Fiona, since it was their only task in the show.

"Yes, I think that would be smart. We don't know what we are dealing with, and animals can be unpredictable, domesticated or not," Zeydan agrees, and I hear Lila's sigh of relief.

"That would be great. It's not that I doubt my or Zeydan's skills, but I have no experience with these animals."

I chuckle. "I seem to remember hearing all about how you wrangled Viggy back to the ship by yourself." Xavier told me about what happened when I was feral with bloodlust and the need to bond my blood rose.

"Yes, well, he was easy. I don't know what else we are dealing with at the sanctuary," she replies as I grab a jacket off the hook and pull a beanie over my head. The others do the same. None of us feel the cold particularly badly, but nobody likes to get wet clothes or hair if it snows.

"I've been in there before. It's fun, but I also know where the tranqs are kept if we can't find the worker. Who did William say it was? I've spent some time there during rest periods when I didn't want to return to Vilax," I explain as we head out into the garage and jump into the vehicle. Luckily, it's a hover style one, and we don't have to worry about getting stuck in snow drifts. The roads out to the sanctuary probably haven't been cleared.

"I think William said the guy's name was Connor," she tells me, starting the vehicle and sticking it in reverse before backing out of the garage. Once we're clear, she puts it into drive, and we start moving down the driveway and onto the street. I'm sitting in the passenger seat, so I program the right information into the GPS.

"Cool, I like Connor, and he loves the animals and knows the sanctuary like the back of his hand. He'll be able to tell us if anything is wrong."

The drive out of town is uneventful. Lila tells us about the auditions she and Ghosie watched today.

"It's going to be so hard to decide. I'm only halfway through them and already offered several jobs," she grumbles good-naturedly. She then fills me in on the gossip regarding Magenta and Susie. She managed to grill them between acts. Apparently, things with my ex clan members have cooled off with Magenta. Hale and Velorina have decided to join my brother's clan, which I'm not surprised to hear, but I do feel a pang of sympathy for the Skarrian. Despite her mostly fickle and promiscuous reputation, I think she truly longs to form a family group. Now that she's parted ways with Nixie, Hale, and Velorina, it doesn't look like it will be happening anytime soon.

"It doesn't surprise me that Aura wants to go back to Earth. They've been in charge of Pleasure Inn for a very long time, and it's familiar and comforting for them, but I can also understand Mark and Susie wanting something different. Both of them just walked into their alien heritage, and for someone raised on Earth, the prospect of space travel and discovering new cultures and worlds must be thrilling," I say, looking out the window and watching the frosty countryside slide by, the snow glistening in the bright light of the streetlamps.

"Yeah. Mark and Susie are not sharing a suite with Aura's family this trip. They've requested their own rooms. I think they just want to create some distance so when they part, it won't hurt so much, but then I don't really know how involved they really all were, or if it was a minor dalliance."

"What about Ricky? What happened to him?" I ask, remembering the cyborg who had been sent as a gift to Aura from Deianira Digicon. I'm pretty sure it was a setup, but she's denying all involvement.

"He's opting to stay with Aura and her family. He's quite enchanted with them, according to Susie. I think the fact that Aura protected him when Agent Smith stormed Pleasure Inn made a big impact. I get the feeling he may not have had anyone in his corner before."

"Are your friends going to stay with the circus for a while? I remember when the Celestian heir was kidnapped. It sent shockwaves through the galaxy, and I even heard about it despite being isolated on Husadavia. I can't imagine his parents are ready to let him go when he's only just been returned to them," Zeydan says from the backseat.

I turn my body so I'm angled toward Lila and look at the soft-spoken god. He's nothing like I assumed the gods would be like. I expected them to be loud, arrogant, and outspoken. Maybe they were once, but having diminished power and losing both the goddess of death and life made them more cautious. Zeydan is always watching and taking everything in, and I bet there isn't much he misses. I could tell how frustrated he was that he couldn't help Ghosie or Brannock, and I don't think compassion and empathy are something that comes naturally to him, but I also saw his interaction with our children, and he is mildly fascinated with them and in no small way enchanted. I really don't think he means any of us any harm, but I will still keep a close eye on him until I know better.

Lila looks at him in the rearview mirror. "I think they would like to. Susie mentioned that she and Mark were going to talk to Link about joining the medical crew, which isn't a bad thing now that we have the children and are possibly adding a few more acts."

The god nods, turning his attention to his window. "That would probably be smart. It would free up Link more often for our family too. The children are going to need to start their schooling soon, and he would be an excellent tutor with his wide database of knowledge. From our conversations, I think it would be something he would enjoy as well. I would be happy to assist him in educating our offspring."

Lila does a double take at his statement, and I just smirk. Oh, so she noticed how he used the words "our family" and "our offspring." I guess the god's all in, and he just has to work on convincing my wife.

"Oh, ah, yes. I guess I hadn't considered that, but they are growing rapidly. Starting their education, even if it's the basic stuff, is probably a smart idea," she agrees, turning her attention back to the road, but I continue to stare at him. His head swivels very slowly so he's looking at me again, and he gives me a slow wink, one side of his mouth ticking up in a smirk.

Oh yeah, he knows exactly what he's doing, and he's playing the long game. I give him a small nod of acceptance and turn my attention back to where we're going. The navigation system tells Lila to turn into the sanctuary, and we park in the few public spaces that are available.

There's one car here, but apart from that, the lot is empty. When we get out, a shrill alarm is blaring, and a blue light flashes over the entry of the sanctuary.

I frown and reopen my door, reaching into the glove compartment and pulling out the laser pistol in there. "William never said there was a break-in?" I frown at Lila, who is biting her lip and stomping her feet, trying to keep warm in the cold. Her breath mists in front of her.

"No, just a disturbance. I assumed there was a problem with one of the animals," she replies as I move toward the entrance, gesturing for them to stay behind me.

"Wait," Zeydan calls, and we freeze while he releases his tails, sending them ahead of us to scope out the problem. It sure is handy that he can see through their eyes. His irises and pupils turn white as he concentrates on what information the nine creatures are feeding him. I hold the door open for them to stream through, but I stiffen when the smell of blood registers in my nostrils. It's only seconds before Zeydan also gains that knowledge from his creatures.

"Someone is injured, but they still have a heartbeat. It's the only one in that building, but it is behind a closed door." He gestures in front of us.

"Let's go." Zeydan grabs Lila's hand and tugs her forward. I can sense her hesitation in our bond, but at the touch of his hand, she relaxes. I'm grateful he can do that for her as I take the lead, my gun up and ready.

The front part of the sanctuary is the ticket kiosk and gift shop. It is open to the public and school groups a couple of times a week. You can wander through it and see all the animals from Reccedea that they raise for use in the circus. They also house animals that have been seized from illegal traders that can no longer be returned to their home planets for whatever reason.

There's also an administration and security office, and that's the place that has Zeydan's creatures on alert. They yip and whine, scratching at a closed door to get in. I turn the handle and push it open before stepping back and waiting for their assessment.

"There's a man on the floor. He's been hit on the head, and there's a small pool of blood under his skull. It doesn't seem to be life-threatening. Apart from that, it's clear."

Lila gasps. "Can you conjure me up a robe with wing slits?" she asks the god, who quickly does as she asks, holding it out to her. She strips and changes into her Celestian form before quickly shoving the robe on and gesturing for me to move out of the way to let her through. Instead, I lead the way just in case Zeydan's creatures missed anything.

Lila kneels and activates her healing power. A bright light washes over the man whom I recognize as Connor. He groans and returns to consciousness as Lila heals the wound on the back of his head. "Easy," she cautions him when his eyes blink open. "I healed you, but don't get up too quickly."

Zeydan puts her discarded clothes on a nearby desk and opens another door, then he disappears before returning with a wad of damp paper towels—that must be a bathroom. He passes it to Lila, who uses it to clean the blood off the back of Connor's head. He just blinks at her as I tuck my gun into my waistband.

"You're an angel," he murmurs, and I can hear the awe in his voice.

I snort. "Hardly. She's definitely more of a devil. All her husbands say so."

He blinks and turns to look at me, recognition in his eyes. "Saxon. What are you doing here?" He stumbles as he tries to stand up, and Lila steadies him with a hand on his arm. Again, he looks at her with hearts in his eyes. "Who are you? Why are you here?" He hasn't even looked away to notice the nine creatures who are sitting patiently to one side, and Zeydan has a knack of making himself appear inconsequential.

"William said there was a disturbance, and he couldn't get a hold of you, so he sent us to investigate. This is Lila, their granddaughter and my wife. Lila, this is Connor, the head zookeeper for the sanctuary," I introduce them.

She smiles at him, and he looks even more dazzled. Poor bastard, Lila really doesn't know her own appeal, and with those giant wings and glowing aura, she really is spectacular.

"Hi." She waves at him. "Did you happen to see who hit you? I'm assuming that's what happened," she asks him, gesturing at his head.

This works to get him back on track, and he frowns and shakes his head. "No. I had just finished my last rounds, and I was going to sit down and eat something when I was struck from behind." He gestures to a container on the desk in front of a whole heap of monitors.

"Do you want to have a look around to see if anything was disturbed here before we walk through the zoo and check it out?" I suggest, and he agrees and disappears out into the foyer gift shop.

I step over to the monitors and study the video feeds. The ten screens continuously rotate through all the cameras in the park. Nothing stands out to me, but I haven't been here in a while, so I wouldn't know for sure.

"Why don't you change back?" Zeydan suggests to Lila. "It's too cold to wander around in that robe out there, despite your tolerance for the weather." He nods to the snow-covered video feed, and she grimaces.

"What if we come across someone else who's injured? I think I'll just put my other clothes back on, and we can cut some space in the jacket for my wings. We should have brought Maxsim and Echo, they would have been good at tracking out there," she muses thoughtfully.

"My creatures will be just as helpful," he promises, not taking his eyes off her as she redresses. She doesn't look away from him either. It's like a weird game of naked chicken, and I can't stop the chuckle that leaves my lips, but thankfully, Connor returns before they make me explain.

"Everything looks fine out there," he tells us, and I gesture to the video feeds.

"I can't see anything on the screen, but maybe you can take a closer look," I say to him, and he sits down and his fingers fly across the console. He brings up a map of the sanctuary, and there are red lights flashing on two enclosures.

"Fuck. The steggy paddock has been breached, and what's even worse, it looks like Htaed is also out." He returns his attention to the cameras, programming the right ones to appear.

One shows a wide open gate that doesn't look damaged, just like someone opened it. "That's Htaed's paddock. He and Viggy usually share one since they have been with the circus, but he's been even more deranged since he returned to the sanctuary, so we had to separate him. I think his mind is broken, and I have no idea why."

I exchange a glance with Lila. Allegedly, her cousins are supposed to have some kind of animal control power, which is why they got the job in the first place. What if they tried to control his mind and broke it instead? They aren't very gentle with their techniques, and with a mind as primitive as a dino's, it probably wouldn't take much.

Connor changes the view, and we see a wide open space. I gape as we watch terrified mini steggies running from a crazed raptor. "Fuck, he's in the steggy paddock. How did he even get in there?"

# CHAPTER THIRTY

## Lila

"Holy shit," I mutter as we watch the live footage. Adorable miniature stegosauruses run around in a blind panic while Htaed chases them. Luckily for them, they are quite agile, so he hasn't managed to kill any of them, which makes him even madder, but I'm sure it's only a matter of time.

Connor jumps up and hurries to a nearby cabinet, opening it and pulling out two big tranq guns. He passes one to me.

He pats his pockets and frowns. "Shit, my swipe key is gone. Whoever attacked me must have stolen it, but why?"

He starts to leave, but Zeydan pushes off the wall. "Wait. Is there a way to see if anyone else accessed those gates?" he asks.

"Sure, just let me run the employee logs." Connor returns to the console, placing his gun down before bringing up another screen.

"What are you thinking?" I ask him, and he points at the park map.

"There's no way he would have made it from one side of the park to the other without getting distracted by something else." He points at the two flashing beacons. He's right, they are on opposite sides of the park.

"We had Htaed in containment because he was upsetting the other animals," Connor explains, frowning at the information he's reading.

"You're right, someone must have herded him to the steggy paddock, and that would not be an easy task. Only someone who knew what they were doing could manage it," Saxon says.

"So you think the break-in was staged to cover their tracks?" I ask, and Connor gasps.

"You're right. Phillip used his card two hours ago. I'm not sure how I missed him when I did my rounds, but it looks like he was working in the steggy paddock, and Fiona was also with him." He brings up some footage, showing them in a large, open, snow-covered space, kicking a ball around with the miniature steggies. It looks innocent enough.

"What are they doing?" Zeydan leans in to get a closer look, and Connor smiles. The time stamp shows it was an hour and a half ago.

"It's weird. Ever since the circus went on hiatus,

they've spent a lot of time here—a lot more than in the past. They taught the steggies to play a version of what they called Earth polo, riding on their backs and hitting a ball around." He looks to Lila for confirmation, and she nods. "I think they were quite shaken when Htaed failed to perform and Viggy got out, and they were worried about losing their positions. They kept talking about needing to present you with another option."

"Seriously?" I'm skeptical, and Connor swings around in his chair and looks at me.

"Yes, I overheard a conversation between them. They said they didn't want to remain on Fluxx because they would be at their grandma's mercy. I think Fiona's exact words to Phillip were, 'I'd rather live in Lila's shadow than deal with Grandmother's fury.'"

"If that was two hours ago, then they couldn't have been the ones who hit you on the head," Zeydan says as we leave the office and head out into the cold, Zeydan's creatures leading the way.

"No, I don't think so. But where are they now? I couldn't see them in the footage," Connor argues.

"If Htaed is truly uncontrollable, then they probably found somewhere to hide the minute they saw him. He is an intelligent creature, so he might hold a grudge," Saxon suggests as we all run through the park, following Connor's lead. We hear sounds of distress the closer we get to the enclosure. Luckily, it's not too far from the sanctuary entrance.

"I've loaded the guns with tranqs, but if he is so far

gone, maybe it would be kinder to put him down," Connor says, looking at me.

"I can't make that decision," I argue, but Saxon disagrees.

"Lila, you are practically the CEO of Galaxy Holdings now. These are decisions you can make."

"Well, it's too late now. Let's tranq him and get him back to his enclosure, and I can see if I can heal him. If his mind can't be healed, then I'll approve euthanasia." My Celestian powers should extend to animals as well, but brains are tricky, which Link never fails to tell everyone when they question when Grandma will wake up.

I can't stop the sob of distress that bursts from my lips when we enter the steggy paddock. There are injured mini stegosauruses everywhere, and unfortunately, Htaed succeeded in killing one and is making a meal of it.

"Shit, he's definitely going to need to be put down now. He got a taste for them," Connor mutters as he and Saxon take aim at the red and orange raptor. He's so distracted by his meal, he doesn't even notice us. Both of them fire two fast-acting tranqs into his flanks. He whirls around and snarls at us, but as he lunges, he stumbles and goes down hard, his eyes rolling back into his head as he collapses to the ground.

"There's a sling in the enclosure there," Connor points to a nearby building that looks like a barn. "We should be able to roll him into it, and the three of us can relocate him with your strength, Saxon, and your…" He trails off, looking at Zeydan, and I realize we didn't introduce him.

"Shit, I'm sorry, this is Zeydan," I tell Connor, who looks at the god with interest.

"Oh, hey, cool, like the god of earth. Did you know he created the animals on Reccedea? How appropriate to be named after him." He chuckles, and Zeydan nods.

"Yes, I did. They are some of my favorite creations." He crosses his arms, stares across the field, and whistles, calling his tails back to him. "It pains me to see them hurting. I will do what I can for the injured ones."

He stalks off, and Connor's mouth drops open, and he pales slightly. "*The* Zeydan?" he asks, and I smother my smirk.

"Yup! Pretty impressive, right?" I don't wait for his answer before I follow Zeydan, and together, we use our powers to heal as many of the steggies as we can. Before we get through too many, I hear Saxon call us from the barn.

"Lila, come quickly." The urgency in his tone has me using my Vilaxian speed to race to him, Zeydan easily keeping up.

"I couldn't smell them over all the dino blood," Saxon tells me as he steps aside, and I gape in horror at the beaten forms of my two cousins.

I rush over to them. Both are unconscious and have deep lacerations. Phillip has a large, three-clawed gouge across his chest, which is oozing blood, and

Fiona has the same across her face, through one eye and over her mouth. I feel nauseous just looking at her, and I'm not sure even my powers can fix her.

"Are they alive?" Zeydan asks as my healing powers activate, and I hold them over Fiona. Hers look more dire than her brother's. Saxon strips off his shirt and passes it to Connor, who is kneeling next to Phillip, and he presses the cloth to his wounds.

"Barely," Saxon growls in response. "Those are not the only wounds. Look at their arms. They are covered in bruises and small abrasions, like they were beaten by hand first before Htaed got to them."

The power drains out of me, and Fiona's wounds slowly close. Zeydan pushes Connor out of the way and tries to heal Phillip, but he only manages to stop the bleeding with his diminished powers. I'll have to seal the wounds.

My well of power still drains very quickly, and I know if I heal Fiona completely, I won't have enough left in the tank for the rest of the steggies and Phillip, so I cut off the power and look at Saxon.

"Call Xavier. Get him to teleport here and bring them both back to the mansion so Link can monitor them, and I can heal them fully after recharging. I need a few more of my battery chargers on hand for that."

Saxon rolls his eyes playfully but pulls out the communicator to contact our warlock while I shuffle over to Zeydan and Phillip.

"I'm sorry I've been so unhelpful. I bring nothing to this family with my powers diminished so much,"

Zeydan laments, staring at my cousin with frustration. I give his hand a squeeze before activating my healing powers and working on Phillip.

"That's just not true, and I'm sure once Liliana wakes up, she can shed some light on that problem." I think we've all resigned ourselves to the fact that my grandmother was once the goddess of life and has answers to a lot of our questions.

Once I get his wound to stop bleeding and I stabilize him, I try to wake him, but like Fiona, I have no luck. I release my power and sit back on my heels, looking at my new potential mate.

"Did you happen to notice that both Phillip and Fiona seem to be in the same kind of stasis that Liliana is in?" I ask him, wondering if he noticed when he was helping heal them.

"Yes, I noticed. It has the same magical signature. It's like whoever did this doesn't want them to be able to talk."

"Why not kill them outright then?" a voice asks, and I startle, standing up to see my mist-covered warlock standing in the entrance to the barn.

"Holy shit, that's the warlock," Connor mutters. "You really do have some powerful friends." He looks at me with awe, and I roll my eyes when Xavier corrects him.

"She has some powerful husbands." He walks over and looks down at my two extremely injured cousins. "Someone worked them over good. I'm assuming the wreckage is all because of Htaed?" he asks. "You might want to move him. I think the smell of steggy blood may rouse him sooner than you hoped. I saw a talon twitch when I walked by."

Connor jumps to his feet. "Fuck, I'll tranq him again, and we can move him." He hurries out of the barn, and Xavier lets his mist dissipate before he raises an eyebrow at me.

"Why don't you just teleport him to where he needs to go?" he asks, and I frown.

"Because I don't know where he has to go. I've never seen it."

He shakes his head in disappointment, tapping the side of it with his finger. "Take the image out of his mind." He nods in Connor's direction.

I wince. "Yeah, but then I have to strip and change forms, and it's cold." I'm not ashamed to admit I whine. Sometimes these powers are more of a pain than they are worth.

"Babe, you've practiced accessing other powers of different forms, not to mention Celestians can teleport and read minds," he reminds me, and I feel stupid, but then I double down.

"But I don't want to run out of power and be useless." I really do worry about this. Instead of having unlimited power, it seems to run out very quickly.

"Well, you have a husband and another potential mate who can help you refuel." He nods at Saxon and Zeydan.

"But Zeydan can't power me up because we're not

bonded." I'm being deliberately stubborn now, but he's pissing me off. I cross my arms and glare at him.

"I'm sure you can manage five quick mutual orgasms. He's a god, so his recovery period has to be spectacular."

"Why are you being like this?" I demand, getting really pissed off now. His tone is flat and bordering on annoyed.

"Because, Lila, your human sensibilities are limiting your potential." He stabs a finger at the injured Skarrians. "You need to fix all your bonds and level up. What do you think the chances are that they should be dead so they couldn't tell us who did it, but the attack was interrupted by a rampaging dino? What's to say this isn't all related to everything we have going on? Who's to say you or, God forbid, the babies aren't the next victims?"

"Why would they be involved?" I argue, but my heart starts to race. I haven't even considered motive yet except they were assholes. I'm sure I'm not the only person they were nasty to.

"Lila, they are Adams adjacent. Until you appeared, they were touted as being next in line to inherit the circus. We've already suspected them of some dubious behavior, and their grandmother is highly suspicious as well. I think we would be stupid to dismiss this as some random attack. Just think about it."

He is clearly pissed at me, because he doesn't even

wait for a response. He just teleports himself and my cousins.

I gape at thin air and rub the ache in my chest that I feel whenever one of my mates is angry at me.

"Ouch," I whisper, too embarrassed to look at Saxon and Zeydan.

"While he was unnecessarily cruel in his worry, he's also not wrong. It's all been heaped on you, and the fact that you haven't devolved into a gelatinous mess in the corner is admirable. You need to adapt quickly, though, and finally make that decision to assimilate to your new life. Part of you is holding onto the past. Zeydan says you are mates, and there is some piece of you that recognizes that, even though you are reluctant to admit it. It's time to embrace it and become the woman you need to be to take down the Syndicate and Agent Smith."

"I didn't ask for any of this!" I shout, and I want to rage, but arms wrap around me, and I'm pulled against a hard chest, my wings pinned against me. Zeydan gave up his half naked ways to assimilate with the family, and I am sad to feel a couple of layers between us now.

"Deep breaths, Lila," he whispers. His tight grip on me soothes me, and I sync my breathing with his. My eyes drift closed, and I listen to our hearts beat in unison.

"We know you didn't, but that doesn't change the truth," Saxon says quietly. "I'm going to help Connor move Htaed and give you two time to heal the steggies." I know what he's saying without him saying it.

He's not only giving us time to heal the dinos, but also to fuck. God, why can't they understand a girl likes to be wooed? I'm almost certain they all know this. So far, Tirrian is winning in the wooing stakes with all my new treasure. Who would have guessed that the asshole dragon would be at the top of the list?

"Can you manage without us?" Zeydan asks him when I stay quiet.

"Yes, we can use that." He points to a small ATV with a trailer attached. I'm sure it's probably used to clean poop or transport food for the mini dinos, but he's right, they should be able to manhandle Htaed into it. He jumps on it and soon disappears out the double barn doors, leaving just the two of us.

"Are you okay?" Zeydan still has a tight grip on me, and I melt into him, enjoying the feeling of being held. Since day one, I've barely had time to stop and just take everything in, so I really cherish the few moments of peace I get between all the chaos.

# CHAPTER THIRTY-ONE

## Lila

I close my eyes, retract my wings, and lean my head back on his chest. I breathe in his unique scent and decide that Xavier and Saxon are right. It's time to let go of old Lila and finally embrace this new life.

I whirl around and press my lips against Zeydan's. He gasps in surprise, opening his mouth slightly, so I slip my tongue in and caress his. He eagerly responds, and one hand slides into my hair to angle my head for better access, while the other cups my ass, bringing us closer together. I moan my approval as we make out for a few moments.

I pull away from him, breathless with desire and wanting more. I look around the barn and spot a ladder leading up into a hayloft. That's good enough for me. I teleport us there, and we collapse onto a soft pile of hay. Our hands tear at each other's clothes—we could both use magic, but there's something more satisfying about doing it manually.

Once we're naked, my hand brushes against his pelvic region, and I freeze and pull back, staring down the length of his body.

"Holy fuck." I can't help but gape at what he's packing. "Is that even legal?" I stammer inappropriately.

Zeydan doesn't just have one member, he has three. They aren't as thick as some of my other guys', but they are long, and they seem to move independently of one another, very much like tentacles do. I stroke a finger over one, and he groans as it curls itself around my finger much like a monkey's tail. The other two try to get in on the action as well.

"It is fine, Lila. As my fated mate, you will be able to take it all when it's time," he murmurs before he sucks one of my nipples. He rolls his tongue around it then nips, and I fist his hair with one of my hands.

He moves farther down my body, and my hands slide to his ears as he reaches my core and breathes deeply before sweeping his tongue through my folds. It's way longer than I'm used to, much like Silac's, but unlike his thin appendage, this one is thick.

"You smell and taste like heaven," he mutters before flicking it over my clit a couple of times, making my body spasm like it's connected to a live wire, before thrusting into my cunt. I shout and use his adorable fox ears to pull his face deeper into my cunt. He goes to town, licking and sucking, alternating between fucking me with his tongue and rolling it over my clit.

I'm a sweaty, swearing mess by the time my first orgasm explodes out of my body. He's edged me for far longer than I usually like, but now I want more. I use his ears to yank him up my body and kiss him, tasting myself on his mouth.

"Mate me, Zeydan. I want you to be mine, and I want to be yours, and I don't want to wait any longer," I mutter against his lips, but instead of slamming home, he pulls away and leans back on his heels, looking down at me.

My heart aches, and I can't meet his eyes. Did I make a mistake? Is this not what he wants?

"Lila, look at me," he commands in that voice that gives me shivers, and I'm helpless to do anything but obey. "I want nothing more than to tie our lives together, but there are a couple of things you need to know first. Mating with me will change you on a fundamental level, mostly so you can stand my power, but also to take my cock deep into your body."

"Okay, I mean I've taken tentacles before, and those don't look that different," I reply with relief, shrugging off his concern. I'm almost grateful that he's worried about me and not rejecting me.

"And I need to change into my god form to make it happen."

"Dude, I have fucked in cat, dragon, and kraken forms as well as many different half forms, I've seen you; you don't have anything that I'm going to run from."

"Yes, but you won't change forms, and you cannot mimic me. It will have to be done in that form."

I still don't understand what he's saying. "You don't scare me. I saw you when you tried to fix Ghosie," I remind him. He looks skeptical still despite my reassurance.

"Okay, don't run from me, it will only turn me on," he cautions, standing up.

I keep my face neutral and nod my agreement. His body starts to shimmer, and I feel the throb of his power as he grows taller and wider and his face elongates, shifting to a fox-like countenance while his body remains mostly the same. Yup, just like I remember, he looks like Anubis. I've always been fascinated with Egyptian history. I feel my cunt drip as I let my eyes drift further down.

I stop and stare at his cock. The three individual members have twined together much like a lollipop, and they form a long, thick, ridged corkscrew. I turn my head to the side.

"I am not sure that is going to work," I point at it, desperate to give it a go, but my pussy is not shaped correctly.

"The fronds at my back will sprinkle you with my godly essence, thus fortifying you to be able to take both my cock and my seed and survive, transforming you to have a small sliver of godly essence."

"Okay, I'm down. Start spreading the godly

essence." I hold out my hands, wanting to feel all that deep inside me. I guess kissing is out now.

"I don't disgust you?" He sounds surprised, and I shake my head.

"Not in the least. I think you're fucking sexy. I'm sad we won't be able to kiss, but get down here and wreck my pussy with that thing."

"Huh, Link said you'd enjoy the challenge," I hear him mutter as he kneels and situates himself between my spread thighs.

The new frond appendages lift up and over him kind of like an umbrella, and then they start to shimmer, and green and gold glittery dust drifts down over my body. I feel it as the dust absorbs into my skin. It's like a pure shot of liquid ecstasy, and I orgasm on the spot without him even touching me. My pussy gushes a thick liquid, and I worry I peed myself.

"Good, your pussy is preparing for my member," he mutters, sliding a finger in. It's thick, and he feels around. "And it's changing shape to accommodate me."

I pant through the pleasure. "Will it stay like that?" I ask him, slightly worried that I'll never be able to give my other mates pleasure again.

"No, it will return to normal once my seed is absorbed." He shakes the fronds again, and another shower of dust washes over me. I scream as an even more powerful orgasm rips through me.

"Oh fuck, it's too much." I grasp the hay below me and thrash my head back and forth. "I can't do it." I try to squirm away, but it's too late. He notches his cock at my entrance.

"You can, Lila. You are doing so well. Soon, we will be connected, and when I paint your womb with my seed, I will shove a small sliver of my soul inside you, making you part god."

He slowly pushes in, and I literally feel it turning like a corkscrew, burrowing into my changed channel.

"No more." I push him away from me. He's fucking huge, and I am just not equipped to take him, but his body is enormous, and he has me pinned. I can't escape. "Please," I weep, my body shuddering with the onslaught of pleasure and pain.

"Still more to go. You're doing so well." He strokes my clit. "Next time, I will breach your ass with one of my members as well and stuff both of your holes." He's hitting all my kinks as his cock literally screws deeper into me. His fronds shimmer once more, and as the dust rains down on me, he slams forward, stuffing me completely. I scream as another orgasm washes through my body. He bites into me with his muzzle as I feel his hot cum burst inside me. His bite throbs, and a piercing pains seems to go from there to the center of my chest as I feel our bond click into place. It's all too much, and it overloads my body, and I black out.

When I wake up, he's in his normal form, and he's wiping me over with a damp cloth. When he notices me watching him, he smiles at me with a look of awe. "It worked. We are mated. You are part god now. Actually, you feel more powerful than I expected, considering my own diminished powers. You probably won't need to use your husbands to power up your mimic powers."

I pout at him. "But that's my favorite part," I tell him, and he chuckles.

"I don't think you'll have any arguments from any of us."

I look away, nervous to ask the next thing. "I feel you, but you don't feel me, right?" I ask him, and his smile drops. I feel sick with disappointment.

"No, but I'm hoping that might change if we join in the Skarrian way." I try to think about how many orgasms I had, but he only had one. We need to try that four more times.

I smile at him and hold out a hand so he can help me up. "Okay, I can get down with that. Now let's go see what I can do for those steggies."

✳

We finish healing the adorable mini steggies. I'm quite enamored with them and like the idea of adding a steggy polo act to the show. Maybe we can get volunteers from the audience to be the players. It's something to think about. Connor and Saxon return, confirming they contained Htaed in his enclosure and changed the security so that only me or my grandpas can let him out again.

We leave Connor combing through security

footage in the hopes he can find who was responsible for the chaos, and we return home to our own brand of chaos. Dinner has been eaten, and board games are being argued over and distributed.

"Mama, will you play the twisty with us?" Cordelia asks, pointing at the mat on the floor. Nik is sitting with Typhoon and Hali, and they are in charge of the spinner. They are a little too young to join in with the game. Cas is in half kraken form, and I frown.

"I'm pretty sure that's cheating," I tell him, pointing to all his extra limbs, and he grins.

"The kids have something they want to show you," he says as I look around the room to make sure everyone is okay. "There are instructions, Lila. They will be fine," he assures me, and I relent and join him. I giggle when I see that Echo and Maxsim have chosen to play Jenga. I'm not sure how they are going to manage that with their paws, but it should be entertaining.

I get down on the floor, and I'm swarmed by the older children. "What do you want to show me?" I ask after smothering them all with kisses and enjoying their delighted giggles.

"Look, Mama." Jack puffs out his chest proudly, and my mouth drops open as he changes into half form. The girls are quick to copy him, and I clap and cheer and celebrate their new milestone.

"So we're all going to play in half form. You need to shift," Cas tells me, his eyes sparkling with more than just fun.

"Well, as long as all tentacles stay inside the vehicle while the ride is operational," I tell him, using code, and he bursts into laughter at my suggestive words.

"But of course, my dear. There are children present," he replies, giving me a wink.

"We made a few moderations to the spinner." Nikos holds up the new spinner, which has eight numbered tentacles on it. Link comes over and starts writing numbers on each of the children and Cas. When he gets to me, he gives me a kiss and waits for me to shift.

"How are the twins?" I ask him.

"They are alright. They are pain free and in the same kind of stasis as Liliana. Spend time with your family, and you can finish healing them when the children go to bed."

"I can go now," I argue. "I actually got a huge burst of power from Zeydan while we were at the sanctuary, and I feel the strongest I ever have," I tell him, and he looks intrigued.

My gaze slides to Xavier, who is pretending not to pay attention, but I know he heard.

"Huh, that's interesting. I wonder why you can absorb power from him. Did you mate in the way of the gods? Or do you think that it worked because he is a god?" Link asks as I strip and shift, and he numbers each of my tentacles.

"I mated him. I decided it was time to embrace my new destiny. I think maybe there was a part of me that hadn't completely accepted everything, and it was making things difficult. I'm hoping things will be different from now on. I shouldn't be fatigued so quickly, according to what Oshan told me."

"Well, that's great. Alright, you're all set. Have fun," he tells me before moving over to a table with Brannock, Tirrian, and Silac. Tirrian is dealing cards, and bets are being placed.

"Ah, I think you're missing the point of Go Fish," I call out, but Brannock waves a hand.

"Hush, woman. I am a Go Fish champion, thanks to Chloe's fascination with the game. I'm about to win big. Don't slow my roll."

I smirk at my Aaz'axian, the last one remaining to seal the mating bond. I will be concentrating on him and making sure Zeydan is locked down as soon as possible, but now is not the time or place to be thinking about it. I'm just thankful my grandpas can't smell how horny I am.

I leave them be and turn my attention to the others. William, Eric, John, Ghosie, Xavier, and Zeydan are all sitting around a Clue board, and William is dealing the cards and explaining the game to everyone.

"No mind reading allowed. Work out the murderer by playing the game," I call out to both Zeydan and Xavier, who look at me with suspiciously innocent expressions. Xavier winks at me, so hopefully he's over his little snit. We'll have to talk about it, but it can wait.

"Where's Saxon?" I ask, looking for my final mate

who seems to be missing. I didn't see where he went when we arrived home.

"He went for a shower and needs to feed. He grabbed a bag and said to tell you to stop feeling guilty," Caspian says, waving for Nikos to spin the spinner. "He said he'll join in with cards on the next round."

I do feel incredibly guilty and have to count my blessings that he's a patient and understanding male.

Playing Twister with five eight-legged krakens playing is not an easy challenge. We aren't even supposed to have five people playing at once, but the kids didn't want to hear it, so we do our best, but the five of us end up tangled so badly that when Saxon returns, he has to physically help us unknot. The children are revved up and beside themselves with giggles by the end of it, so when Eric solves Clue, Zeydan stands up.

"How about we go run some of that energy off outside before we go to bed?" he suggests, pointing out the patio doors where it has started snowing.

The children cheer, and it takes us another half hour to get them bundled up in their adorable snowsuits, hats, gloves, and boots. The two cats go out with them, and I lean against the doorframe and watch as Cordy, Cally, and Jack try to teach Ty and Hali to roll snowballs. They only end up throwing tiny fistfuls, so they abandon that and make snow angels instead.

A knock on the front door brings my attention

back inside. "Are we expecting anyone?" I ask, but everyone looks as bewildered as I am.

John gets up and goes to see who it is, and I blink in surprise as he returns with Vivian in tow.

"Vivian, what a surprise," Eric greets his sister-in-law sarcastically. There's no love lost there. "To what do we owe this visit to?"

I deliberated whether or not to contact her and let her know about Phillip and Fiona, and in the end, I had chosen not to out of caution, just in case she is mixed up with all of this.

I turn my attention to Vivian, surprised at what I'm seeing. Unlike the perfectly put together woman I met the first time we came to Skarr, this woman is completely different. Her smile is forced, and she looks rough. Her clothes aren't as perfectly pressed as they were the last time she was here, and she has dark circles under her eyes. She wrings her hands together, drawing my attention to them, and I notice her knuckles are bruised and one of them is split and oozing.

Saxon's nose flares, and he zeroes in on the same thing I do. That's interesting, considering we found my cousins barely hanging on to their lives at the dino sanctuary, beaten to within an inch of their lives before being attacked by a rampaging raptor.

She takes a deep breath, and it's like she pulls herself together, straightening her back. "I heard that you found Liliana. I wasn't waiting for an invitation to visit my sister. I want to see her," she demands haughtily.

"Well, she's still hasn't regained consciousness yet," William explains coldly.

"I would like to sit with her anyway." Vivian doesn't seem inclined to take no for an answer.

Link stands up, abandoning his hand of Go Fish somewhat reluctantly. I'm pretty sure he is winning, looking at the pile of cards next to him.

"I'll just go check on her if you give me a moment." He hurries in the direction of my grandpas' wing, where Liliana and my two cousins are. Hell, how are we going to explain that? Maybe Link is going to move them into another room until we can learn the truth from them. It's better that she doesn't know they are here.

*Xavier, can you help him?* I ask, sending the thought to his mind, and he stands up and wanders subtly in the opposite direction, but I know as soon as he is out of sight, he will teleport to help Link.

Vivian looks around the room, unable to hide her disgust as she takes in all my remaining mates. "Quite the menagerie you have here, William," she sneers at my grandpa, who leans back in his chair and just grins.

"Yes, our Lila has mated some of the most powerful beings in the universe," he replies, acknowledging her slight and turning it upside down. "We couldn't be happier that our legacies will be continued for many years to come. We have two new grandbabies —two more Adams to take on the mantle of the circus." He is not so subtly rubbing that she is not an Adams in her face while gesturing to the children playing outside. She follows his gaze, and I watch as her mouth drops open, and she pales considerably before she starts to back out of the room.

"You know what? I don't have time to wait for permission to see my sister. I'll come back another time when you aren't so inundated." She quickly turns and hurries back the way she came, leaving us to exchange confused looks. I follow where her gaze had gone and see Zeydan's nine tails bristling with excitement as he watches the children play in the snow.

Was it Zeydan who sent her scurrying? Before I can ask anyone else what they think, Xavier appears in the middle of the room, looking frantic. His gaze stops on my grandpas, who are on guard.

"John, William, Eric, come quickly. Liliana is awake."

**The End... for now.**

# AFTERWORD

I can practically hear your screams from here. I know, I know, that was a doozy, but it was the best place to leave off. But you can order the final stunning conclusion of the Galaxy Circus series on Amazon.

I am aiming to have it out hopefully end of October. But I am going to Edinburgh so I left the place holder date until I can be certain.

In the mean time why don't you check out one of my other series. You can find everything you need to know here.

www.lexiewinston.com

# ACKNOWLEDGMENTS

To my cover designer Jessica, of Raven Ink Covers. Thank you for making the covers exactly what I envisioned, you nailed it and all of them.

Thank you to both Jess at Elemental Editing. My book is pretty and readable thanks to you.

My ever reliable and faithful beta readers Kerry and Tegan... You da bomb xxx

So we're almost there. I hope you loved Spectacle. I was super proud of the Nikos birth scene and all the kinky fuckery through out this book. The final book will be called Ovation and it will answer all those damn questions you still have. Hopefully to everyone's satisfaction.

Keep an eye on my Facebook Group - Lexie's Ladygarden for news of when it will release.

And lastly to you guys the readers. I love what I do, and probably would do it regardless if anyone read them or not, but you guys make it that much sweeter so thank you.

Until next time, happy reading

www.ingramcontent.com/pod-product-compliance
Lightning Source LLC
Chambersburg PA
CBHW051320190726
48290CB00001B/242